Hellalyle and Hildebrand is Tagai T:
There are two others of a comple
unfinished, awaiting inspiration.

He has worked most of his life i
interest in Arts and Humanities. Things that are beautiful and
appealing play an essential part in his imagination.

Besides travelling in West Europe, he has journeyed to the far
South Atlantic, and European Russia, anxious to see parts of the
world that are for many mystical destinations on a historical map.

HELLALYLE AND HILDEBRAND

Tagai Tarutin

SilverWood

First published in 2019 by SilverWood Books
This edition published in 2020

SilverWood Books Ltd
14 Small Street, Bristol, BS1 1DE, United Kingdom
www.silverwoodbooks.co.uk

ISBN 978-1-80042-025-0 (paperback)
ISBN 978-1-80042-026-7 (ebook)

British Library Cataloguing in Publication Data
A CIP catalogue record for this book is available from
the British Library

Page design and typesetting by SilverWood Books

To Her Royal Highness
The Princess Hellalyle, Princess Of Eydis And Orn
this book is dedicated.

In acknowledgement of the illustrious services she rendered to the
world, by means of her cordial nature and cultivated taste, unsurpassed
in the annals of history, nor dimmed by
the passage of time.

Contents

Author's Note

History has left a legend of the infinite beauty of Princess Hellalyle, a quality present in her person which gave intense pleasure and profound satisfaction to the mind, arising from her sensory phenomenon, and a personality in which the summit of spiritual nature was manifest. There is a depiction of this lady within the pages of this book that was not created by drawing or brush strokes of the human hand, but by its agency – a machine. It is sad to recognise that the masters of art, present or long dead, could only recreate the mien of this noble woman as imagined in their mind's eye; so, let it be not a real picture, but leave such things to the mental image of the reader.

My father gave me a glorious guard
Twelve noble knights were my watch and my ward
Eleven daily served me well,
But oh, I loved the last — I fell,
My true love's name was Hildebrand,
And he was prince of Engelland.

Hellalyle and Hildebrand
(extract from a Danish Ballad, translated by Whitley Stokes, 1855)

1

Young Hildebrand

One mid-winter's day in mediaeval England, a mantle of snow covered the land – temperatures low, branches of trees unable to shed the white blanket. The flakes, large as crowns, fell in silence, no wind to disturb their descent from the clouds. A lone figure on horseback emerged through the poetry of light: a young nobleman, a teenage prince called Hildebrand, disturbed from his slumber by the sweet voices of seraphims, subconsciously spurring him to travel the byways and woodland trails surrounding his castle abode. Heeding without question their beguiling sound, he set out at first light, guided along winding tracks by a strange influence on his mind and body, to arrive unerringly at soaring, vertical cliffs that rose out of the sea of trees. The fall of snow ceased and it was now he heard the plaintive bleating of a little lamb; looking up he saw to his dismay the diminutive creature trapped on a narrow ledge, high above, unable to move, so perilous its situation. He could make out, further up, the face of a sheep, its frantic mother looking down over the precipice, crying out in extreme distress for her offspring.

Unhesitatingly Hildebrand dismounted, and in complete disregard for his safety, with no artificial aids to assist him, he set out to scale the immense wall of stone, treacherously covered in ice and snow. Fearlessly, onwards he climbed, hands freezing, frequently slipping but always managing to cling on. The natural inclination of humankind to accept failure as the norm did not apply to this individual doggedly pursuing his goal, until, triumphantly he reached the newborn. Standing precariously on the narrow ledge, he fashioned a make-do harness from his belt and outer clothing, and then gathered up the little innocent, securing it firmly to his upper body. Resuming his ascent, the lionhearted young man doggedly inched his way upwards, and against all the odds, finally reached the top of the icy crag. The parent ewe cautiously approached as Hildebrand gently placed the lamb on the ground, and he watched with satisfaction the uniting of a mother with her progeny, only then for her to turn away; and with the little youngster following they passed through a visionary gateway, a change of state, that opened in a space between two trees, a short distance from the edge of the precipice. Hildebrand dropped to his knees, astonished and humbled by the classical conception he saw before him, of celestial attendants costumed in white, welcoming the agent and servant as they returned to the Divine Father. In the background of the utopian reality he could make out a municipality perched on a promontory – the Holy City of Jerusalem. The spectacular scene then abruptly vanished before his eyes in a vivid flash of light, leaving Hildebrand perplexed at the meaning of the presentation. Perhaps that is how it should be, for there are some things in heaven and earth that are beyond the wit of ordinary mortals to comprehend.

Unbeknown to the young nobleman, his dangerous assignment was a test: the first of two, set for him by metaphysical forces of the wilderness, testing his mettle, moulding it, and he passed their trial with conspicuous gallantry – a person prepared to scarify himself for that of the sacrificial. A dutiful enactment he would make in future years, but this time his offer would be taken up, much to the distress of a loved one looking on.

As he made his way back down avoiding the sheer face of the cliff, descending via its margin to his horse waiting far below, he had the uncanny sensation that someone, or something, was observing him. Stopping intermittently, he would look round searchingly; only an accidental slippage of loose scree noticed by the knight betrayed the presence of unseen onlookers; but dismissing it as a natural consequence, he shrugged his shoulders, unable to discern what it was that aroused his suspicions, a temporal man, blind to the secret shadows covertly watching over him. Not until he reached the safety of the valley floor did the witnesses retreat into the wilderness. The courageous youth had been ignorant in his climb that, if his hold had broken, plunging him to the earth far below, the angels would have saved him.

Three months later, the advent of spring brought three mounted figures: the young Hildebrand, fourteen years old, escorted by two knights riding their horses at walking pace through forest meadows in the greenery of middle England. The weather was fair with a fresh feel to the breeze. The sky above was predominantly blue, but blemished with high, delicate, wispy clouds, which, from their bosoms, gave the appearance of what looked like mare's tails – ice crystals, falling, and trailing away in the direction of the wind – indicating how cold it was in the upper atmosphere. Also, the pure air, bright with clarity so sharp it was if the snow-anointed hills of the distant Welsh Borders could be reached out and touched. Altogether then, an exceedingly glorious day to be borne along in the saddle. Legend has it, the renowned artist Peter Paul Rubens painted this iconic scene in the manner of his picture titled Summer – also known as Aurora – which resides in the present-day Royal Collection of Queen Elizabeth II. It was a companion piece: the season of spring. However, if true, the composition can be considered a lost masterpiece, displaced by the mists of time.

It was a point in the late twelfth century – a youth, a blonde-haired prince of royal lineage, was perfecting his equestrian skills, schooled in the craft by the soldiers mounted on steeds either side of him. As they rode along they passed blooms of daffodils emergent on the woodland floor, and it seemed they waved, dancing in the breeze as Hildebrand sauntered by. Then, as if by chance, they came upon a holy dwelling in a forest clearing: the domain of nuns, an Augustinian house called the White Ladies Priory, so named by locals because of the light-coloured vestments the ecclesiastical women wore. Its location set against a backdrop of dark, thick woodland.

A no more sibylline setting could be imagined, so enigmatic its situation in the landscape. (The distant image of the nunnery visible in Ruben's painting.) The building, caught in the forest's dark shadow cast by the afternoon sun, exuded a mysterious ambience of the biblical; especially so when a raven flew in to settle high on the pinnacles of the sanctuary, curiously focusing its gaze on the prince, regaling him with a dolorous cry. The corvid with its lustrous black plumage presented a mysterious presence, for it was the very one that brought sustenance to the prophet Elijah in the desert – now resurrected to this time present, by the spirits of the forest to watch over the unsuspecting Hildebrand from the day of his birth. The bird's totemic presence brought a poetic nuance to the convent of the White Ladies, reinforcing the importance of this religious house, for, by the end of the day, the prince would learn of his destiny from a member of the sorority.

The knight, Henry Guiscard, suggested to his comrade and the young prince, "Let us see if the prioress will furnish us with refreshment and we will rest in the quietness of this idyll." Both readily agreed, and the three dismounted. Henry Guiscard walked up to the main entrance and rang the hanging bell. After a short interval, a little hatch opened in the door, and the face of a nun peeped out.

"What is your purpose here?" she said to the visitors, prompting the knight to reply with a request for refreshment, and permission for him and his comrades to be allowed to rest outside the walls of the convent. "Wait here, and I will get the prioress to speak to you." With that, she closed the hatch, leaving the prince and his escort resting on the grass while their steeds grazed around them. Eventually, the main door opened, and two nuns emerged, one being the Mother Superior, Eustacia de Sumeri – an elderly woman radiating singular omniscience. The three horsemen jumped to their feet in deference to such an eminent-looking ecclesiarch.

"Well, what have we here?" said the prioress. "We do not get many visitors, as this location is so far off the beaten track, carefully chosen to ensure utmost privacy. Rumours abound accusing us of being anchoresses, but I can assure you that is not the case. However, now you have found us we are duty-bound to offer you comestibles. Bread, cheese and wine – will that suffice?"

"Excellent," said Adam of Hereford looking at the others while rubbing his stomach. (This man-at-arms had previously relinquished his modus operandi to take holy orders under the Bishop of Hereford, but reverted; an apostate, garnering a nickname that had stuck ever since.) Before the prioress turned to depart, it was noticeable she observed the young nobleman with a keen eye and turned away frowning, deep in thought, the vision of Prince Hildebrand occupying her mind. The two accompanying knights noticed this, and looked at one another and then at the boy, curious of the Mother Superior's odd behaviour, while the youngster acted dumb and said nothing, allowing the adults to do all the talking. After finishing their refreshment, the equestrians lingered awhile admiring their surroundings, marvelling at the dedication of the nuns in their isolation.

That evening it started to rain, and back at the castle, Hildebrand, in his private chamber, practised his swordplay in front of a massive log fire. Every so often he would stop and listen to the rainfall beating down.

A knock came at his door and calling out, "Enter," a servant appeared saying, "Prince Hildebrand, there are visitors to see you downstairs in the great hall."

"What! On a night like this?" said the perplexed young man. "What is so vital that it induces people to venture out in weather such as this?"

"It is two nuns from the priory," replied the attendant. The incredulous prince strode athletically down to the hall, and there stood the nuns, wet through, warming themselves by the fire. Turning, they curtsied.

"Young sir," exclaimed Sister Lescelina, "our prioress has inexplicably fallen ill, shortly after you and your comrades departed earlier today. Old and frail, we fear she is dying, but in her approaching quietus, keeps asking for Prince Hildebrand, saying she has a portent to reveal, but it must be to him, and him only. Master, we earnestly beg you to come quickly."

Hildebrand, the two messenger nuns and the same two knights that accompanied him before, duly arrived, just before midnight, at the White Ladies Priory. The bodyguards and the sisters diverted to the warming room to recuperate with victuals. The prince, now on his own, was shown through to the private quarters of the prioress where a welcoming, warm log fire burned brightly in the hearth. In the flickering light thrown by the flames, the youth witnessed a decrepit woman swaddled in sheets lying on her bed. The feeble lady motioned to the attendant nuns to leave the room, wanting to be alone with the young prince.

As Hildebrand stood, looking down at the prioress, she smiled and raised her hand to him in a gesture of wonder and exclaimed with quivering lips, "I never thought a day like this would come – I cannot believe my eyes, to see you standing there just as the Angel predicted that you would." He knelt at the side of Eustacia, the prioress, who grasped his hand surprisingly tightly in her own scrawny, arthritic clasp, and pulled him closer. "I have something profound to say to you, my young man, pay close attention," she gasped, as Hildebrand brought his ear nearer, to glean her quietly spoken word. "In the not too distant future, you will receive a message from a world so different from everything that abounds. It will be a request to travel to a land beyond your imagination; to command a guard of eleven knights, reincarnations of super-warriors from the eternal kingdom that lies beyond; to protect the daughter of a king, now a girl, dwelling in her father's dominion, a mysterious region of terra firma. She will become a most beautiful lady – features that will draw your breath away, a special person, possessing femininity to delight the senses of men, an inspiration to all of womankind, but a figure invested in the kindness and wisdom of the Almighty. Her purpose on this earth to sweeten bitter waters."

Hildebrand, enwrapped by the old woman's soliloquy interrupted, "But, Mother Superior, why am I indicated in this extraordinary prophecy?"

The prioress held up her finger for silence and continued, "Hildebrand, you cannot know it, but divine providence has singled you out from other mortals, possessing qualities far above that demanded by the knightly order." She foretold that the magical noblewoman she had described would intertwine with Hildebrand, sweeping away the dark forces of a nether world, adding, "When your summoning comes, it will be from the spirits of the hinterland. In what form I cannot say, but it will be on your thirtieth birthday and be unmistakable; so on that day make haste, for this exquisite woman will be the last prophet of Christendom until the Apocalypse of Revelations puts an end to the world."

The knight, his innocent young face lit by the glow of the fire, earnestly inquired, "How do you know of such things – where did you learn of them, please tell me?" But the old prioress descended into a deep unconsciousness and did not respond. Thwarted, Prince Hildebrand, releasing the grip of the dying woman, crossed himself, and leaned forward to kiss the cold forehead of the wizened Eustacia de Sumeri breathing her last. Rising to his feet and feeling overwhelmed in body and mind by the occasion, he respectfully backed up, leaving the room. Outside, waiting, was the tearful young nun, Juliana Bauceyn. "Sister," uttered the stunned Hildebrand, "your superior has revealed to me a most extraordinary prophesy, a narrative that I cannot divulge, but, can anyone here throw light on how she became the messenger for such an augury?"

"Dear prince," said Juliana, "I know you have been coming here in secret since you were a little boy. The sorority believed your father, for whatever reason, sent you to receive knowledge from our polymath Eustacia; a learning that was outside the normal bounds of rectitude.

"During your formative years, some of the sisters were privy, witness, to a benevolent phenomenon emerging from the hinterland – a magical wind that breached the walls and closed doors of the priory to swirl around Eustacia, enveloping her in a divine cloak of an incorporeal nature. When we tentatively broached the subject the prioress swore us to secrecy, admitting just one thing: strange voices drove her onwards in her teaching of Hildebrand, developing his reasoning and judgement, preparing him for his ultimate role as protector of a beautiful deity. But, unforthcoming when we tried to pry further into the strange world that had visited her, one member of the sorority suspected the Mother Superior harboured a knowledge not of this sphere – that of Prince Hildebrand, chosen by the Immortals.

"It was on the evening last, when I, and sister Beatrice, came upon the prioress alone in the chapel and were mesmerised to see an apparition, a gilded, ghostly outline in human form, heavenly and serene, conversing with her. The whole scene was lit by a golden glow that seemed to come from the 'other side'. Its mellow ambience blended the pillars, vaulted ceilings and masonry walls in extraordinary pastel shades with umbral shadows thrown heightening the drama: a spectacle Beatrice and I will remember all our lives. In this blessed building, we felt the sure presence of something wonderful, hearing a beautiful choir of female voices, softly, harmoniously, as if serenading the conclave of the prioress and the manifestation. Then, abruptly the apparition disappeared, and all returned to normal, and we scurried away, lest the Mother Superior should discover us.

"The next morning, you and your companions descended upon us. Not long after your departure, she unaccountably fell ill and sent for you. I feel it deeply that her demise is preordained, somehow linked to your presence here tonight."

What the sorority and the prince did not know: Eustacia de Sumeri's commitment to Hildebrand had come to an end, called away from the land of the living to higher echelons.

The years passed; the young man grew to be an accomplished knight, his adventures came and went, becoming a seasoned warrior and veteran of the Crusades – some say a virtual mercenary. Legends grew around his accomplishments as an undefeated fighter, enjoying prowess that was acclaimed throughout the known world. However, his dynastic considerations seemed not to concern him; many liaisons with favourite females Prince Hildebrand experienced, but to his eternal credit never consummated, unknowingly guided by an all-seeing eye.

It was late eventide; Hildebrand slumbered in his chambers at the castle fortress. On the stroke of midnight, the soldier turned thirty years of age, causing the silence to be disturbed when there came three loud bangs at the door. The prince, startled by the sound at such an unearthly hour, arose from his bed, donned a cloak, and carrying a lighted candlestick went over to unlock and open the door. He was taken aback to see in the faint light a tall man of foreign appearance standing there. Slavonic-looking, strongly resembling a Boyar; holding a staff in one hand, sporting a dark, ample beard; apparelled in clothes sympathetic of the region: conical hat encircled by fur at the rim, wearing a long caftan like coat nearly reaching the floor, heavily brocaded, edged in sable fur with large cuffs; but his exact facial features indistinct, ghostly in the dimness. The prince beckoned him to step into the room; the visitor bowed and advanced two paces, and exclaiming in a deep voice with a thick accent, introduced himself as Athanasi.

"Sir, I am instructed to give you this important message. Please give it your earnest attention," handing over a scroll to the edgy Hildebrand. The Englishman turned away, holding the roll of parchment closely, perusing it by the light of the candle he carried, noticing how the wax seal was impressed with a cypher unfamiliar to the knight.

Rotating it dextrously, curiosity aroused, the prince inquired of the mysterious individual, in a matter-of-fact way, "How have you arrived at my door without being challenged by the night guards?" Getting no reply, he looked up, and to his surprise, the mysterious individual had vanished. Darting to the doorway, he looked this way and that, along both passageways, but only emptiness and silence presented itself.

Hildebrand started to question his sanity. "How could anybody disappear so quickly? It is physically impossible!" The prince moved quickly along the passages and came upon a guard fast asleep, curled up in the corner. "Wake up! Wake up!" Hildebrand said, vigorously shaking the man's shoulder.

The guard stirred from his stupor, rose to his feet and apologised profusely, "Sire, I do not know what came over me, this has never happened before, I cannot understand it." Hildebrand, exasperated, dismissed his protests and excuses with a wave of the hand and carried on to search out the other guards, and likewise, he discovered them asleep at their posts, arousing them by prodding the soldiers with his foot. When interrogated, all blurted out apologetically that they had no recollection of any strange visitor passing them in the night! Mystified, shaking his head, the prince made his way back to his chambers, shutting and firmly bolting the door behind him, hoping not to be disturbed again.

He stood there, looking across at the scroll lying on the table, mulling over what to do. With a start, he went across and picked it up, unfurling the parchment and read its missive. A request from a monarch, by the name of Thorstein, appealed for Hildebrand's services as a bodyguard to the sovereign's daughter. The script detailed how another eleven knights, unique in their calling, had answered the summons and were making their way to his kingdom of Baltania. It was a destination unknown to the prince: a name that conjured infinite mystery. He noted, in the finality of the writing, how it explicitly mentioned the strength of the bodyguard would be twelve men strong but left the reader in no doubt that Hildebrand's acceptance would be assumed. The prince, puzzled by this, reflected on the sudden disappearance of the courier departing without formal acceptance or refusal. Staring into the darkness, a faraway look came into his eyes as the memory of his final encounter with Eustacia de Sumeri at White Ladies Priory came flooding back. The prognostication she had made all those years ago had come true.

Hildebrand slept fitfully for the remainder of the night as the agencies of the Creator played upon his subconscious mind, so that, in the morning, at first light he became resolved in his determination to be the protector of an unknown lady in a distant land. With a few cursory farewells, typical of his nature, and keeping his destination and reasons secret, he set off – to leave once again the shores of England, but this time never to return.

2

The Castle of Preben

This impregnable fortress of stone, atop an intimidating, unyielding escarp, dominated the surrounding hills. Because of its strategically important situation, it was the principal stronghold of King Thorstein, whose secondary seat at Yrian lay many leagues north-east. A forbidding edifice, its four massive central towers soared above a chapel and the royal apartments. From the ground floor rose a magnificent great hall and a well-stocked armoury, sizeable barracks, ample kitchens; while outside a vast courtyard extended, abuzz with clamorous activity. This area contained granaries, a smithy, and stables – all adjacent to the perimeter walls, with access to delightful gardens; the pleasure grounds of the nobility.

The stronghold's crenellated curtain was of considerable thickness, with mighty, flanking drum towers. The main entrance, over a drawbridge, spanned a defensive ditch, hewn out of solid rock, leading to a portcullis in an imposing twin-turreted gatehouse.

A steeply sloping road descended to a busy, expanding village, at the centre of which was an impressive timber church; here thrived a community which had grown out of the influx of traders from undeveloped frontiers, taking advantage of the commercial opportunities the kingdom offered.

On the outskirts of the little town, the cultivated countryside gave way to the wilderness, the preserve of, amongst other creatures, aurochs, bears, bison, wild boar, elk, lynx, and wolves. In marked contrast to the tract of featureless forest lay a shimmering expanse of inland freshwater sea, the aquamarine jewel of Lake Eydis; and beyond, the broader prospect of distant icy crests of the Orn Mountains.

In this part of Europa, the monarch's realm had come to define the march of Christianity, which for centuries had forged a path through lands of the infidels. Here, paganism was fighting to survive, to hold at bay religious forces bent on suppressing heathen veneration of the spirit of nature.

In Thorstein's kingdom, a change was in the air when the queen, proud mother of his seven sons, gave birth to a daughter: an unusual child, who, as she grew up, would become a legendary figurehead of exceptional beauty, wisdom, and gentleness. Her presence would help lighten the weighty shadow of Preben's forbidding fortress, and instil into its people feelings of benevolence and courage. The princess would vigorously oppose one of the tenets of Romano-Christian doctrine – that humankind was the culmination of existence, for she judged it to be only part of a circle, expressing her abiding love of all living creatures. Even hostile tribes of the region came to revere this remarkable woman.

Her name was Hellalyle, the Princess of Eydis and Orn.

3

The king enlists the service of twelve brave knights

Two crows flew side by side from Preben castle,
unerringly straight their path, as they crossed the terra firma.
With steady wing beats the pair pressed onwards,
league after league,
skimming the tallest trees,
bearing an urgent message to the spirits of the hinterland.

King Thorstein requested the presence of Queen Gudrun (his second wife), the Abbess Princess Amora (his sister), ministers, and representatives of the church.

Once they had gathered in the great hall, the king announced, "In the aftermath of the victorious, decisive battle in my territory bordering Kievan Russia, my presence is required there to settle pressing political matters. I will leave shortly, escorted by Prinz Paulus" – his stepson – "and a strong detachment of soldiers from the castle. I have been reliably informed, all my seven sons" – by his deceased first wife, and all knights – "have miraculously survived the military engagement. A message has been sent, ordering them to join forces with their father en route."

As the audience listened attentively to the king's exposition, he paused for a few moments, before exclaiming, "However, the safety of Princess Hellalyle" – younger sister to his sons and stepson –

"concerns me, given I will likely be absent for many months. After much deliberation, I have decided my daughter should remain at the castle, pending my return."

A ripple of voices was audible, as those present expressed alarm at his plan, considering the fortress would be inadequately defended, at a time of increased instability stemming from the war in the east. Everyone was aware parts of the kingdom had become vulnerable to incursions by marauding bands. One of his councillors, Erland, the chancellor, who stood out from the rest, resolutely raising his arm to catch the king's attention, was invited to speak by the king.

"Your Majesty, I cannot praise your daughter enough – we hold her in the highest esteem. Some might regard her as a young, inexperienced woman; yet far and wide, people had become susceptible to her beauty and intelligence. In the event of her engagement to a foreigner of royal blood, the loyalty and devotion she inspires in the monarch's subjects would prove advantageous as it would surely be replicated in the kingdom of her betrothed. I respectfully request you do not put her at risk in this way."

Hellalyle's aunt, Princess Amora, interceded, lending weight to these sentiments, saying, "May I remind my brother, the princess, very shortly after her mother's death, had willingly accepted, and fulfilled, all the duties befitting a queen, in addition to supporting her brothers, displaying maturity and responsibility beyond her years. Why! Even His Majesty's own advisors on occasion, chose to seek her advice in difficult negotiations, grievances at court, for her very presence would soften the hearts of men, ward off ill will, on the strength of her good nature."

When Amora had expressed her views, Abbot Jurian, the authoritative cleric, took the opportunity to voice his impressions of the princess. He was a tall man, height accentuated by the mitre on his head, and with an impressive crozier in his right hand, he presented a commanding figure. With a booming voice, he addressed not only the king but all the assembled, saying, "Hellalyle possesses, in addition to gifts already mentioned, many other remarkable

King Thorstein

qualities, elevating her above ordinary human beings. She retains a purity of spirit, and emotional serenity – even the wild creatures of the natural world instinctively respond to her as if accepting her into their domain. Your abbot knows, for I have seen it with my own eyes. I humbly beg the king to ensure his incomparable daughter is not put at risk during his absence."

Signalling the assembly to be silent, Thorstein, summoning his authority and reserve, declared, "Do not concern yourselves, this matter I have given considerable thought. In the interest of Hellalyle's safety and wellbeing, I have recruited twelve of the finest knights in Christendom, and their sole task will be to protect the princess from danger during my time abroad. Even as I speak, these warriors are traversing the land, closing in on this fortress."

While the king tried to concentrate the minds of his audience on the significance of his announcement, his thoughts strayed following the course of these courageous warriors, riding towards Preben, as if their arrival would alleviate his anxiety and bring about Hellalyle's salvation. The abbot, trying to disguise his misgivings, spontaneously raised his eyes to heaven, praying that Thorstein had made the right decision.

The meeting at an end, the king stepped down from the rostrum, and on his way out from the hall asked the abbot to accompany him to the monarch's private quarters. On entering, the servants and retainers were commanded to leave. Now on their own, Thorstein said to Jurian, "Please be seated," while the monarch remained standing looking out through a window.

The abbot, sixty years of age, with piercing green eyes set in a long, kindly face cleanly shaven, gazed studiously at the monarch, curious of what the king was about to say. This respected man of the cloth was possessed of a high forehead emphasising his acute intelligence, atop tonsured grey hair. The trim frame of the cleric when seated in the king's chair, the drapery of his cassock, presented an all too familiar image to those painted by the venerated Matthew Paris, official chronicler to the Abbey of St Albans in England. It is suspected by many that when Paris created his acclaimed work, *The Chronica Maiora*, it contained oblique references to the Abbot of Sunniva, such was Jurian's legacy to the sciences and spiritual world. It gave rise to an extraordinary and intriguing theory: that pilgrims from Thorstein's kingdom, having crossed Europa, must have visited St Albans, imparting knowledge to the recorder, Paris.

After a moment of uncomfortable silence, Thorstein started to speak with a slightly tremulous voice, indicating high emotion, "My learned abbot, what I am about to say must not go beyond these four walls…earlier, I detected your ambivalence to my plans for the protection of Hellalyle in my absence. People would think I am of unsound mind if I told of how I came to choose my daughter's bodyguards." There was a long pause. "For it was on a morning, a short time ago, when alone at prayer in the chapel I had the most unforgettable experience. There came, what I can only describe as, a strange presence borne on the wind, which blew forcibly through the windows and beneath the door. It brought the faint sounds of the multitudinous voices of women singing in the most beautiful harmony as if heaven itself was serenading me."

This revelation from the king caused the astounded abbot to cross himself in deference to the Almighty.

Thorstein continued, "Its bearing surrendered up to me the names of twelve knights, and so compelling was its influence, I knew then the soldiers were destined by Providence to be the protectors of my daughter. Many times, I have wondered, how Hellalyle – although my offspring – sometimes gives the impression she is not of this world, but from another sphere, somewhere special, and the visitation I received lends credence to these suspicions. It also pleases me that one of them is a knight of royal blood, a prince of England."

"What is the prince's name?" Jurian enquired in a hushed tone.

"It is Hildebrand," came the reply.

The appellation caused the abbot to abruptly rise from his seat in alarm, exclaiming, "Hildebrand? Hildebrand? I have heard of this man. Word has it, he is the most acclaimed fighter there has ever been, but also totally ruthless, and I also know of him to be a mercenary, and no doubt the other bodyguards of Hellalyle will be. Your Majesty, are you sure what you experienced was not a warning? I say this, because mercenaries cannot be trusted. If these twelve men were to renege on their contract with you and decide to go on a rampage, they would leave a trail of destruction. With respect, sire, to imagine your daughter being shadowed from dawn till dusk by this man, Hildebrand, leaves me in a state of unease."

"Fear not, I know what I heard. Your concern is misplaced," the king assuredly replied.

4

Hildebrand travels to Castle Preben by way of a great lake

Summoned by Thorstein, Hildebrand, a knight adventurer, made the long and arduous journey to Preben; there to meet the king and the eleven warriors he had enlisted from the length and breadth of Europa, to serve and protect his beloved daughter. Astride his mighty warhorse, the dauntless figure of Hildebrand was reduced to an insignificant dot, such was the vastness of the land, from which, unknown to him, the creatures of the wild were keenly but secretively following his progress.

Far above, a flirtatious cupid peeped from a mass of fleecy clouds, keeping a sportive eye on the horseman. On observing the knight's impenetrable armour, he resisted firing a golden arrow from his unerring bow before vanishing into the empyrean. The winged youth had been sent to ignite in Hildebrand an inescapable yearning – for love, both human and divine. His unfulfilled mission would now fall to another messenger from a hidden world beyond mortal existence.

The warrior, a prince of England, thirty years of age, and of aristocratic bearing, stood six feet three inches tall, fit, muscular, with powerful shoulders, blond locks and a broad, high forehead. Wide-set eyes, icy blue, emitted an intense expression. His jaw was square, with firm mouth and full lips, his manner determined; his unique voice compelling, mellifluous, resonant. The knight's resolute features were marked by the vicissitudes of war, and he was unmistakably recognisable as a doughty soldier, a master planner. It remained a mystery why he left his homeland; rumour had it he had been anxious to test his revolutionary military tactics on the broader expanse of a foreign battlefield – the countering of flexible command structures within formations of massed cavalry; a bold strategy, ahead of its time. However, was it just coincidence? For such an army was due to wreak havoc throughout Asia and beyond!

A born leader, strong-willed but principled, he was believed to be a direct descendant of the ruthless, warlike Sweyn Forkbeard, the despot who had ravaged vast swathes of England in revenge for the massacre of the Danes on St Brice's night, over two centuries earlier – his mysterious ancestry was confirmed by heraldic devices on shield and surcoat, depicting a Danish axe above three golden lions.

His journey that day eventually led him along the edge of a vast body of water, named Eydis, sparkling azure-blue in brilliant sunlight. Awestruck by the picturesque setting, he decided to break his journey by the banks of the lake for refreshment and rest. Gazing at the glittering expanse, Hildebrand marvelled at a magnificent panorama, and, inspired to stay longer, lay down, his arms folded behind his head. Dozing in warm sunshine, he was soothed by the gentle lapping of wavelets brushing the shoreline. Closing his eyes, he mused on the nature of his assignment and began to conjure images of the princess's physical appearance. Would she turn out to be some plump, cosseted, and characterless young girl?

During his reverie, he was unaware of being observed, offshore, by a mysterious woman swimming in the lake, her head immersed, then visible above the surface. All at once he froze, startled by the eerie, hypnotic sound of her voice, appearing to summon him, incessantly chanting his name across the water.

"Hildebrand, Hildebrand, come to me, Hildebrand..."

The knight felt as if his body had been jerked bolt upright, at the vision of a seductively attractive woman wading waist-deep through

Hildebrand

the eddies, her supple figure enhanced by the soaked gossamer dress she wore, the matted mane of her long chestnut hair clinging to her shapely back and shoulders. As her haunting figure beckoned him, he narrowed his eyes to gaze again at her outstretched arms enticing him to move ever closer. Powerless to resist her alluring smile, the spellbound Hildebrand stumbled into the shallows, inescapably drawn towards the temptress waiting to embrace him.

At that moment, thundering hooves in the distance heralded the arrival of another body of knights, a band of warriors riding at speed, also travelling in the direction of Castle Preben. The deafening noise served to distract Hildebrand, breaking the siren's magnetic power over him to such a degree that with a tormented cry of utter despair she plunged beneath the waves, vanishing from sight.

If Hildebrand had been unnerved by this unearthly encounter, he did not show it when he heartily greeted his comrades – the other enlisted bodyguards, who only casually dropped a hint they might have witnessed a mysterious figure as they approached the lake. Glancing at each other and shaking their heads, they reacted as though he were playing a joke, and to humour him one of the knights said, "We must have glimpsed the spray from a diving catfish."

However, this spectral encounter at Lake Eydis still preyed on him, until his peace of mind would renew in the presence of a remarkable princess.

5

The bodyguards' first glimpse of the princess

All the knights – save one – reached Castle Preben late morning for an audience next day with the king. They were intrigued to learn that the monarch would be leading a procession from the castle to the church and that the king's daughter would be present.

Determined to catch sight of the woman they had been engaged to protect, they set out on foot to survey the ceremony, but on reaching the portcullis were startled to see a warrior on horseback, clattering across the drawbridge. Aggressively turning about, the rider blocked their passage, straddling the gateway with his charger. They noticed the face of this giant, intimidating man to be partially obscured by a cloth, his one visible eye glaring at them fiercely and defiantly. Hildebrand alone recognised the figure as his friend, the Teutonic Knight, the twelfth bodyguard Karl von Altenburg.

When he dismounted, he was greeted enthusiastically by the Prince of England, "May I introduce, Karl von Altenburg, the protector of the Emperor Barbarossa. It has been my privilege to have served with this imposing fellow. Although he was struck dumb by an opponent's sword, there is no better man to have with us, fighting at our side."

The Teutonic warrior, standing head and shoulders above them, grasped the hand of each knight in his mailed fist, vigorously shaking a greeting, prompting one of them to reply on behalf of the others, "It is an honour, von Altenburg, to have you as our comrade-in-arms."

The strength of his handshake could not but give the impression of exceptional power. The knights waited while he stabled his horse before moving on in search of a suitable vantage point from which to view the parade, already hemmed in by a clamouring crowd. The towering, outlandish figure of von Altenburg caused some people to step back in fear and move away.

It was noticeable to Hildebrand the ethnic makeup of the crowd: predominantly Scandinavian, Germanic, and Slavic, but there were also Turkic types, and lesser still others of the Mongoloid race.

On the king's arrival, the crowd's excitement swelled to a crescendo, as the eager multitude duly applauded Thorstein's entourage – including Queen Gudrun but, noticeably, not Prinz Paulus – advancing in stately fashion towards the imposing timber church. Now, the acclamation of the throng quietened as the hooded figure of a young noblewoman was spotted, and the refrain of the name *Hellalyle* was audible above the hush. The twelve knights, who were keenly awaiting her arrival, craned to catch a glimpse of her.

Even though they could not see her face, they were conscious of an intense stillness, an aura of profound reverence, heightened by the expressions of the onlookers pervading the scene as she passed. Some stretched out their arms, trying to touch the hem of the princess's cloak, while others, overcome with emotion, eagerly pushed their children forward to be closer to her presence. The princess appeared to speak to them, but her words were drowned by the excitement it caused.

Once she had entered the church, the knights, returning to the castle animated by her fleeting appearance, exchanged their impressions. One of them was heard to say, "Well, what a surprise that was. Never for one moment did I assume we would be a bodyguard to such a figure, and what a woman she appears to be! From what we have been able to see of her, Aphrodite could not do her justice."

Karl von Altenburg, Teutonic Knight

Hildebrand, in a more pensive mood, reflected on the profoundly affecting character of a woman whom the king's subjects venerated as if she were a divine personage, and said, "Let us not be hasty, reserve our judgement until we meet her. I am sure there is no woman on earth who could be that sublime."

During that afternoon, the twelve guards familiarised themselves with the layout of the castle. As they moved towards the stables, they saw what they thought was the same young noblewoman they witnessed in the parade earlier, standing with her back to them, in conversation with a blacksmith. Unaware of being watched, she chatted briefly (the knights were unable to hear what she was saying) until the farrier, accompanied by a stable lad, led a frisky, wild-eyed, but handsome stallion from its stall. A towering destrier of seventeen-and-a-half hands; golden-brown, deep-chested, of muscular build, with an eye-catching, sturdy frame. It had been fitted out with an unusual saddle the knights had not come across before, featuring what seemed to be an extra pommel, an altered seat, and, surprisingly, a single stirrup. How an equestrian could use this accoutrement and control a horse puzzled them, but their curiosity was satisfied by the unfamiliar spectacle of the woman they were observing, confidently preparing to mount the potent steed. It astonished them that she was disposed to ride such a combative, unpredictable animal – a warhorse more suited to a knight in armour, trained to bite and kick out in battle. Incredibly, responding to her charismatic influence, the mighty creature became docile, as relaxed as a contented foal in the presence of its mother.

The intriguing way in which she came to acquire this singular saddle, believed to be of Eurasian origin, is worthy of explanation...

Several years before, an equestrian traveller from East-Central Asia arrived unexpectedly at Castle Preben, having trekked across continents from the foothills of the Sayan Mountains, then across the Mongolian plains and over the Altai, leading a pack-horse, which, like the animal he chose to ride, was of small frame, but hardy, characteristic of the wild herds of its native region. The stranger had brought with him a saddle of unique design and craftsmanship, which he zealously guarded as if entrusted with a precious object. No one could understand the purpose of his visit, for he gabbled in a foreign tongue, smiling inanely, even laughing deliriously in a melodramatic manner, as a man possessed.

A mass of people had gathered around this eccentric figure, and in the confusion that ensued, the king summoned a young princess, who he thought might be able to throw some light on this strange character's unexpected appearance.

There followed an extraordinary incident, in which the stranger, setting eyes on the princess for the first time, prostrated himself at her feet in a rapture of adulation, as if in the presence of a holy leader. At first taken aback by his reaction, then regaining her composure, she courteously assisted the man to his feet. He responded to her kindness with many exaggerated bows, babbling excitedly. All at once, a gust of wind drove a small, spinning column of dust across open ground, propelling it in her direction and brushing the skin beneath her raiment. She raised her hands instinctively to protect her face, until, as abruptly as it sprang up, the turbulence inexplicably stilled.

The startled onlookers were not aware, during this freak of nature, that the young woman had experienced sensations of paranormal energy pulsing through her, investing her with increased powers of understanding and a feeling of inexpressible fulfilment, changing her life forever. Speechless with astonishment, the crowd now witnessed her engaging the strange fellow in conversation, speaking fluently to him in his native tongue, the Mator language; utterances that to the throng sounded more like gibberish.

The king and his sons looked on in wonderment, proud of her intellectual skill and her remarkable, persuasive gift of communication. At the culmination of this bizarre spectacle, the foreigner, in a flamboyant gesture of homage, effusively presented the princess with his prized saddle. Deeply touched, she drew him aside to offer refreshment. Away from the public eye, he used the opportunity to disclose the purpose of his visit.

She learned that the saddle, so skilfully crafted in supple leather, had long ago been the dedicated achievement of the most accomplished horsemen of the Altai; yet, surprisingly to her, the workmanship looked brand new as if it had been made yesterday. These superstitious nomads came under the influence of spectral forces, known to them as the Ghosts of the Steppes, bearing orders to the riders of the plains to conceive a new style of saddle: one suitable for a lady of royal birth, yet unborn, to ride with dignity and in comfort. For one day, she would have to travel alone into the wilderness and become the "bridge" between two worlds.

Fearful of the implacable phantoms, the craftsmen fulfilled their instructions, leaving the finished artefact at a designated spot by the wild headwaters of the Ishim river. That very night, the saddle vanished without a trace, invisibly removed from the river bank by the apparitions, who then, from the summit of Mount Sutai, unleashed a storm of such violence that it swept everyone away. Any witnesses to the unfolding unearthly happenings were eliminated.

An entire tribe rendered extinct.

Enthralled by this fascinating narrative, the princess still wondered how the stranger had come by the saddle, and why he was so sure she was the character he referred to in the story. Having reflected deeply on everything she had seen and heard, she vowed not to divulge the secret to any living person.

The enigmatic wanderer devoted a single day to instructing the princess how to ride her mount on a twin-pommelled seat, until, confident she was proficient in its use, he took his leave, avoiding attention by stealing away from the castle at nightfall, never to return.

The burly shoeing-smith, standing at the horse's head, held the bridle while the stable lad gripped a lock of the mane and handed the reins to the rider. Cupping his hands, he helped her into the seat, and although unseen because of her dress, she hooked one leg around the upright pommel, the other raised up against the lower horn, and placed a foot in the single stirrup. In that position, she was seated *aside* her mount – conspicuously unspurred.

Horse and rider set off, making their way at a walking pace, in the direction of the main gate of the fortress. Drawing alongside the knights, who were looking up at her, she smiled politely, acknowledging them with a slight tilt of the head, and murmured the words, "Good day, gentlemen," which prompted all the soldiers to reply in unison "Good day, madam."

What with her coming so close, they were momentarily transfixed, and at the same time, overawed that she should have spoken to them. As the horsewoman passed by in a dignified fashion, she was seen to be carrying a large bag over her shoulder, and with a mantle serving to conceal part of her face, the knights were intrigued as to her identity.

As she crossed the spacious courtyard, the knights marvelled at her accomplished horsemanship, equestrian skills that coordinated with the destrier's measured tread, her free arm held loosely at her side. Her bridle hand did not move across her front, but through the action of the wrist, her arm from the shoulder a continuous spring, responding to the motion of the horse's head, slipping backward and forward as the creature proceeded.

As she drew closer to the twin towers, a group of the king's cavalry appeared, ready to escort her. The riders left the castle, traversing the sward towards the Wildwood, leaving the knights with a compelling impression of having been, if but briefly, in the company of the king's daughter, the princess, whom they would soon have to pledge their life and honour to defend. As for Hildebrand, he found it impossible to rest that night, such was his state of expectancy at the prospect of being formally introduced to her.

6

Hildebrand's trial of strength

On the second day, awaiting the king's call, Hildebrand was in a contemplative mood, with time on his hands. Strangely motivated to explore some of this unknown country, he set out, riding for some hours until he reached a bright, tumbling stream, where he dismounted for refreshment and rest. His tired mount, cooling itself in the rapid current, suddenly reared its head as if pricked by some paranormal force. It bolted and then galloped away out of sight. The knight looked bewildered, and shouting aloud with little purpose, tried to summon the creature back.

Having followed the horse's tracks, Hildebrand found himself in a wild place surrounded by cliffs, forming a natural amphitheatre. To his relief, he stumbled on his missing steed, swishing its tail, browsing peacefully on a single patch of lush, green grass. Baffled by the animal's capricious behaviour, but overcome with emotion at their reunion, he gently stroked its mane to reassure it of his presence.

Yet his relief would be short-lived. A warrior of superhuman stature and power came striding out of the woods, bearing down, hell-bent on attacking him. Chillingly, at a cursory glance, no head was visible under the giant's helmet, no eyes glinted through the slit of his visor. Hildebrand shouted out to the aggressor, "Identify yourself." But there came no answer, only the wielding of his sword as if to strike.

Forced to defend himself, Hildebrand retaliated fearlessly, with great bravery and skill. There ensued a violent gladiatorial struggle; a seeming fight to the death, the fierce clash of their heavy weapons reverberating through the gloomy chasm. The two combatants fought amain, neither soldier gaining the upper hand as the action continued relentlessly, hour after hour, until dusk fell.

Then, without warning, the supernatural assailant broke off the engagement, sheathed his sword, and, drawing back while ignoring his opponent's astonishment, appeared to favourably assess Hildebrand's superlative performance in armed combat, before mysteriously moving away and disappearing into the fading light. The knight was left standing alone, confounded but still defiant.

Meanwhile, not far away, unaffected by the savage encounter, the knight's untroubled steed contentedly cropped the verdant turf of an imaginary field, patiently awaiting his master's return.

Unknown to Hildebrand, the Spirits of the Wild, concealed high on a rocky ledge above the canyon, had been monitoring the extraordinary confrontation. They had summoned this phantom fighter – a Hyperborean – from the lands beyond the North Wind, to test the prince's mettle, needing to satisfy themselves of the unrivalled valour, prowess, and intrepidity of a knight they had elected to be Hellalyle's gallant and the heroic commander of her bodyguard.

7

The knights present themselves to King Thorstein at the castle

The assembled knights had selected the English prince, Hildebrand, as their leader and spokesman. Knowing that the sovereign had already singled out one of the warriors, an imposing individual whose face was obscured but for one eye, Hildebrand requested an audience with the king.

In a small chamber near the great hall, Hildebrand explained how this knight, Karl von Altenburg, came to bear such a savage facial wound.

"Your Majesty, it was inflicted by a two-handed broadsword, causing such a devastating injury that most of his features were sheared away – yet as if by some divine intervention, he had survived. However, the Teutonic soldier lost the power of speech through his disfigurement, which is so unsightly it repelled all those with the misfortune to catch sight of it. The warrior will not expose his face, unable to endure the public revulsion his lacerated countenance might cause.

"I, Hildebrand alone, have seen von Altenburg's horrific wound, for we had fought side by side at the siege of Constantinople, where the two Varangian defenders who had just butchered the German had been on the point of dispatching him. Until I intervened, killing both adversaries and sparing the injured knight from certain death."

However, the king was resolute, insisting that he needed to scrutinise any soldier offering his services to be a guardian of his daughter. As a concession, though, he would interview this knight in private.

Hildebrand took von Altenburg to one side to confide Thorstein's demands, "Karl, I am so sorry, but the king is adamant that you must agree to his request and expose your face if you want to serve him."

The tragic figure baulked at this obligation, turning away from Hildebrand in a fit of despair. Leaning against a stone wall, he shook his bowed head in the defiant expression of refusal.

The other knights rallied to their comrade in support of him in his ordeal. After some persuasion, von Altenburg accepted the king's condition resignedly, and, encouraged by his friends, made his way to an anteroom.

Meanwhile, Thorstein, accompanied by Hildebrand, followed the line of the ten warriors, each bowing to the sovereign before he engaged them. After the monarch had inspected the last soldier, he and Hildebrand approached the room where von Altenburg was standing.

A slender shaft of light from a small window high on the stone wall disclosed the centre of this chamber, and around it, all was in semi-darkness. Thorstein stood before the giant figure of the Teutonic Knight, who had tried to conceal himself in the shadows. The soldier cautiously removed his mask as the king spotted his vague outline through the gloom, squinting to survey the warrior more closely.

The monarch's features visibly stiffened when he caught sight of the man's gruesome lesion, while Hildebrand merely stared down at the floor. In undisguised horror, Thorstein half turned and then dismissed the German, who, concealing his face once more, hastily re-joined his comrades. The king, in a state of shock, gazed up at the window. Then, in a distressed tone – just about audible to Hildebrand – he exclaimed, "How can one imagine the despair and frustration of a man forced to hide his face from his fellows?

Denied the pleasure of a woman's attention, the comforting touch of her hand, through an inability to respond naturally to the regular intercourse of daily life? Human kinship severed, at a single blow, by the savage cut from a two-handed sword! What is God's purpose in condemning this unfortunate man to endure life bearing such a terrible injury?"

Hildebrand respectfully urged Thorstein to look on von Altenburg as a knight of honour and a formidable warrior, appealing to him thus:

"Only the faithful companionship of his fellow knights would inspire in him stronger purpose and the will to live. Now, rest assured that he will serve Your Majesty faithfully, and disguise his disfigurement from the king's daughter."

After a moment's reflection, the king replied, "I do not doubt the loyalty of these men, but please bear in mind that the needy and unfortunate have always been at the forefront of my daughter's concern. Why, even now she has conjured some idealistic scheme in her innocent way, with my sister Amora. It is their ardent wish to establish an infirmary for lepers! God knows what she will think of next? There are rumours that the princess even cares for the wild creatures in my kingdom. Perhaps one day her bodyguard might find proof of this – and what a discovery that will be! You, twelve courageous warriors, will be guarding her, and she, in turn, will care for you all. The sore affliction of your friend will concern her deeply, and from her sympathy and reassurance, he is bound to derive much comfort.

"Her bodyguard will quickly discover that she has the most appealing and innocent nature, but keenly intelligent and erudite, so, I warn you not to try to outwit or take advantage of her, as you will be left floundering. The intellect that she possesses is beyond her father's understanding. From what superhuman source she has gleaned this prodigious gift remains a mystery."

Thorstein stroked his beard reflectively and continued.

"My daughter was only a girl when she lost her mother, Queen Rigmar, in a tragic accident during a visit to the castle armoury. One of the guards had carelessly left a loaded crossbow unattended.

It accidentally fell to the floor, its ricocheting quarrel piercing the Queen's head and killing her instantaneously. Such was the unfortunate demise of this endearing figure, daughter of King Magnus of Norway and his spouse Estrid Byrdasvend.

"The princess, now in her mother's place, has become indispensable to her father and her brothers, who value her guidance in all matters. Everyone in my kingdom loves her dearly, and it would be difficult to imagine life in her absence. You will notice that my daughter, when meeting strangers for the first time, always covers her head – the reason for this will shortly become apparent, as you shall see.

"There is one more thing…you might have already noticed how my stepson, Prinz Paulus, shows a marked antipathy towards my daughter. It has not always been so. Why this has started, so near to my departure, is a mystery, but it is now so worrying I am compelled to take Paulus with me. I need Hellalyle to be free of distractions, to assist in the running of my kingdom from this castle."

Hildebrand, thoroughly intrigued by these tales of the extraordinary young woman he had yet to encounter, heartily congratulated the king on being her father, but Thorstein had heard many such plaudits before and did not respond, merely saying, "Let us enter the hall, where I shall invite Princess Hellalyle to meet her bodyguards."

8

Princess Hellalyle meets her protectors for the first time

From an imposing stone doorway at the end of the great hall emerged a slender young woman of medium height, accompanied by a lady-in-waiting. The face of the princess was part-hidden beneath the hood of a dark-blue cloak of luxurious velvet edged with a brocade of gold, silver and silk, superlative English needlecraft of *opus anglicanum*, the most accomplished in Christendom. This unrivalled craftsmanship achieved the acme of artistry; iconographic images worked on the front and back of the garment depicting creatures of the Wildwood, intricately entwined in foliage; garnets and pearls delicately threaded into the pattern. Because Hellalyle's brothers had commissioned this special gift to their sister, she had felt it appropriate to wear it on this auspicious occasion.

As she approached, her garment unfastened, the eyes of the soldiers became drawn to her distinctive attire. A crimson, long-line dress, with a decorative belt to gird the waist, the drape of the gown hugging and enhancing her bewitching figure. In the presence of her bodyguards, she lifted the hood, revealing no wimple or coronet on her head – only her flaxen plaits, gleaming like precious metal. Around her graceful, smooth, swan-like neck hung a simple silver chain, with an elegant sapphire-mounted pendant, a jewel to complement the azure hue of her sparkling eyes.

The princess, blessed with a flawless Scandinavian complexion, her countenance so faultlessly conceived, attained the very zenith of female perfection – a young woman of incomparable beauty.

To capture her image for future generations, the king had commissioned a portrait from the sovereign master, Dyonisius of Sicily, a revolutionary artist who had severed the matrix of the stylised convention of Byzantine practice by introducing an extraordinary degree of naturalism and perspective.

However, the maestro discovered that the longer he studied the sitter, the more perplexed he grew, unable to come to terms with a strange spiritual quality radiating from her face, affecting him like a hallucinatory dream. For the first time in his vocation, he admitted defeat, finding himself incapable of capturing the mien of this extraordinary young woman seated innocently before his easel. Despairing of his inadequacy, he abandoned the commission as initially conceived, and, of his volition, altered the composition of the portrait to that of a lady, whose features, obscured by her robe, were captured reclining in a woodland setting by the shores of a great lake.

The artist, on returning home to his Mediterranean island, never recovered from this experience, and renounced his work. The image of the princess would haunt him for the rest of his days, and his reputation declined, eclipsed by the art of Cimabue and Giotto.

King Thorstein, hugely disappointed, used the picture as a study for a cartoon, from which a sumptuous tapestry was woven and displayed in the great hall. This hanging would come to intrigue the viewer, for it depicted the story of an esoteric woman in a magical landscape, yet its narrative appeared somehow incomplete. Dyonisius had unwittingly created a sibylline masterpiece, both mysterious and prophetic.

When the soldiers first caught sight of the physical features of this woman whom they were under orders to protect, they became struck by her elegance and charm. They tried, as discreetly as possible, to spruce their appearance as they lined up for review.

The king motioned his daughter, accompanied by her lady-in-waiting, to inspect the assembled knights. The warriors were to declare themselves and salute the princess, who was keen to observe each soldier in turn, but at close quarters some looked apprehensive, sensing an inexplicable aura about her.

The first knight to present himself was Frederick Schtauffen, claiming descent from Arminius, leader of the German tribes who had defeated the Roman Army at the Battle of the Teutoberger Forest. Then followed Nienhault von Streitz, apparently descended from Ardaric, King of the Gepids, scourge of the Huns at the Battle of Nedao.

Thirdly, William de Chartres, allegedly descended from Charles Martel, leader of the Franks; victorious at the Battle of Tours. Then Phillip Guiscard, scion of the Norman, Robert Guiscard, who had conquered Southern Italy and parts of Sicily, and had distinguished himself at Civitate. After him came William de Bures, a descendant of Count Roland, Charlemagne's most accomplished warrior.

Uggi Bergfalk was next, the direct descendant of the fierce Haakon Bergfalk, senior bodyguard to Rurik, founder of the Rurik dynasty; rulers of Kievan Rus. There followed Heinrick von Tieffen, a descendant of Arnulf, Charlemagne's bodyguard; and then Richard de Chartres, descended from Raymond, Count of Toulouse, leader of the first Crusade.

Andre Grenier presented himself, a professed descendant of Eustace Grenier, Crusader Lord and conqueror of the Egyptian army at Yibneh. He was followed by Siefer von Reuss, claiming descent from Otto the Great, triumphant over the Magyars at Lechfeld.

As Hellalyle slowly moved along the line, the warriors were unable to take their eyes off her, transfixed by her magnetic presence. When the princess was about to approach a much taller and more imposing warrior, a Teutonic Knight of Herculean build and strength, she noticed his face partly hidden, and that he remained silent. Hildebrand, standing next to him, stepped forward to

Hellalyle

explain that this was Karl von Altenburg, once bodyguard to Kaiser Rotbart, Emperor Barbarossa, but had lost his power of speech after sustaining a severe injury in battle. This inscrutable character wore a stained cloth as a mask, obscuring his visage but for one eye. It gave him the disturbing appearance of a leper, which caused the encouraging smile of the princess to freeze momentarily.

Once she had overcome her initial shock, and the knight had saluted her, she moved closer. Looking up, she reassuringly whispered to him, so quietly that only he could make out her words:

"Rîter, vürhtet iuch niht vor mir." ("Knight, be not afraid of me.")

The giant warrior, overcome with emotion in the presence of this comely woman, was conscious of an intense feeling of liberation in reaction to her considerate and tenderly spoken words.

When Hellalyle reached the last knight, named Hildebrand, the English prince, she appeared to show no favour. She greeted him amiably, but as formally as she had treated his comrades.

Excepting Hildebrand, who was of mixed ancient British and Scandinavian origin, all the other soldiers displayed noticeable signs of Germanic and Nordic ancestry, bearing similar features. Their faces were long and narrow, their cheekbones indiscernible. One man showed characteristics of the Alpine race.

With skin tones rosy and fair, eyes of variant blue and grey, those of Scandinavian forebears tended to be stiff, slender, and erect. They moved with controlled strides, unruffled in temperament. The knights of Germanic stock were powerful, thickset, freely moving and self-possessed. The princess seemed pleased with the inspection, but for Runa, her lady-in-waiting, it had proved an unpleasant encounter; the burly soldiers gave the impression of being cold-blooded, pitiless and prone to violence. Each bore the scars of injuries in battle, their feelings hardened by the grim experience of military service. She had felt threatened by the presence of these men, with their savage and ruthless appearance, even, she imagined, heedless of the random slaughter of women and children. Finally, she recalled the sinister figure of the towering and grotesque Teutonic Knight, Karl von Altenburg.

While she was prepared to accept that these formidable fighters might be more accomplished than the king's soldiers, she shuddered at the thought of the innocent femininity and physical beauty of the princess set against this brutal, combative body of mercenaries.

Nevertheless, Hellalyle, with her distinctive, exceptional personality, warm-hearted and magnanimous, displayed such an instinctual perception of people that she had induced these knights into believing that all their problems had been lightened and resolved.

However, those gathered in the hall were unaware of the princess's confused state of mind. At that moment, she had divined an astonishing revelation concerning the bodyguards, who, excepting Hildebrand and von Altenburg, were not of the ancestry they claimed.

They were, instead, the very reincarnation of those illustrious figures from history, miraculously manifested to protect her.

Conscious that her father would not know their real origin, Hellalyle tried to grasp what mysterious forces were responsible for summoning these knights, and the reason for this inexplicable visitation. It comforted her that these warriors appeared unshakeable in their dedication to the chivalric code and the Peace of God, and with her acute discernment, she endeavoured to placate and reassure anyone who lived in fear of them, without revealing their actual identities.

As she prepared to leave, she paused and drew Hildebrand aside.

"My father informs me that you are the commander of my bodyguards, and their spokesman, so please bear in mind that I shall hold you personally responsible for their welfare. The appalling hideousness of that gruesome wound I witnessed haunts me, and there must be no recurrence of such appalling injuries. Tomorrow, I shall make plain my role and duty, your expectations of me, and what I require of my knights – to fulfil my father's wishes."

Hildebrand, confused by her equivocal manner, bowed to her request as she inclined her head, seeming to deflect his manifest unease. She delayed her departure from the hall to have words with her aunt, Princess Amora, and her stepmother, Queen Gudrun, attended by her ladies-in-waiting. Closely surrounded by these people, the twelve warriors' vision of the princess was obstructed, causing them to break rank. With Hildebrand's attention momentarily distracted, Hellalyle cast him a fleeting glance of appraisal.

When the soldiers had regrouped, they remained vigilant, watchful of the princess as she left, each reflecting deeply on his first encounter with this enigmatic luminary.

Runa, following Hellalyle out of the assembly, observed a miraculous subtle change had appeared in the embroidery of the princess's cloak. Images of knights were now clearly visible in the design. This magical alteration confounded her lady-in-waiting, and when she and Hellalyle later came to examine the clothing, to their astonishment, they saw the profiles of twelve warriors meticulously introduced into the artistic work.

9

The princess absents herself from court

Finally, the day came when King Thorstein, his stepson Prinz Paulus, and the entourage departed on their long journey to the east. The monarch planned to return in the second quarter of the following year. The responsibility for the security of the castle now lay with the deplete castle guard, the sheriff, and, primarily, Hellalyle's twelve knights.

In the first few days of the bodyguards' deployment, the princess showed her displeasure at the soldiers' close attention and appeared unwilling to cooperate. She always insisted on leading the party, sufficiently far in front as to escape the idle talk of the men.

The hooded princess, mounted side-saddle, cut a lonely and obscure figure, seemingly absorbed in a world that she cared not to share with others. When Hildebrand attempted to draw alongside her for a consultation she would show irritation, the princess's hand emerging from under her cloak and waving a finger from side to side, warning him to keep his distance. It gave the impression she was a prickly, insular individual, much to Hildebrand's dismay, and it set him wondering how long it would take to gain her confidence.

However, fortune rewarded the brave, for Hellalyle quickly warmed to these soldiers of war, and they eventually became a replacement for her absent brothers. The bodyguards in return came to realise that this extraordinary woman was not susceptible to man's empty flattery. The princess possessed not the slightest trace of feminine foibles, only interested in carrying out the essential responsibilities her birthright had bestowed on her – especially now she was virtually at the helm of the kingdom, steering it through calm waters in the king's absence.

The inspirational stories the soldiers had heard about her rang with echoes of truth when it became apparent to them how spiritually pure she was, possessing immense capabilities and imbued with a disposition of supreme kindness and understanding. Never once would the knights fail to be impressed by the genuine affection and respect the people showed in their greeting for Hellalyle as she rode by, and she in return acknowledged them with a simplicity of manner, her searching blue eyes critically surveying all before her.

One morning soon after the king left, Hellalyle inconspicuously absented herself from the royal court, declining to inform the bodyguards of her whereabouts. The knights, assuming she had not left the castle precinct, divided the force to reconnoitre its extensive and intricate layout. Hildebrand informed his comrades, "I am going to explore the garden. It's a plausible place to find her – from what we hear she has a passion for tending plants in her tranquil oasis."

The soldiers were told how the princess was not averse to getting dirty and dishevelled, assisting the labourers in various seasonal tasks, even resting in some sheltered corner to share lunch with them.

His quest to no avail, Hildebrand moved further afield, unaware he was followed by a tiny, observant songbird skipping from one vantage point to another.

The Englishman, intent on tracking her down, neared the blacksmith's forge where he detected strains of conversation above the routine noise of beaten metal. He caught the unmistakable voice of the woman he sought. On entering the workshop, he was stunned to see the princess, her features transformed in the fierce glow from a forge hearth. In such a striking contrast between light and dark, she might have been a figure in an allegorical painting. With the white linen bonnet of a servant woman partly concealing her golden locks, her sleeves rolled up, and a thick leather apron about her waist, she struggled to wield a heavy hammer, endeavouring to fashion a white-hot bar in the form of a horseshoe.

Mesmerised, he watched her face lit red in the glare, as softened metal gripped by a pair of long-handle tongues held in the swarthy fist of a muscular farrier, was rotated around the horn of an iron anvil while he bellowed stentorian instructions.

"Bend the centre to staple shape, now shape the ends of the bars to form the heels of the shoe." The metal was reinserted into the furnace, and at the critical temperature quickly removed, and the process continued. "Curve each of the staples to make each side of the shoe," he loudly commanded.

Then once again he thrust the shaped metal into the intense heat of the coals.

Nature had bestowed on Hellalyle a naturally compassionate quality, and a perfect form to match, but she was also cultivated, fluent in many languages, conversant with the sciences, and accomplished in music and dance. With innate curiosity about the ways of the world, she had always been keen to familiarise herself with the crafts and talents of her father's subjects, particularly regarding the art of a blacksmith's handiwork; she had made up her mind that the experience would help her gain insight into the daily struggles of the ordinary people.

With the king and her brothers away, Hellalyle had taken the opportunity to visit the forge, which her father insisted was out of bounds – he vehemently disapproved of any manual activity that might put her at risk of injury. The notion of his daughter sweating and toiling in a smithy, subjected to intense heat, acrid fumes, and the danger of flying red-hot scale disfiguring her flawless complexion, horrified him. Thorstein and his sons had implored her to abandon such rash ideas, but, while appearing to bow to their judgement, Hellalyle's heart remained set, determined to shoe one horse – at the very least.

What inspired her, beyond this noble animal's physical beauty, was its significance in the human world: the delight and exercise of riding, bearing soldiers to battle, transporting goods, facilitating the trade of every country. Now bent on fulfilling her ambition, she swore friends and associates to secrecy.

The remaining knights from the search party, reassembled with Hildebrand, were captivated by the unlikely spectacle of a comely, slender young woman at hard and hazardous labour, so unlike their impression of the gentle, discerning Hellalyle, admired for her dignity and intelligence, conversant with all the affairs of her father's kingdom.

The soldiers, preoccupied in their astonishment, had failed to notice the same little bird that had earlier trailed Hildebrand, perched on a rafter overhead. It keenly observed them, mysteriously influencing the singular events unfolding in the farriery.

The pretty apprentice feigned to disregard the blatant attention of the men around her, knowing if she blushed, her face smeared with smuts and grime would camouflage her bashfulness. Pluckily, she pursued her arduous work, forming the round edge of the horseshoe, and then once again the farrier speared the metal back into the burning charcoal. At the appropriate temperature, the farrier withdrew it and shouted:

"Now, quickly, using the stamp and pritchel I showed you, make the nail holes..."

After which, Hellalyle, exercising the uncanny power she seemed to hold over animals, induced a mighty warhorse tethered nearby to shift its enormous weight onto three legs, and voluntary raise its huge limb, to enable the princess to trim the hoof. The smith was amazed by this, as he had experienced flattened toes, broken bones in the legs and ribs, and the tip of a finger bitten off, all caused by these unpredictable creatures.

As she applied the heated metal, the creature seemed utterly at ease, reassured by her presence. Amidst clouds of smoke and the hiss of burning horn, she impressed it, allowing the shoe to form a perfect fit, to the smith's marked satisfaction. After a few deft strokes with a hammer and file, he handed the finished shoe to Hellalyle, commanding in a serious vein, "This, Princess, is the most crucial part, so listen to me carefully. I am now going to position the nails for you to hammer them in, for a spike driven in at the wrong angle could maim this horse for life, do you understand?"

Hellalyle, feeling inhibited to speak with all the men watching, nodded, and following the farrier's every word, turned her attention once more to the prominent destrier towering over her, and courageously swung the hammer, to safely secure the shoe to the animal's foot.

Her handiwork accomplished, the princess caught her breath, showing strong emotions of relief and satisfaction, blowing a curl of hair out of her eyes. Her instructor turned to the audience and triumphantly yanked his student's arm aloft, proud of her achievement.

There followed a spirit of light-hearted entertainment, as the knights watched with amusement the princess distractedly mopping the perspiration from her spattered brow with a filthy rag. With restrained clapping and murmurings of approval, the whole company gathered round her to warmly applaud her prowess and outstanding craftsmanship. Hellalyle, acknowledging their praise with an engaging, enigmatic smile, perceived this an opportune moment to engage her knights.

"My dear soldiers, do forgive me for keeping you in the dark about my appearance at the forge. I feared the innocent farrier would take the blame for collaborating, in what my father considers is a stupid, foolhardy action on my part."

The knights, however, seemed more concerned about her present physical state, Uggi Bergfalk in particular.

"Your Highness, for such fragile beauty to have accomplished what you have just done, is without parallel, but you could have seriously injured yourself, and then what would have become of us? We, twelve knights, have done nothing but talk of the good fortune that has brought us here, to be your guardians, so please be careful. Otherwise, your father will skin us alive."

Their disquiet touched her to the core, but putting on an

unruffled, stoical front, she replied, "Please do not worry on my behalf – we ladies are not as delicate as we appear, but I thank you for such kind words."

It was Hildebrand, tossing convention to the wind, who impulsively grasped her swollen wrists, "Let me see what damage you have done." Easing open the palms of her hands he said, "Now look at them: blotched, bruised and infested with raw blisters; if ever they burst…!"

The sudden sensation of Hildebrand's touch had a startling effect on her, like a lightning strike, causing her to break his hold self-consciously. Only their eyes connected fleetingly, as she turned briskly away from him. The knights, confounded by this curious contretemps, stood back, lost for words, but the imperturbable princess was quick to regain her characteristic composure and decorum, and quietly, but firmly, said, "Gentlemen, it is time to go, and I must return in secrecy to the privacy of my chambers." She gracefully donned the long, grey, hooded cloak she had brought with her, and calmly slipped away through the shadowy lee of the castle walls.

When the princess returned to her apartment, the tiny bird that had diligently followed Hildebrand and so patiently observed the scene at the smithy now alighted on her windowsill, about to fulfil its role as emissary of all the benevolent spirits of the natural world.

Runa, the lady-in-waiting, was quick to notice the dramatic change in Hellalyle's appearance. The princess, seeing Runa's open-mouthed stare, said, somewhat scornfully, "I have been shoeing a horse, slaving away at the forge – do I have to justify everything I do?" (she was angry with herself, reflecting on her rebuff of Hildebrand, realising his only concern was her physical wellbeing).

Immediately, she apologised, bringing a hand up to her furrowed brow, "I am so sorry Runa, I didn't mean that, please forgive me," and went on to explain what had happened.

When Runa learned what had been going on, the lady-in-waiting reproached Hellalyle for undertaking tasks unbecoming of a lady, particularly a princess. Holding a polished brass mirror to her mistress's face, she reprimanded Hellalyle, "How can you have displayed such undignified behaviour in front of Hildebrand?"

The princess was at a loss for words, looking almost ashamed. Now, it was Runa's turn to apologise abruptly, holding her fingers to her mouth as if doubting whatever had prompted her to make such remarks.

Runa, who was older than the princess, came of humble peasant stock – unconventional for one in the service of a noblewoman. She was the widow of a ploughman, who had died unexpectedly of an unknown illness. Disabled from a hip injury sustained years before, Runa was unfit to take on her late husband's hard labour, leaving her homeless, in a state of penury.

It chanced now that the king's daughter required a new lady-in-waiting, for her attendant – the woman who had once attended her mother, the queen – had passed away recently, and when the compassionate Hellalyle learned of Runa's desperate plight, she offered her the position. Runa became the princess's royal servant and confidant.

It is a story worth retelling: Runa's husband, with death beckoning, lay on their bed and with supreme effort, lifted an arm to reach out and softly caress the peach-like skin on the cheek of his wife, and with a gentle sigh breathed his last. Runa, weeping, desperate in her sorrow, bowed her head, holding his lifeless hand to her face. The childless woman, her movability compromised by a broken hip suffered years before, faced an uncertain future. Homelessness beckoned. The roof over her head, the humble dwelling of thatched roof and mud walls, likely to be taken away.

The day after her husband's untimely death, Runa valiantly attempted to carry on her husband's work ploughing the land, for to occupy the simple dwelling was inextricably linked to its occupants being able to work the ground. Lacking the strength of a man and severely hampered by lameness, she struggled interminably with the wooden plough, valiantly calling out encouragement and instructions to the pulling oxen. The forsaken peasant woman cut a sad image, stumbling along, intermittently falling in the muddy earth, as the draft animal, without the familiar command of a man's voice, went along in its monotonous drudgery, virtually dragging Runa along after it, leaving a crooked, uneven furrow scarring the soil. With no children to help her she had yet to sow the seed; the hopelessness of her situation stared her in the face: a future of penury – dispossessed of house and home.

Quite by chance, Princess Hellalyle, in the vicinity, seated high on her destrier warhorse, witnessed the scene. Signalling her father's escorting soldiers, she moved closer to observe better this unequal struggle between the weaker sex and the resistance of stubborn earth. Then, having seen enough, she prompted her steed to engage and present itself in front of the unfortunate woman.

Runa, catching sight of the king's daughter approaching, managed to pull up the obdurate oxen; an inspired setting then ensued: that of a comely princess, side-saddle on a knight's charger, imperiously looking down on a disabled, dispirited widow standing before the plough; the image of juxtaposition resplendent in the suffused amber light of a golden sun as the orb approached the horizon.

The peasant woman, not much older than the princess – conscious of her dishevelled, threadbare appearance and embarrassed in the presence of the renowned, royal beauty – curtsied, avoiding eye contact with the female equestrian. The flustered Runa attempted to tidy her auburn hair and brush down her ragged clothes, such was the effect of Hellalyle's stare, but, especially, fearful of the discovery of no spouse to work the ground and maintain its productivity. However, it was obvious to the king's daughter that what the landed lady was attempting was beyond this unfortunate female's capabilities.

"Am I addressing the person known as Runa?" inquired the princess.

"Yes, that is correct, my lady," Runa nervously replied.

"Where on earth is your husband?" asked Hellalyle, before going on to say, "Surely it cannot be that he would leave his disabled wife to undertake such demanding work? You are of the gentler sex and heavy labour for one such as thee is not in thy remit."

A quavering voice responded, "My lady, my husband, Olaf, passed away two days ago; the Lord took him from me, and now I am alone, endeavouring to carry on his work lest I will be cast out," and broke down crying. The princess, in a compassionate vein, dismounted, let go of the reigns and led the tearful Runa from the field, her horse faithfully following, while instructing the soldiers to bring back the oxen and plough. As they did so, the king's men paused and watched, intrigued, as the royal princess went arm in arm with the wretched woman. As they strolled to Runa's lowly abode, the monarch's daughter chattered away with words of comfort, and retreating further away the two figures became silhouettes, mystical like, in the landscape. At that moment of visage, a small cloud passed in front of the solar disc, causing, momentarily, beams of bright light like lances to emanate forth, penetrating the sky from one horizon to the other, as if the heavens were celebrating the end of a taught melodrama played out on the earth below.

Once in Runa's simple dwelling, the two sat down to talk. Hellalyle broached the problematic subject of Runa's uncertain future.

Expressing her concern, she ventured, "Runa, it would be dishonest of me to allow you to carry on with your impossible task. Forgive me for saying so, but you are faced with the unattainable if you persist in living here with all the other responsibilities it holds."

Before the Princess could say more, Runa stood up and burst out sobbing, saying, "But what will become of me? I have the assistance of nobody – who will want to care for a cripple?" Hellalyle rose to comfort the distressed in a consoling embrace, as Runa sobbed on the princess's shoulder.

"Runa, you must not give up – all is not lost, for I have a proposal to put to you. Now please be calm, sit back down and listen to what I have to say." The peasant woman dabbed her eyes dry with the piece of coarse linen, gathered herself and with an attentive ear awaited the noblewoman's proposal. "Only a few days ago," said Hellalyle, "my lady-in-waiting died. Whom, if you did not know, previously attended my dear late mother. Her departure from this world means I am looking for a replacement. The person who takes up this post must, above everything else, avoid gossiping and keep their counsel." With a slight pause she continued, "I have learnt from reliable sources that you fall into this category, am I correct?"

Runa nodded, her mouth open in astonishment, covering it with both hands at what the princess was alluding to, only to exclaim despairingly, "I have not had the noble upbringing for such a position, my lady – knowing nothing of courtly matters and I can neither read nor write!"

"Do not concern yourself of such things," interjected Hellalyle. "With the Abbess Amora's permission, the nuns from the scriptorium at Thorbjorg monastery will teach you literacy, and I will induct you into the world of the royal court and its proceedings. Fear not, Princess Hellalyle will always be at your side, someone to turn to when you feel overwhelmed. You need not decide on my offer immediately, but think on it for two days, and do not concern yourself with the rigours of the plough – that is not for you."

The princess stood and prepared to depart. Runa – euphoric, overcome at the unbelievable offer from the princess – knelt before the king's daughter and kissed the royal hand, even holding the back of it to her face; reluctant to let go, so thankful of her saviour. Hellalyle smiled in sympathy, assisted Runa to her feet, and departed, with a passing comment that she would return in due course for an answer.

That night, outside, an uncommon silence reigned. No one could imagine the marvellous scene unfolding as two mysterious beings from Arcadia emerged out of the hinterland; one, a shadowy apparition in black, like some umbral figure in human form from a nameless part of a hidden kingdom. It took out the oxen and plough, and in ghostly deed tilled the land to completion – a feat that so defeated Runa. Following the phantom with the plough, the spectre of a sower, depositing the rye seed upon the freshly tilled earth from a basket that hung around the neck. Within the pervading darkness, the facial features of these two figures were indiscernible adding further eeriness to the supernatural event.

Hellalyle's intervention in Runa's plight had prompted benevolent spirits – those ever-present since the nascent beginnings of the universe, who, in secret to all, had watched over the noblewoman since a little girl – that now manifested the incorporeal to come to the widow's aid.

Abbot Jurian once saw them working together at harvest time, helping the labouring women gather ears of corn left in the stubble, a backbreaking, humbling task the princess would sometimes undertake. The monk, pondering the surprising scene of a pious, noble lady with her dutiful servant, toiling as gleaners in the field, casting long shadows in the evening sunlight, recalled the compelling Old Testament story of Ruth and her mother-in-law Naomi.

Runa prattled on artlessly as she prepared a soothing salve for Hellalyle's blistered hands. The princess, ignoring Runa's banter, gazed in wonder at her own delicate wrists. As she brushed the surface of the skin, she felt a strangely pleasing sensation at the very spot where the knight had touched her. Experiencing feelings of intense emotion, she was unaware that some preternatural power was at work, drawing her closer to the Prince of England.

The princess, entranced by this strange incident, became conscious of being watched. Glancing up, she saw the now familiar little bird staring fixedly at her from a window ledge. When Hellalyle responded with a gentle, quizzical gaze, the bird fluttered away.

In a meadow below the castle, where a knight's stallion quietly grazed, stood Hildebrand, a puzzled expression on his face. He flexed his fingers, examining the open palms of his hands, affected by intense feelings and sensations identical to those the princess experienced. He never noticed that same, mysterious bird – an ortolan, which had flown down to perch on the cantle of his horse's saddle, studying him intently. A few minutes later, as if satisfied its mission was complete, the winged messenger broke the silence, suddenly giving voice to the sweetest song imaginable, before it took off on a journey to deliver blessed tidings to the untamed inhabitants of the earth, the sea and the sky.

The presence of these knights was no coincidence, for an enigmatic spirit, bearing the names of twelve mercenaries, had sprung out of the primaeval wilderness. Moving invisibly, it breached the impregnable bastion of Preben. Once inside the castle walls, it seemed to infiltrate Thorstein's emotional state of mind to such effect that it persuaded the king to engage these very soldiers as his daughter's bodyguards. The phantom courier represented God's other kingdom on earth, that of nature, and they regarded the prodigious Hellalyle as their princess, even though she was unaware of it.

Acutely conscious that evil forces of the underworld were conspiring to kill her in the monarch's prolonged absence, they had chosen these superlative warriors to be the phalanx of her protection, singling out their leader Hildebrand to be her brave gallant. For they had also foreseen that the time would come when her father gave his daughter's hand in marriage to the eligible heir of a distant kingdom, and they would lose Hellalyle forever.

10

The bodyguards' disquiet over Prinz Paulus

With Hellalyle's stepbrother now absent, the bodyguards discussed Prinz Paulus's motive for showing such a pronounced aversion towards the delightful princess. They had particularly noticed his habit of never looking her in the face, as if from fear or repulsion. The knight William de Chartres, of the entire escort the most pious, and often mocked for his devoutness, caused some unease when he remarked, "The woman we are protecting appears to be of an almost saintly disposition, guileless and unworldly, in marked contrast to Paulus, who was but a trader from Ghenna."

Expanding his argument he said, "I believe there is a dark side to the prinz, hell-bent on thwarting Hellalyle's excellent work in her father's realm. This vexatious fellow might not be the only sinister force trying to obstruct the princess; there could be others from the underworld preparing to strike, in an unimaginably horrible way. Why, even her future offspring could be in danger, for these malevolent spirits will always try to ensure that she will be the last of her kin. We must all remain vigilant."

This revelation, if hard to credit, aroused suspicion all the same, but now the knight Uggi Bergfalk spoke:

"Thus far I have held my tongue, for had I spoken you would have scorned me. But, on hearing what our comrade has just divulged, I now feel able to reveal what has troubled me in recent days, even though I could scarcely believe what my eyes beheld. Do you remember when we escorted the princess to the Abbey of Sunniva, where, seated in a patch of wildflowers, she sketched the surrounding orchards? Well, when we were leaving, and the princess was strolling out of the meadow, I reached down to retrieve her cape and noticed that the plants had turned their stems and blooms in her direction – as if like the sun itself she was a source of natural energy. It is uncanny that she appears not to be aware of her extraordinary powers."

The knights regarded each other with a shared sense of uneasiness, but in wonderment as well. Some of them made the sign of the cross, believing that these revelations must hold divine significance.

Acutely shy and introverted, Paulus was ill at ease in the company of women. He would become embarrassed and tongue-tied whenever he caught sight of an attractive girl, and therefore, his peers would make fun of him. Because of this, the prinz harboured bitterness and resentment; his prospect of forming a lasting relationship was doomed from the beginning.

No one could have been aware of his clandestine flirtation with an attractive, dainty young lady, who dwelt in an unknown part of the wilderness. He kept this attachment close to his chest, for fear of further ridicule. Travelling through mountainous country, he was bewitched by this beautiful siren; the ardour and infatuation of his first romantic entanglement consumed him to such a degree he was prepared to endure hardship and inclement weather to reach her.

At the end of his journey, still preoccupied and oblivious to his surroundings, he would enter inhospitable, forested lowland, oddly devoid of living creatures. In dramatic contrast, far above, the skies would change to billowing cloudscapes, piled up to form vaporous silhouettes of hooded figures, transformed from a netherworld. Huge, ashen blankets hung like shrouds, tinged with glowing golden light, the crimson complexion of a dying sun low on the horizon. What struck the eye most – through a jagged break in the canopy –

was the remarkable sight of a giant ringed planet, tilted on its axis. At highest altitude, icy fibres of an unusually dark red discoloured the atmosphere, like stains of blood; yet no motion was discernible in that sinister, celestial sphere.

Down below lay dense woodlands, oppressively still, through which flowed a mysterious river fed by the persistent snows of the legendary Riphean Mountains. It was here that the prinz, seated on the decaying trunk of a fallen tree, would wait with his back to the water's edge, the intriguing setting of his strange assignations. In secret, his lover would rise, invisibly, from the silver eddies of the current. To his delight, she would creep up to tease him in seductive whispers, her long fingers playing over him in sensual caresses. She leaned over his shoulder, her soft cheek pressed against his, whispering enticingly, "My dearest Paulus, how I have yearned for your return, you occupy my dreams to the expense of all others, for without you I cannot live."

As her luscious red lips brushed his, she toyed with the locks of his hair, exciting his senses in the most carnal fashion.

Little did he know this temptress was the water sprite who had lured Hildebrand by the shores of Lake Eydis.

The prinz was besotted with her, blind to the threat this seductress posed for him in her masquerade of allure and feigned devotion. This malevolent femme fatale held Paulus in thrall, her cunning evil nature concealing a striking likeness she bore to that all too persuasive serpent, writhing in the undergrowth of Eden. How deviously she schemed to tear apart the frayed fabric of the prinz's vulnerable nature by exploiting the fact that he was no blood relation of Thorstein or his family. With her beguiling demeanour, a litany of falsehood was laid before the unfortunate man. "My darling, why do you accept the authority of Thorstein, for you are better than he, superior to his sons, and as for that daughter of his, take away her beauty, and there is nothing, a vacuous, shallow individual. She is the king's favourite, listening to her every word, her brothers defer to her manipulative nature. This woman holds the key to your future. Remove Hellalyle and the monarch's power crumbles, delivering to you his vast kingdom, for his sons will surrender to your authority, this I swear."

As she spoke, there was a stirring in the demonic sky, for the shroud-like clouds moved, and through a rent in their cover, the ghostly faces of Satan's disciples could be seen leering down upon Paulus.

The Prinz's features darkened, his eyes intense in their stare as he spoke. "Yes, yes, now I see it all, for you speak with knowledge that is the truth of the world. You have opened the door to an axiom hidden away, that the king and his family will never accept me as their equal. His daughter despises me for what I am, an outsider, not worthy to walk with her brethren in the corridors of power."

The seducer from the water, continued with her cajolery. "Don't you see," she said, "The inconsequential man that is Thorstein, administers his realm from the comfort and safety of his fortress, sending his sons into battle, while your father died a glorious and honourable death at the battle at Iconium."

She continued with her cruel exposition, wounding the prinz's heart, hardening it further.

"Did you know the king thinks ill of you? Regarding you as an interloper and an imposter."

The more she cajoled and insinuated, the more his mind fractured into fits of hysteria and madness, causing him to break down, sobbing on the breast of the evil woman. As she stroked his bowed head, comforting him, she wore a malicious smile knowing his willpower was now defeated; he was a pawn in her hands, defenceless and pregnable. Struggling to overcome his emotions, the poor man uttered the frightening words, "Unto you; I surrender my spirit; guide me on the path I must take, to obliterate the abominable Hellalyle."

Now, snatching her opportunity, she swooped, capturing him in one last irresistible embrace and summoned the Devil which rose from the bowels of the black earth, to take possession of his soul, in a satanic bond.

From that moment, the innocent Hellalyle – the water sprite's premeditated target – would be stalked by a deadly adversary, this unfortunate man possessed by Lucifer, intent on striking her down.

The remarks by William de Chartres regarding Paulus's malevolent personality induced the bodyguard to strengthen its observation of their charge. In one instance, the princess left her private chambers and was surprised to see two knights positioned at her door. She paused, addressing one of the soldiers, Richard de Chartres:

"Why are you standing guard outside my door?"

"On Hildebrand's orders, Your Highness," came the reply.

"I appreciate your attentiveness, but you agreed that no body-guards would be on station outside my rooms."

The two men glanced at one another and fell silent. They looked straight ahead as the princess beheld them with eyebrows raised in an expectant stare. Hellalyle perceived these battle-hard-ened warriors were now deliberately acting dumb as if caught in some misdemeanour. Getting no response, she let the matter drop, and with humour in her sparkling eyes turned away, followed by her lady-in-waiting. Immediately, the two knights jumped into action, one placing himself in front of the two women and one to the rear, so that now a procession formed. Hellalyle stopped still and demanded an explanation.

"What is going on?"

"We are only obeying Hildebrand's commands, Your Highness. To escort you wherever you go, never let you out of our sight," the knights replied in unison.

"This is intolerable. I shall have something to say about this when I see your leader," she exclaimed, in a tone of utter frustration.

As they reached the hall, the leading bodyguard issued a com-mand, "Halt, please remain here."

Both soldiers edged forward, and cautiously entered the doorway, one checking his left side and the other his right, the princess looking at her lady-in-waiting with an expression of acute exasperation. The soldiers satisfied themselves that all was clear, and then silently they returned, backing up towards the doorway, which caused them to collide with each other. They jumped in surprise. Furiously, they began to blame one another for this embarrassment in front of their charge.

As she witnessed this unfortunate comedy, a broad smile appeared on Hellalyle's face, which she immediately covered with her hand. But her lady-in-waiting gave away her hilarity with shaking shoulders, and hid behind the princess, head bowed, trying valiantly to stifle laughter.

Another new security measure Hildebrand imposed was to instruct the corps of knights that if anybody requested an audience with the princess, they had to avail themselves of a search – an imposition that Hellalyle considered ridiculous, as it eroded the trust between her and the people. However, she decided not to object now. Instead, she let Hildebrand and her bodyguards embarrass themselves, for she suspected it would not work. She was to be proved correct, because of what later transpired.

These men-at-arms with their hard-bitten features were masculine, possessing vigour, courage, and a commanding presence, but now far from home. They were completely unaware of an unseen consequence that this enactment would have when news of it reached the attention of the unattached women in the surrounding populace. There was an immediate increase in the number of people seeking an audience with the princess, because nearly all were females, wanting to be bodily frisked by the bodyguards.

Some of the knights, egged on by the women, attempted to search them, but when it became evident they could not go further due to the delicate nature of such a search, they were bewildered about what to do next. With red faces and desperate for guidance they hurriedly sent a message to Hellalyle, who by reports erupted into laughter when she received it, commenting that since the arrival of her bodyguard at the castle, her days had been immensely entertaining. She ordered an end to this well-meaning but absurd security measure of Hildebrand's while assuring the soldiers that she would have a meeting with him in the next few days – to the satisfaction of everybody concerned…

11

Hellalyle confronts Hildebrand

The bodyguard of mercenary knights had dispensed with the services of squires long ago; these duties were now their responsibility.

Hildebrand, alone in the knights' armoury attending to such tasks, heard a gentle rap at the door. On opening it halfway, he was surprised to catch sight of the princess. She wore an inscrutable look, intimating that she would like to enter. For a few moments, the knight stared at her, his mind preoccupied in disbelief at his good fortune, before a tactful cough from his visitor broke his trance. He courteously invited her to enter.

Almost furtively, Hildebrand sought to tidy the quarters as the princess got her bearings. She seemed curious to be in her bodyguards' domain but did not attempt to draw his attention. She gazed like a child at an eye-catching array of armour and weaponry. Polished helms, an assortment of mail, the glint of sharpened swords, shields for the mounted warrior, racks of bright lances, and bridles with saddles on display ready for equestrian use. The Prince of England, uncomfortable in the silence, defied convention by speaking first.

"Are you well, Your Highness?"

Except, there came no reply. Instead, she unexpectedly chose to single out a weighty cleaver-like weapon with a broad curved blade.

"What is the name of this menacing object?"

"It is a falchion, Your Highness," Hildebrand informed her.

When she persisted by asking its purpose, he added, "It is a destructive cutting sword, and dangerous in the wrong hands."

At this disclosure, she visibly paled. Hildebrand did his utmost to steer the conversation, but the princess responded in her way. Deeply engrossed in thought, she ran her delicate fingers over various implements as she continued to survey the scene. At one point, he could not help but notice how the young woman shrank away from the site of a cluster of crossbows, the lethal instrument that had been the cause of her mother's death.

Her enigmatic presence mesmerised the knight, who was unable to avert his eyes.

Spotting an open barrel, Hellalyle leaned over to take a closer look and noticed a dark brown, pungent-smelling fluid. Stepping back abruptly, she asked, "What is this nauseating substance?"

"It is a mixture of sand and vinegar for cleaning mail, and is unduly harmful to the skin, my lady!" he explained, with a forceful gesture of the hand.

With awe, the princess noticed what a large and powerful hand it was, grasp firm and secure from the wielding of heavy weapons, calloused, hardened, and leathery in texture, which left a favourable impression on her. Continuing her inspection, the king's daughter turned her back on him, stopping at a line of glinting spurs to ask a surprising question.

"Can it be true, as people report, that you directly descend from the belligerent warrior Sweyn Forkbeard, who fought and won many battles in your homeland, more than two centuries past?"

"Yes indeed, Your Highness, but I refrain from mentioning it."

Hildebrand responded somewhat apprehensively, aware that her interrogation had become more intrusive.

"When your assignment finishes, let us pray that you do not lead your fellow knights to cause havoc in my father's kingdom, in the aggressive fashion of your forbear!" she retorted.

The knight, trying to fathom her motives behind this visit, felt unable to press her.

As she approached a large crucifix on the wall above, she crossed herself, whispering a short prayer. Further along the masonry she came across a Russian Icon, depicting the Virgin Mary and Child, mounted there by the bodyguard, Uggi Bergfalk. Hildebrand became intrigued at the princess's reaction as she grew transfixed at the image before her. Hellalyle appeared overcome and reached forward, to touch the Holy relic, only then to jolt backwards with a dramatic look of astonishment, beholding something so extraordinary, as to be out of this world. Unbeknown to the English prince, the king's daughter with her unique Disposition of Providence perceived that the icon – a virtuous woman with child – was sending her a message. It induced in the royal personage a glimpse into the future that, as Mary was with child, so the princess will eventually be, with Hildebrand, the father of her offspring; now close by, solicitously watching her.

She lingered for a few moments deeply absorbed in thought, before, with a perceptible change of mood, she turned towards the broad-shouldered Hildebrand and, gazing at the scarred visage of this virile knight, she admonished him for failing to consult her concerning his new-fangled security measures at the castle. As they searched each other's faces, the princess formed the impression that he was not listening to her. He was like someone rapt, beguiled, his countenance complete serenity as he beheld her. Hellalyle seemed powerless to deter the intense chemistry growing between them, her expression of deep seriousness suddenly transforming into an authentic smile. Now, in exasperation and confounded by all their familiarity and intimacy, she shattered its spell and rushed out of the room.

In the open air, her hands tightly clenched, she all but despaired at her lack of earnest purpose when dealing with the soldier, her struggle to resist the extraordinary effect this man had upon her.

Hildebrand, though, perplexed by the significance of this situation, merely shrugged his shoulders and carried on honing the blade of a broadsword, whistling to distract himself. The princess, standing under the window of the armoury, overheard his idle tune.

Peeved by his apparent insouciance, his nonchalant reverie, she emitted a sharp outburst of annoyance and frustration.

That very evening, as a mark of appreciation, she surprised her bodyguards by arranging a banquet in their honour. Von Altenburg chose not to attend; his injuries would prevent him from consuming the dishes at the feast. At the event, it became noticeable to some of the guests – and painful for Hildebrand to perceive – that Hellalyle was studiously ignoring him throughout the entire proceedings. Although it was not in her nature to be unkind, and this change of sentiment had troubled her profoundly, she had resolved to suppress any repetition of the flirtation that had occurred between them earlier that day.

12

The Island of Svanr

One day Princess Hellalyle summoned the leader of her bodyguards; she had an unusual request to put before them.
Hildebrand presented himself bowing politely, while saluting her
with his sword, voicing, "Princess, I am at your service."

Avoiding the familiarity of names, she addressed him, "As the
leader and spokesman of my bodyguard. I wish to visit an island
on Lake Eydis not far out from its southern shore. A location of
choice because it is there I meet two delegates, where it affords their
identities remaining secret.

"Are you and your comrades au fait with the rigours of the oars,
for it is that skill you will need in transporting my lady-in-waiting
and I by boat across the water? If not, there are other men I can call
on, having undertaken the trip numerous times."

Hildebrand, somewhat taken aback by this request, fumbled
slightly in his reply and, anxious not to relinquish the responsibility
put upon him by her father, replied, "Of course Ma'am, we would be
extremely honoured to undertake such a mission."

To which came a sceptical reply, "Come now," said the princess,
"Are you sure my guardians have experience for such a task?"

The Englishman's face coloured, reluctant to admit his complete
ignorance of seamanship but endeavoured to assure all would be
well. Hellalyle had to turn away, hiding her face from the prince,

as a knowing smile broke out on her features, for she suspected her soldiers had no boating skills: only experienced warriors of the land, not of the water.

Hellalyle was known by the king's subjects to sometimes exhibit a friendly, mischievous nature and this was one of those occasions. She had created an uncertain situation for her knights, hoping it might serve to relax a little, the tight, formal atmosphere they displayed towards her.

Back at the knights' quarters, consternation ensued when they learned of what Hildebrand had agreed.

"You must be mad consenting to such a thing. None of us has ever picked up an oar; what must you have been thinking of?" said the Teutonic knight, Frederick Schtauffen, looking around at the others for confirmation.

The mumblings of trepidation continued to assail their leader's ears, until finally, in a display of contrition, he exclaimed, "Well, it is done now, I cannot rescind my words to her, so let's make the best of it, you never know, we could all do with a laugh."

"Drown, you mean!" came a voice, causing a chuckle to break out among the group.

Early next day, Hellalyle let it be known now would be the ideal moment to venture out over the lake, as the weather was set fair; no appreciable wind to disturb the surface of the water. It was all too soon for the twelve bodyguards, with no time to learn and practise oarsmanship.

The time came as the party arrived ready to go aboard. With a morning mist obscuring the vistas and the sky above, the twelve knights stood at the ready, like Viking warriors at the water's edge, with their oars held vertical, assembled, willing and waiting to take their station in the rowing boat.

For Hellalyle's island quest, she wore a gown quite unlike the fashion of the times: garments referring to antiquity in style; an ivory-white dress of pure silk, closely resembling a Roman stola, expensively woven cloth of luxurious sheen, fixed with a clasp at each shoulder; sleeveless, exposing the bare arms of a flawless and perfect tone.

The garment's neckline richly decorated, the consummate apparel catching the light; two grey cords, one tied around and under the bosom increasing the folds over the attractive upper torso, the other girding her middle pulling in the fabric stressing the narrowness of her waist. The lady's costume was exemplifying the perfect symmetry, the joyous contours of the innocent wearer.

Overlaying her gown, partly covering it, and coloured royal blue, an exquisite wrap corresponding to a Roman palla, but worn this time like a cape, instead of swathed over the left shoulder, adjunct on the arms. This appendage richly embroidered by *opus anglicanum* in white thread. Verily a picture painting, producing the images of swans with wings outstretched, wings folded, visions of cygnets, some half-hidden in the plumage of their progenitors, their regal majesty depicted in flight; others portrayed on rippled water, while the star constellation of Cygnus shown as background to the whole composition. A gorgeous creation that pleased the Almighty, skilfully rendered in subtle split stitch by the needle of artisans of more than one generation.

The textile was rumoured to have made its way centuries later to the workshop of the Stroganovs at Solvychegodsk in Northern Russia. Its association with the legendary figure of Hellalyle, the Princess of Eydis and Orn, rendered the artefact priceless, so it was placed securely behind glass, a source of inspiration and teaching to the school of embroidery established there, but unfortunately its whereabouts now unknown.

The noblewoman's hair, arranged in braids that encircled and surmounted the head, gifting the noblewoman the image of a subtle, golden crown, while the intense blue of her eyes mirrored the ultramarine of Lake Eydis, and its Slavic old name: Krasivoye Sineye More (Beautiful Dark-Blue Sea). Then, as if on cue, the sun broke through, dispersing the obscuring veil, its rays bathing the scene in its ascendency; the brilliance of the emergent sun sparkled on the water in a vector of bright light, drawing the eye as it trailed away to the true observable horizon. Visible, all around her, the land, sea and sky: the three constituents, embodying the planet Earth. It was a spectacle encapsulating the wonders of the cosmos.

Just as Princess Hellalyle contemplated the distant view of the isle, two swans magically emerged out of the blinding reflection, to swim alongside the wooden vessel – a foreshortened Norse longship. It appeared a random visitation by two birds meandering on the water, but the pair were acquainted with the king's daughter, and their visit had a purpose: the inspection of the craft. At one point, as they slowly encircled the clinker hull, the cob could be heard hissing at the knights, but they lingered for a moment alongside the noblewoman, issuing subtle, indistinct sounds to which Hellalyle appeared to listen intently and then acknowledge with a gentle nod of the head, mystifying those attendants standing nearby. As if satisfied, the aquatic birds glided away in the direction of the island. Nobody knew, save Hellalyle, that as the creatures proceeded, their presence and wake in the water contained magical powers, removing any threat to the boat in its mission, smiting the destructive spirits that might dwell beneath, or over, the surface of the inland sea, on the course the craft must take.

Before boarding, Hellalyle requested her guardians to follow the line of the swans and try to keep them in sight. William de Bures asked of the princess if their destination had a name; she beheld him with a searching, inquisitive gaze before answering.

"The Isle of Svanr," said she.

The knights one by one took their position at the boat rowlocks. Hildebrand took the princess's hand and assisted her aboard, the same for Runa; then he too placed himself at the oar.

The lady-in-waiting, anxious to guard her mistress against the attentions of the burly soldiers, fussed over her charge, attempting to quickly settle Hellalyle on the seat at the stern facing her guardians. But then a stricture arose when the maid noticed how the line of the princess's legs was visible to the crew, as the drape of the dress's smooth fabric emphasised in its delineation the excellence of Hellalyle's lower limbs. Ignoring the protestations of her mistress she produced out of their belongings a delicate lamina of light green velvet and laid it over the princess's lap, obscuring a sight which Runa believed aroused in the men lascivious thoughts. How wrong she was, her mistress privy to the warriors' secret: they were, save one, from another sphere; the distractions, temptations of worldly existence were inconsequential to them. As the boat cast off, the princess, an experienced passenger in a rowing boat, watched the proceedings covertly, expecting to be entertained by her soldiers lack of nautical skills. Immediately, the novice rowers struggled hopelessly with the oars. One of their number upended himself, falling backwards with his legs in the air as his blade missed the water, causing Hellalyle to burst out laughing, only to stifle uproarious gaiety behind her hands, appearing anxious not to prolong the embarrassment of the fellow's predicament. Runa joined in the merriment of the occasion as the boat went around in circles, the rowers seemingly unable to come to terms with control of the vessel. Gradually, however, they persisted, and soon the craft was fairly skimming over the surface of the lake. As the distance to the island fell away, a keen observer would have noticed the numerous times Hellalyle's eyes fell on Hildebrand, toiling away at the oars, only to divert her gaze instantly when she thought Runa had seen; the princess duly narrowing the eyes trying to maintain an impassive stance, befitting her royal station. While Hildebrand, absorbed in propelling the vessel, seemed unaware of how his presence aroused curiosity in the princess.

Eventually, the boat came upon the island, catching up with the two birds and beaching itself by the bow on the foreshore, allowing the swans to break off, swim quietly around a nearby headland and disappear.

Now mid-morning, the party disembarked, making their way up to the edge of the greenery.

It was here Princess Hellalyle, after a moment's deliberation, addressed them all, "I am going on my own to meet two important emissaries, and all of you wait here. At the highest zenith of the sun, I will return. Do not worry, I shall be quite safe, for no harm will befall me – it is something I have done many times. Runa will confirm this." Hildebrand attempted to protest, but Hellalyle countered irritatedly, "Will you, please, do as I say! You have my assurance – what more do you want? Let me hear no more of it!" At that admonishment, she turned and quickly made her way across the island, soon disappearing, taking with her a troubled conscience; her put-down of the Prince of England, a man that aroused in her the complicated feelings of human attraction – her snapping at Hildebrand a sign of confusion. A situation not lost on her lady-in-waiting, acutely sensitive of the young lady's emotions, for Runa, watching the receding figure of Hellalyle, held a clenched hand to her lips, in a sign of concern and sympathy.

When out of sight, her protectors, perplexed by the princess's secrecy, and sudden inconsistency of character, sat in a circle around Runa and deluged her with questions, hoping she could shed some light on the enigma, but Hellalyle's confidante remained steadfast in her loyalty and remained silent on the intrigues of the heart.

With a slight change of tack, William de Chartres asked of Runa, "Where did the princess obtain her wardrobe, so comely but so rare, am I right?"

Runa contemplated for a few moments whether to reveal what she knew of that subject, but noting the earnest, expectant faces on the men, she relented, "My mistress can be very unbecoming at times to any questions she thought pried into her private, secret life: changing the subject, sometimes walking away, depending on how her mood took her. There are many rumours about the king's daughter, of the many admirers she has, those near at home and those at the farthest ends of the known world; some she acknowledges, but others unknown to her. Take those items of clothing arrayed on her today; her dress could have been a gift from one of these, but it continues to be a source of speculation whenever she wears it. One story has it that the apparel originated from Thrace centuries ago, but we will never know, for as I say, Hellalyle never speaks of it. However, I can reveal with certainty the origins of her exquisite cape, as one day the princess took me into her confidence. It was a tribute, she said; a present from a woman called Eustacia de Sumeri, a Mother Superior of an Augustinian nunnery, called the White Ladies Priory, situated in that faraway country called Anglia. The princess disclosed to me that she knew nothing of the English lady, only that an acknowledgement came with the garment, describing how its creation was aeons in the making, designed by the artists of the Holy Martyr, St. Dunstan, and that the object possesses prescient significance."

The knights listened intently, marvelling, whispering to one another at Runa's disclosures. However, Hildebrand, stunned at the mention of Eustacia de Sumeri, got to his feet, and in silence moved away to stand on his own, staring motionless across the water, recalling the dying words of the notable prioress, all those years ago.

Runa continued, "This meeting she now attends; the Princess and I have been to this island many times, and it is the only occasion she wears those exquisite garments. When I enquired why, she replied, 'Out of respect for those that I meet,' and that is all she would say. What a strange world it is when a young lady wishes to prevent humanity, even the king and her brothers, from knowing who it is she beholds face to face on this island. All that I have told you is the truth. However, rest assured, she will return; wait and see."

Hildebrand abided awhile and then suggested to the other soldiers that half of the detachment reconnoitre another part of the island, so a party of six knights set off, leaving the remainder in the company of Runa.

When out of sight of the lady-in-waiting, Hildebrand voiced his concerns to the others, "Look, King Thorstein has entrusted the safety of his daughter in our hands so we must honour our commitment, never mind what the princess might say. We will double round, keep our distance, and maintain her under observation. If we are adept, she will never know we are there. What do you say?"

The others readily agreed, Charles Martel exclaiming, "Of course, we must – the monarch has ultimate faith in us, so carry on, Hildebrand, and lead the way."

As they traversed the compact but small island it presented itself as a place of a mysterious oddity; a profusion of cedar trees the same as those that clothed the Old World, but now only found in a few isolated places of the Mediterranean, namely the Troodos mountains of Cyprus. The views all around were curiously like those of the Aegean: light-coloured cliffs, and rocky promontories that terminated at the edge of sparkling water, pebble and sand inlets giving way to secret caves.

They never came upon Hellalyle, for she had descended a narrow pathway out of sight into a rocky cove. There, divested of her cloak, she sat on a boulder by the cerulean sea, resembling a goddess from Ancient Greece in her resplendent dress. On the translucent blue-green water before her, poised on its surface, the cygni; the same two as seen before, with the 'Hellenic' maiden listening to them, as they delivered a secret narrative passed from the spirits of the hinterland to their Princess Hellalyle – tales from the natural world informing the lady of its triumphs, tribulations, and enquiries to the princess's wellbeing.

Next occurred something beyond the bounds of physical law, as the woman on the rock produced, out of nowhere, a lyre; and in her gratitude to the snow-white messengers, rhythmically plucked the instrument's strings, performing a romantic tune, resonating softly in the sheltered inlet, to the delight of the majestic birds. They responded, serenading her with song sympathetic to the music. Derived from a world beyond human comprehension, the secret strains of the musical notation was an unusual but beautiful sound, organised in time to stimulate creatures from the other division of the earth and issue forth poetical strains of a melodious song. It was, indeed, a composition worthy of a king's ransom.

The image of the female potentate with the stringed instrument of turtle shell in hand, engaging the ambassadors from Arcadia, recalled mythology of Ancient Greece. A study to surely invigorate the imagination of a future, great, Renaissance artist, and endear him to a create a masterpiece with overtones of the classical world; *a composition of six thirteenth-century knights searching in vain a mystical island for a beautiful swan maiden, ensconced out of their sight in a secret lagoon.*

In time, the twelve guardians of the young lady would come to realise she possessed faculties far in excess of their ability to understand: able to understand the murmurings in the divine wind, and the lexicon of all lesser mortals; thus it was propitious they made their way back to the boat to await the princess's return.

It was not long before Hellalyle, with palla again about her shoulders, nonchalantly came into view humming an idle tune while swishing a stick – giving the impression she had just been for an innocent stroll – never portraying, giving away, the slightest indication of her incredible experience which remained concealed deep within. Nearing the temporary camp and noticing everybody's eyes were upon her, she faltered in her steps, and in an embarrassed vein, discarded the stick, only to gather herself and reimpose a stately bearing. Even so, as she walked into the midst of everyone an awkward silence reigned.

To lighten the occasion, she allowed her demeanour to relax and announced excitedly with a single clap of the hands, "We will now have a meal. Stay seated my boys, us ladies are going to wait on you." The soldiers valiantly protested a princess should do no such thing; it is they who will attend to her. "Nonsense," she said, waving away the objections, indicating them to stay where they were. "Come on, Runa, we have work to do – let us hope I have prepared sufficiently for all these hungry mouths." Astonishingly, it appeared the victuals they were about to consume had been prepared earlier by the king's daughter with the assistance of the castle cook, demonstrating her mastery of the culinary arts now her father was away. Their humility and respect for her all too evident as they graciously accepted food and drink from the enthusiastic noblewoman – handed to Hellalyle by her lady-in-waiting – taking the items from a large basket carried by the rugged figure of Karl von Altenburg, the one-eyed colossus towering over the apprehensive Runa.

To observe a royal princess of the Middle Ages, classically attired, demonstrating compassion to others of lower rank, in the manner of servant provider, while on the foreshore of an enchanting sea, with its clement waves dribbling in on golden sand, presented unforgettable theatre to the human eye.

Von Altenburg, delighted with his distinctive, nourishing and tasty gruel, consumed the meal away from the others. It was poignant to observe the inimitable fighting man of grotesque, but hidden, facial features, sitting on his own so as not to be off-putting to the others, struggling to pour the liquid sustenance into the blooded fissure that had been his mouth. Holding his head back, face-cover aside, slurping, gagging noises audible if one were too close.

As the party prepared to leave, Hellalyle, with Hildebrand and some of the knights at her side, walked down the edge of the shallows. She pointed to the far shore from whence they came, saying, "Gentlemen, the boat must keep to the course that we took to get here. Do not deviate from it. I must stress this: do not stray from that line." Some of the soldiers standing behind her could not help but note the images on her cape, and then to where she was indicating, surmising some unknown connection between her and the earlier presence of the swans. Noticing the quizzical expressions on their faces, she said, "Please do not query my instructions again – it may appear I am a dominating harridan giving orders, but, in this instance, it will be appreciated for my knights to carry out the instructions of a woman."

Hildebrand, curious of her directive, looked at his comrades and shrugged his shoulders, replying to the princess, "If this is so crucial, then your wish is our command. Perhaps one day you might enlighten us as to why?" Hellalyle pursed her lips, frowned, and turned away to assist Runa in her preparations, keeping to herself the secrets of their safe travel.

The boat set off, and with the oarsmen rowing in smooth unison, they presented an orderly ship. Far out over the lake, too distant for the craft's occupants to make out, two eyes, just above the surface, intently scrutinised its progress. The eyes belonged to a being from the underworld endowed with sinister intentions, but unable to venture closer, prevented by the protective forces left in the wake of the pathfinder swans. The Russian warrior, Uggi Bergfalk, remarked to his comrades – between heavy intakes of breath – how this part of the great lake seemed strangely denuded of all living things. The knights, unaware that its inhabitants had departed, harboured superstitious fear of an entity that had entered this aqueous region of Eydis.

The vessel summarily reached the original point of departure on the south shore, leaving all satisfied at such an engaging day out on Lake Eydis. At the same time, the malevolent entity far out, disappeared, extinguishing itself in the depths, spurring nature's inhabitants to return home to the water.

As soon as Hellalyle stepped ashore, uncannily, a breeze got up, and a minor swell ventured in, lapping at the wooden quayside, causing the clinker-built longship to bob at its moorings, while billowy clouds came into sight scudding across the blue sky. The regular cadences of the weather, the rhythms of life resumed, on Hellalyle's safe return to the sanctuary of the mainland.

In the air, the spectre of two large white birds flew in and out of the cloudscape, across heavenly pastures, rising ever higher into the wild blue yonder, returning to those celestial spirits who dwelled in the remote regions of the empyrean.

Hildebrand perceived the enigmatic duo, and shouted "Look! Can you see them? High, high above! It must be the Princess's swans! How can anybody not be humbled by such a spectacle." The rest of the party craned their necks, shielding, focusing their eyes on the remarkable tableau, now barely perceptible to the human eye. Hellalyle cast a glance over her knights and, in a guarded moment, a pleasing smile swept her face; witnessing the souls of hardened men, experiencing a symphony of emotion, their imagination stirred by the ranks of the lower order – two creatures traversing the great arch of the firmament in no finer majesty.

Before they could make tracks, a phantom figure appeared in the atmosphere, unnoticed by the party, hidden from their sight by a cloud; the divine embodiment in human form of the Breath of the Universe. It looked down on the group, puffed out its cheeks and with rounded lips blew with all its might; causing the breeze to momentarily strengthen with much force; causing the trees to rock and sway; whipping up spray from the lake, dust from the land; and blowing the drapes of the noble woman's costume against her frame: profiling with exactitude the immaculate female form. An embarrassing situation for the princess which the two ladies struggled to hide, glimpsed momentarily by Hildebrand alone, and this time the captivating vision aroused his pleasure, but, ever the gentleman, he looked away concealing his feelings, and, at that, the mighty wind suddenly abated. The sky-born deliverer, noting the events below, and satisfied with the intended outcome, smiled and disappeared into the unknown. What occurred was a unique event: a subtle contrivance by the natural world to arouse desire in the Englishman and bring closer the union between the Princess of Eydis and Orn, and the greatest knight in Christendom.

13

Ethla

One morning, Hellalyle seemed uncharacteristically withdrawn. She paced distractedly about her chamber before crossing the courtyard to the gateway of the castle. Reaching the drawbridge, she stared vacantly at the ground and then, mesmerised, involuntarily raised her head, fixing her eyes on the distant horizon.

Observers, intrigued by the princess's unusual behaviour, were unaware that in the hours before dawn, tossing and turning in her bed, she had, under an extrasensory influence, received an instructive message. Extraordinary was its persuasiveness, for it had resurrected in the princess's mind mental images of Ancient Greece as taught by the polymath, Abbot Jurian, in his education of the child Hellalyle. She imagined seeing the Greek god Hephaestus towering into the sky above, pounding away in silence on a great anvil, then pausing in his hammer blows to point at the boundary between the earth and the sky, as if showing the direction the noblewoman must go. The spectacle faded from her mind to be followed by a mysterious voice, that was all too real, instructing her to set out immediately to a said village some five leagues to the east, protected by her soldiers – but unaccompanied by Runa, her lady-in-waiting.

The connotation of the anvil in the heavens with the rare sight of the princess toiling upon the same in the farriery would have been intriguing enough for any observer, but now, to have implanted in her subconscious, Hephaestus, the only immortal who was ugly... What was the mystery about to unfold for the king's daughter?

One of the duties she undertook following her mother's death was visiting tenants on her father's estates, an obligation that now bore greater significance.

The princess, unconventional for a noblewoman, was never seen travelling by waggon, choosing instead to ride side-saddle on a warhorse. Her conspicuous figure now mounted high on a magnificent steed, Hellalyle took leave of Preben, escorted by twelve warriors. On the journey the soldiers followed in close formation until they reached a stopping place, where Hellalyle caught sight of a muster of crows soaring and gliding overhead, some of the carrion alighting in the tilled field. On rising ground, a peasant guided his wooden plough, drawn by a pair of oxen forcefully breaking the compacted soil. They made deep furrows where the labourer toiled one foot in front of the other until the agrarian group disappeared over the crest of the hill.

In the middle distance, plodding far behind, another rustic character came into focus, casting rye seed from a basket. Alighting, Hellalyle released the bit from her horse's mouth, and as inconspicuously as possible stepped forward to get a better view of the beguiling vistas in this enchanting location. From a vantage point beneath an imposing oak tree, while her steed grazed contentedly nearby, Hellalyle gazed, entranced by the prospect of this pastoral scene. Sweet sounds of birdsong filled the air, and white downy clouds suspended in the empyreal blue slowly drifted across the face of the sun, causing brilliant cascades of light to fall across the landscape, adding another striking dimension to the ensemble. The princess, shielding her sharp eyes from the blinding rays, traced the pronounced curve of a spectacular rainbow; precipitated by a heavy shower, its filmy polychromic bands were singularly intense as it overarched the hills, set against a backdrop of snow-clad mountains.

The soldiers, halting a short distance from Hellalyle, remained mounted in a semi-circle. Their horses waited patiently, some grazing on the lush grass, others seeming alert to this extraordinary world of creation. The knights were astonished when crows, flapping excitedly through the leafy branches of the trees, started to cluster around the princess, one or two lightly coming to rest on her shoulders. In the soldiers' eyes, this exceptional woman resembled some prodigious manifestation of nature, silhouetted in its arboreal frame. However, only Karl von Altenburg could perceive in these shifting episodes some weighty, inexplicable portent, although he preferred to conceal his strange presentiment from the other knights.

As Hellalyle and the soldiers began to get on their way, he lingered awhile, gazing in bewilderment at the spot where the princess had been standing – and at the fading, bow bent spectrum of colours beyond. Glancing back, Hildebrand chanced to catch sight of von Altenburg, stock-still in self-absorption. Turning about, he drew alongside, enquiring, "Are you alright, Karl? Is something troubling you?"

Stirred from his reverie, the Teutonic Knight made as if all were well, and, climbing onto his steed, rode off to re-join the line.

Afterwards, he could never fathom why the scene observed that day had so preoccupied him, or why he had been singled out to meditate on its significance; whenever he tried to put the incident to rest, it continued to lie lambent in the back of his mind.

In due course, drawn by intuition, the princess and her entourage reached the outskirts of a village. She had frequently visited it on her itinerary and had developed friendships with many local people. On this occasion, an angry crowd had formed, shouting wildly, the cries of a girl in extreme distress manifest. Only when Hellalyle drew near did the gathering begin to disperse and fall silent, revealing the cause of the commotion. A man, the village elder, wielding a stout stick, had seized hold of the wrist of a petrified simpleton and inflicted a savage thrashing, causing her to shriek with pain. The adolescent girl with light brown hair appeared to be mentally and physically impaired; short in stature, approximately four feet five inches tall; with a shrunken neck, short arms, fingers and legs. The features of the unfortunate creature were malformed – small chin, flat face, slightly protruding tongue, and slanting eyes.

The princess dismounted, the villagers standing aside to allow her access, but as the knights moved forward to form a circle of protection, Hellalyle motioned them to fall back. Addressing the throng, she demanded to know the reason for the waif's punishment, but these people who admired and respected the princess seemed ashamed they might have offended her, and looked down and away in embarrassment.

Removing the rod from the man's hand, she ordered him to explain his action. Conscious of her serious attitude, he nervously replied, "The persistent theft of crops and food bedevils the neighbourhood, no culprit discovered until this very day, when we caught this dim-witted girl red-handed, in the process of stealing from the root crop in the muddy field beyond."

Castigating them for forsaking the unfortunate child, Hellalyle took her by the hand and leaned forward, gently asking, "What is your name?"

Traumatised by her experience and in awe of this woman's presence, the girl remained mute and motionless. Even when the princess reiterated the request, she still seemed powerless to speak. It was while being so close that the princess noticed how the urchin's eyes bore a curious, tiny white spot on each of her pupils. An estimate put her age at twelve to fourteen years, but nobody could be sure as such afflicted children never lived beyond the first two years. Her miraculous survival was as mysterious as it was confounding. It was heart-breaking for Hellalyle to witness how uncomely were the features of the destitute waif, causing the princess to become momentarily self-absorbed, recalling the dream she had the previous night, of the ugly Hephaestus.

The noblewoman perceived a cord around the foundling's neck, partly concealed by her ragged clothes, which on close examination revealed a piece of attached bone engraved with the name "Ethla".

"Is Ethla your name, little girl?"

The princess asked gently, but still, the girl would not utter a sound.

"Well, that is what we shall call you," said Hellalyle with a sympathetic lilt in her voice.

When the princess questioned the local people, and none could shed light on the waif's background, she offered to take care of the hapless girl, informing the village elder she would arrange compensation for any losses the community had sustained.

The knights, concerned for Hellalyle's safety, had watched the young princess fearlessly confronting the incensed crowd, and when she had brought about a peaceful outcome to a tricky situation, and shown compassion for a petty thief, their admiration increased threefold. Even so, Hildebrand felt it his duty to inform his charge, "My lady, may I respectfully say that by ordering your bodyguards to hold back in the face of an unruly mob, your life could have been in danger. You must let us carry out your father's wishes to protect you at all times."

The indignant princess rebuffed the knight, "Your description of the crowd as an unruly mob is inappropriate. Remember, they are humble villagers, where starvation is an ever-present threat from the vagaries of the weather. Any unaccountable loss of food is justifiably upsetting, so please have a care in what you say. I commanded my guard to keep away, for I will not address the king's subjects in the intimidating presence of heavily armed soldiers, even when one of them happened to be a Prince of England!"

Sheepishly accepting her argument, he bowed politely before assisting the princess onto her horse. The knight, standing with his back to her as he secured the girth on her destrier, missed Hellalyle's cautious sign of appreciation, a momentary spark of approval springing from her pretty face. The other knights chuckled at the notion of their leader put in his place by Thorstein's gifted and enigmatic daughter.

Hellalyle insisted the barefoot Ethla should walk beside her on the journey to the castle, tethered to the princess's horse to prevent her from running away. Her armed escort was now made up of two units, one riding in front of the princess, the other following behind. As they progressed, Ethla appeared to limp and stumble. The princess promptly reined in her steed, and after dismounting, urged the girl to sit and rest, so she could physically examine the injured soles of her feet.

The princess, kneeling in front of her, was shocked to observe numerous blisters and lacerations while noting the deformity of a noticeable gap between the first and second toes.

Ethla, gazing fixedly at the face of this warm-hearted woman, saw in the king's daughter the first person to show her compassion and kindness, and was fascinated by her allure.

Hellalyle resolved that, given the poor girl's lameness, Ethla should ride her horse while she accompanied her on foot. Concerned about the princess's social position, Hildebrand suggested the child should travel with him, but, ignoring his advice, Hellalyle motioned to the knight to lift Ethla onto her steed. Hildebrand obeyed, yet, still hopeful the princess would change her mind, he remarked, "If you insist on traversing by foot, then I will walk resolutely behind you, regardless of my aching feet or the weight of my armour."

If Hellalyle imagined he would quickly abandon his reckless action in the noonday heat, she underestimated the resolve of this doughty soldier. Gripping her reins, the princess bore an expression of disguised amusement, as she declared tersely, over her shoulder, "Do as you wish. Knowing your strong attachment to Fortis, your faithful stallion, I am delighted you seem willing to show this noble animal the same consideration you are offering me. Surely your horse will appreciate the significant reduction in the weight it must bear when a strapping trooper renounces his saddle."

Outplayed once again by the quick-witted princess, the knight, leading his charger, stretched his muscular legs. Intent on proving he was prepared to stay the course, at the same time he was impatient to seek some common ground with this intriguing woman. Hildebrand, ordering the other soldiers to remain in their saddles, was determined to protect his charge in any eventuality.

Returning home, as they passed beneath the bent boughs of

a sturdy oak tree, they were oblivious to the furtive presence of the little songbird perched precariously above, concealed in a sprig of acorns as it blew to and fro in the wind. As Ethla went by, the tiny creature, keeping its eye on her, caused the girl to blurt out involuntarily, in faltering tones and indistinct syllables, "Why do you speak hurtfully of a knight who thinks highly of you?"

The princess could understand this garbled speak, and taken aback by this unexpected reprimand, glanced first at her bodyguards (the bird's strange rebuke was not intended for their ears) and then to Ethla, with a sharp riposte:

"Ah, you can talk after all! However, young lady, you pass false judgement! Let me make it plain: this knight has been engaged solely for my protection, and no intimacy exists between us. Hold your tongue, until I permit you to speak."

The princess found the simpleton's first utterance unsettling. Patting her hair self-consciously and casting a sidelong glance at Hildebrand, she wondered whether Ethla had an inkling of the emergent feelings Hellalyle and the Prince of England held for each other, which the princess was trying to suppress.

The diminutive passerine darted away, chirping gleefully in its bobbing flight through a break in the green awning before vanishing from view over the encroaching forest. There, in a remote clearing, the bird ensconced itself in the lower branches of a birch tree and waited.

At once, agents of all the wild creatures of this awe-inspiring land began to assemble. Large and small, predator and quarry – bear, wolf and lynx, side by side with elk and deer; eagle and falcon accompanying dove and partridge. There was a restraint on any instinct to take flight or hunt that they might better digest an important message. Here they gathered, occupying every patch of ground, all the branches of the trees, listening intently as the feathered envoy spread positive word of the propitious plan to keep their appointed princess within the bounds of their domain.

The party was getting ever nearer to the fortress of Preben, and the castle's outlines were becoming more evident. The princess, detecting an anxious look on the face of the knight Andre Grenier – who had been closely watching Hildebrand's flagging figure – ordered the column to stop. The Englishman, overcome with exhaustion, lurched in his tracks. Hellalyle ran towards him, and he slumped into her arms. Just as she was about to collapse under his weight, Nienhault von Streitz came to their aid with the strength to support Hildebrand. The princess, sure Hildebrand must be suffering from acute sunstroke, begged him to continue on horseback.

"Hildebrand, you must remount your steed, and we will return with utmost speed to the castle, where you can rest."

But the shattered warrior groaned.

"My lady, I insist it is you who must ride. Otherwise, my only option will be to stride on ahead unflinchingly, and most likely I will die in the attempt."

Hellalyle, mindful of the seriousness of Hildebrand's condition, tearfully consented.

"I cannot bear to see an obstinate soldier suffer on my behalf. Nienhault will you lift Ethla out of my side-saddle so I can remount, and seat the girl behind me and she can grasp my waist. Karl, please help Hildebrand onto his horse."

Immediately the Teutonic Knight swung down from his charger and effortlessly lifted Hildebrand into the saddle.

Hellalyle cast a solicitous glance at Hildebrand as they cantered away, two of the bodyguards riding close to their leader. The party, passing through the gatehouse at speed, drew up at the entrance to the castle, and as soon as they had alighted, Hildebrand fell to the ground – to Hellalyle's distress. The knights, experienced in treating soldiers suffering heat exhaustion at the time of the crusades, exhorted her to remain calm.

Hesitantly, with backward glances at the Englishman, Hellalyle led the limping Ethla into the castle to introduce her to Queen Gudrun and Princess Amora, instructing the attendants to wash the girl and find her suitable clothing.

That evening, Hildebrand, still confused as he recuperated in the knights' quarters, fancied he overheard his comrades whispering to each other. They stood back, and at that moment he picked up the sound of the rustle of a long cloak as a hooded woman came quietly into the chamber. In dimly flickering torchlight, Hildebrand saw Hellalyle looking down at him, and as he tried to raise himself, she gently restrained the weakened man.

After politely discharging the other knights, the princess drew up a seat next to Hildebrand's bed, and began a conversation.

"You must promise me you will refrain from trying to test my willpower in this teasing fashion of yours when there is little cause for contention between us. You are not in England now and do not have authority over me. Let me explain; I had chosen to walk to lighten the burden of my mount, not much perhaps, but if I can assist one of God's creatures in any possible way then I have a duty to do so."

Then with a surge of emotion she revealed her passion for riding destriers, the warhorses her father's soldiers used. Her face clouded, as she exclaimed, "I can recall how frequently these noble animals have been maimed or killed in the heat of battle. Whether in time of peace or war, my sincere concern had always been their welfare, regarding them as the innocent victims of men's violent actions."

Drawing closer, she confided to Hildebrand, "The ministers of the church, behind my back, maintain I hold misguided views concerning the creatures of the animal kingdom, who they erroneously regard as inferior, devoid of the Holy Spirit. I cannot accept this, or that humankind should hold sway over them."

Using a parable to demonstrate her conviction, she said, "Imagine, if a man were to fall from a soaring precipice, plunge into seething rapids, his professed superiority of mind would not save him. Yet, the creatures of the air and the waters thrive in situations where we would perish. It convinces me the Creator conceived a world in which no living thing had ascendancy over another."

Then the princess's demeanour changed, her character transmuted into that of a great thinker, a prophet. She uttered in measured tones, "I predict that in the distant future, humankind will experience societal changes engineered by themselves either by accident, or pre-planned, but, will be so profound, they will clash with the writings of the Bible that have endured through the aeons. Any laws or guidance from the Holy Book, they cannot live by, no longer find comfortable, will be suitably twisted in a new interpretation, or cast aside. Humanity itself will decide the laws they obey, arrogantly thinking they are the centre of the world, coming before all things as the new deity, replacing God, the everlasting. In their resolve to resist such pressures, the Christian church, knowing the sacred writings to be uniquely inspired by the Creator, will be found wanting, the wondrous diversity of nature depleted, sending the earth spinning out of control towards the day of judgement."

A moment of silence ensued as she gathered herself and returned her attention to the knight. Hildebrand, listening intently to the princess, entranced by her sharp intelligence, grace, and gentle nature, remembered her father's words – King Thorstein's perplexity at the origin of his daughter's extraordinary mind.

The great knight suddenly realised they were now conversing informally, instead of in the official capacity that had dogged him since his first introduction to this magical lady.

As Hellalyle rose to leave, she held his hand, saying, "My dear Englishman, I must thank you from the bottom of my heart for the consideration you showed me in your selfless, chivalrous act, even though it could be thought of as a rash and silly thing to do in the heat of the day." At this, Hildebrand propped himself up in bed on one arm and posed the question:

"What is your true judgement of my action, Your Highness?"

The princess gazed down at him, but with her face in shadow beneath the hood of her cloak, Hellalyle's winning smile passed unnoticed as she stood in silent contemplation before turning away and walking out. Hildebrand, disappointed by her silence, lay on his back. He narrowed his eyes as he watched her leave, apparently stopping outside to thank each soldier in turn. At first, he tried to eavesdrop on her words of gratitude, but then resignedly turned his face to the wall, all but despairing of a woman who had become the sole object of his affection, yet remained elusive and unfathomable.

However, both knight and princess were unaware how benign powers beyond their comprehension or control were influencing events, having already determined that the valorous warrior Hildebrand had been elected to capture Hellalyle's heart, the first seeds of the harvest sown.

14

Hellalyle's banquet

It was early evening at Castle Preben. Guests and company were gathered in the great hall, eagerly anticipating Princess Hellalyle's second banquet. The feast was held in honour of her twelve knights, in appreciation of their vigilance in protecting her; to the extent, she had never been aware of danger. The king's daughter enjoyed the company of these battle-hardened warriors with their wisecracks and rough-edged humour.

Her dealings with their leader Hildebrand, however, she found awkward. As time passed, she realised more and more how drawn they were to one another, and so tried to keep her distance. Ever conscious of her royal position, she endeavoured to appear dispassionate and treat her knights impartially – but Hildebrand, on numerous occasions, had inadvertently induced half decipherable smiles from the princess. She found this both annoying and frustrating, yet was helpless to prevent herself. She was under the influence of this knight's powerful charisma, conjured to the fore by those all-seeing spirits of the sylvan tract.

At the celebration, the comely hostess was keen to maintain her reserve in the presence of the Prince of England, stubbornly refusing to acknowledge any chemistry that might have developed between them.

The princess, with her innate organisational skills, had taken an active role in the planning of any festivities held at the Castles of Preben and Yrian. It was an obligation once performed by her late mother, then subsequently by Queen Gudrun, the king's second wife. Gudrun, a quiet and unassuming woman, had surrendered these royal duties to her stepdaughter, whose remarkable qualities she would have been the first to recognise.

The choice of dishes – to which Hellalyle applied herself with zeal and imagination – was the most crucial consideration in the preparation of a banquet. She visited the kitchens regularly, offering her advice and often lending a hand, proficient as she was in the culinary arts – to the chagrin of her father, who disapproved of his daughter becoming too preoccupied with the functions of his servants. On this occasion, she noticed the young Ethla, whom she had seen fit to promote to the position of working in the scullery. Before approaching the young helper, she enquired of the master cook, Mechislav, what task she was assigned.

"Your Highness," replied the cook, "I have had the most devilish task trying to communicate with the backward girl, so in the end, I left her to occupy herself in the corner of the kitchen. She has taken it upon herself to try her hand at cooking. I have no idea what she is concocting but have no fear; it will not be allowed to pass from the kitchen."

Happy little Ethla, standing over a simmering pot, looked up at the princess as she drew close. A blithe expression played over her anamorphic features, and with her limited staying power, she was puffing as she stirred an odd-looking mixture with a wooden paddle. It was gruel-like in its consistency, with solids floating on top. Hellalyle, placing a reassuring hand on the girl's shoulder, asked with some apprehension, "What is the nature of the ingredients, Ethla?"

Sparked by the princess's interest in her gastronomic endeavours, and to the astonishment of the kitchen staff, the girl, with her simple innocence of court etiquette, led her mistress by the hand, sometimes pulling her, pointing to discarded offal and various other offerings of questionable nutritional value scattered around the room. The girl chatted away with anomalistic words that only Hellalyle really understood, endeavouring to say, "I have put this in, and look, that as well. I even found the guts of chickens over there – someone had discarded them on the rubbish!"

Repressing a grimace, the princess expressed her admiration for the girl's skills.

"Well, young lady, you have impressed me with your competence and knowledge of cookery. I will look forward to sampling your recipes at the feast," she said, much to the consternation of the staff, who had been watching and listening as the princess paid so much attention to the strange waif unexpectedly brought in to work with them.

Hellalyle now abandoned Ethla, who was enveloped in a vaporous cloud of curious smelling odours as she toiled, with her tongue sticking out as she demonstrated a singular fascination for her bizarre and bubbling brew, in the manner of a witch agitating the congealed and curdled ingredients in a murky cauldron.

Deep in thought, the princess had not the heart to upset the girl by disparaging her first dogged efforts. She summoned Mechislav, and covertly said to him, "I do not want to belittle this unfortunate girl's first efforts at useful work, so I want you to serve Ethla's mixture *only* to myself at the banquet. Also, I require that you bring Ethla up to the servants' entrance of the hall where she can get a brief glimpse of her mistress 'sampling' her food. Then, you must return her to the kitchen. She need not know there will be an alternative platter for me alongside her dish."

Hildebrand, concealed in the doorway observing all this frantic activity, was intrigued to learn what the princess might be divulging to the chief cook, until Hellalyle caught sight of him and motioned him to leave.

"Hildebrand, what are you doing here? Please leave at once, and stop following me. Surely I deserve a few moments to myself?"

Like a chastened boy, he turned around and climbed the steps, not aware of the appreciative smile the princess gave to his retreating figure.

At sundown, the lively and incessant chatter was heard coming from the great hall, where the assemblage, including all but one of the twelve knights, conversed excitedly in expectation of the princess's appearance. The animated conversation grew quiet as the eyesome beauty of Hellalyle's majestic splendour became the focus of everyone's attention, especially the men. Hildebrand tried to side-track her, but she gave him the cold shoulder, anxious to set her association with the escort – and particularly their leader – on a proper footing. An observant person, however, might have noticed a quick flash of her eyes whenever she caught sight of him off his guard.

The company stood by their places at the tables, and with a signal from the princess, they all took their seats. Hellalyle had six of her bodyguard knights seated to her left, and to her right, Abbot Jurian, and five of her other knights, all hanging on every word the princess uttered. Queen Gudrun was seated at an adjoining table with other guests, keeping a diplomatic low profile, letting her stepdaughter be the decisive figure of the event. No one knew that future misfortune would engulf the unfolding tale, and this would be the final banquet. The commanding presence of the king's daughter, the beautiful colour of her apparel and adornments to her illustrious figure as presented, could not help but give the vivid impression that a re-enactment of the Last Supper was taking place. Except in this play, the fulcrum was a princess – unique in her time – and there was no traitor within the great fortress of Preben, but instead an enemy that was coming from without...

Dishes appetising and plentiful were placed before the diners, accompanied by the sound of minstrels in the background, acrobats and jesters providing suitable entertainment. For Hellalyle, the pertinent moment soon arrived for her to perform the conjuring trick of pretending to sample Ethla's unusual comestibles. The disabled girl was permitted a brief peep at the princess from the kitchen doorway, where she imagined glimpsing the royal personage taking a delicate morsel of her innocent offering, unaware of a more palatable platter placed next to it.

Suddenly, in the hall, a woman guest spied Ethla and fainted, unleashing panic amongst the diners and causing the princess, momentarily distracted, to make the unfortunate error of eating from the wrong plate. The company looked on as she savoured a mouthful of the mixture while glancing and smiling at Ethla, whose face was just discernible peeking out of the doorway before she was ushered back to the scullery. Hellalyle made every effort not to retch at this virulent assault on her taste buds. Begging excuses of her startled guests, she fled the room, but could not help noticing Hildebrand through the corner of her eye, his elbows on the table, smirking behind his hands at her obvious discomfiture.

After this unwelcome incident, the princess suffered food poisoning and did not reappear for five days. When she was taken ill, she had requested that Ethla should on no account know the source of her mistress's malady. As Hellalyle gradually recovered, and was kept informed of events, at her insistence she received daily visits from Ethla so that she could supervise the girl's welfare and try to shield her from bullying and ridicule.

The princess received a gift of twelve bouquets from her knights. Greatly touched, she listened to her lady-in-waiting Runa as she related the concern and responsibility they felt for their absent charge.

"The Prince of England expressed special solicitude," Runa added with a roguish grin, which Hellalyle feigned not to detect.

On the afternoon of the fourth day of the princess's recuperation, Runa informed her that Hildebrand had requested an audience. Surprised by his appeal, Hellalyle retorted, "What does he want of me?"

Runa merely shrugged her shoulders resignedly.

"Admit him only when I am ready!" responded the princess with feigned hauteur, hurriedly fussing about her appearance as she lay propped upright on her daybed before allowing Runa to let him in.

In reaction to Hellalyle's apparent earlier indifference to him, Hildebrand marched in resolutely. Standing to attention, he looked straight ahead, sarcastically confronting the princess with the words, "How much longer must I, and the rest of your bodyguard, wait while you lie in bed, Your Highness?"

"What a callous thing to say!" the lady-in-waiting exclaimed with a gasp.

Hellalyle, vexed by the knight's behaviour, comforted her companion and tried to reassure her, saying, "Pay no attention to him, Runa! Perhaps it would be best if you would kindly leave us now, and allow me a few words with our genial warrior."

The chaperone cast a contemptuous glance at the knight as she left the room.

When they were alone, the princess castigated her bodyguard, severely rebuking him.

"You dare to antagonise me in this fashion when you know that I have been unwell!"

Hildebrand countered, "If only you would desist from trying to be all things to all people, my lady, you might have avoided consuming that contaminated food! In the kitchen with Ethla, and later at the banquet, I knew what you were contriving. Be firm with individuals and relate to their actual condition, without conjuring some idealistic world of wishful thinking: if reality disappoints, one must learn to live with it."

The princess was stupefied by his audacity, as no one had dared to confront her so bluntly before, but curiously, she did not object to this harsh censure, coming as it did from him.

"So, is this your judgement of me?" she responded in a hushed tone.

The Prince of England tilted his head obliquely in her direction and answered, "Of course not, but the knights who defend you have grown restless, waiting for your return."

The princess, troubled by Hildebrand's offhand and remote manner, declared, "Inform my knights that I intend to vacate my chamber on the morrow!"

"I am glad to hear it!" Hildebrand reciprocated.

Then, averting his gaze, he set off, but paused near the door, and, with head half turned towards her, added his parting shot in an emotional vein:

"It may be but four days since you absented yourself, but this gap might seem like a lifetime to your protectors. They have held you in such esteem that now their emotions have become hollow, their aspirations futile. They long to see you in good health, blooming and resilient at the helm of this kingdom, steering them through any difficulties on the strength of your magnetic presence. For my part, I could wish for nothing better than you to inspire and guide us – you, with eyes so beautiful they have stolen my heart, as there is no woman alive, or who has ever lived, that is as beautiful as thee."

She could not see it, but his eyes were moistened in the emotional moment, for the knight had missed her so much. With that, he left the room.

Runa, returning at that moment, seemed disdainful of the knight as he departed, but also puzzled to notice the princess gazing after Hildebrand with an expression of intense elation and joyfulness lighting her exhausted features.

Retrieving her attention, the lady-in-waiting ventured to enquire of Hellalyle the first task she would attend to when resuming her duties, to which Hellalyle unequivocally replied, "Why, I intend to instruct a young woman in the core competencies of domestic science!"

True to her word, the princess did precisely that.

15

Hellalyle administers to the wounded Karl von Altenburg

One evening, following a prolonged and violent rainstorm, the air was still moist, the menacing rumble of thunder subsiding in the distance. Princess Hellalyle – having sent her attendants away – set out to meet her bodyguards, stationed at strategic points around the fortress. As she took advantage of an opportunity to talk to them individually, in turn, a supernatural incident occurred, unleashing powerful forces from the heavens above. This mass of energy, violet coloured, closely resembled St Elmo's fire, and it suffused in its aura the unmistakable silhouettes of the king's daughter and her knight.

The manifestation bore the inscrutable hallmarks of Hellalyle's astounding nature, her far-visioned handiwork breaching the barrier separating present time from each warrior's perception of the past, enabling her to communicate with them freely, and on their terms. Enveloped in a Pentecostal radiance, Hellalyle would learn first-hand from these brave and honourable men (as if these events were unfolding before her very eyes) the part they had played in titanic conflicts of the past, shaping the world to come. She also learned of the astounding element of these illustrious knights; that, once given cause, they could summon their vast armies of old to crush any adversary intrepid enough to endanger the life of a princess by invading her father's kingdom.

The impact of this extraordinary experience had a dramatic effect on Hellalyle's intellectual power; she had become a virtual pansophy, possessing universal knowledge and wisdom. But it also caused the princess to momentarily lose her natural composure, when, like some wild, over-inquisitive child, she entreated the warriors to reveal the mysterious being who had induced them to become her protectors. Her pleading would be to no avail. She was denied a secret she would never unlock in her mortal existence.

However, that aside, there was one knight she had never met privately, and that was Karl von Altenburg.

"Where would I find Karl von Altenburg?" she enquired of Andre Grenier.

"He will probably be found in the stables, Your Highness, as he finds comfort in the presence of animals. However, my lady, I respectfully advise you to show caution, as he tends to prefer solitude, and if disturbed could be temperamental."

With no comment, she thanked them and left. They gazed after her with grim expressions on their faces but at the same time with a gentle shake of the head, acknowledging her gracious persistence.

Hellalyle descended the castle steps to cross the courtyard and entered the stables. At the far end, there was a yellowish light from tallow candles, safely positioned so as not to be a fire risk to the hay and straw bedding. With slight trepidation, remembering the other knights' warning, she walked light of foot towards the glow. Passing the rows of horses, she calmed them by whispering soothing words, and putting her hand to their nostrils or laying it on their flanks.

Unsure if anybody was there, she stopped to listen and became aware of strange guttural noises. Moving closer, she could see the tall figure of a soldier with his back to her, holding his head against that of a horse, caressing and soothing it. Hellalyle realised then that the strange sounds came from von Altenburg, the few utterances he could muster due to his terrible wounding.

Nervous, but also with steely determination, she uttered a gentle cough to announce her presence.

"Ahem, ahem."

The giant suddenly froze for a few moments. Then he raised himself to his full height and slowly turned, so his one eye could focus on the princess, bathed in the flickering luminescence. Hellalyle held his stare and smiled, hiding her hesitancy about what would now happen.

For what seemed an eternity to her, he stood there like a statue, undecided on how to react to his privacy being disturbed. Still, the sight of this young woman in front of him was something no man, however embittered, could resist, and the knight eventually bowed his head in respect. As if to say, *"Your presence here, in this lowly abode, is a great honour."*

To his surprise, Hellalyle then indicated to him to follow her.

"Come with me," she said, "for I have many questions to ask," and he subserviently allowed her to lead him to two upturned barrels against the wall, where she motioned for both to sit facing each other.

"Now, my little man," said the princess with a twinkle in her eyes to put the knight at ease.

"I wish you to indicate how you are feeling. I have spoken with your comrades, and they assure me everything is excellent and is as it should be with them. However, what about yourself? For the wellbeing of all my bodyguards is of the greatest concern to me."

With sign language, he signalled that all was well, as the imposing soldier held Hellalyle in a virtually hypnotic gaze as she carried on her discourse, dumbfounded that she was enjoying his company.

Eventually, she had to leave, and stood.

"Please, stay seated," she instructed. "Since our first introduction in the great hall by my father, it has been my earnest desire to speak in private with the most enigmatic of warriors to have ever graced this fortress. Having now done so, it confirms my first impressions, that you are an exemplar of fortitude and loyalty. May God be always at your side."

Her evocation prompted a tear to start flowing from his eye. Hellalyle sensed the despair and loneliness his disfigurement had caused, so she paused and took his large hand. Holding it between hers, patting and massaging it, she smiled a gesture of reassurance.

As she went to depart, she could not help but notice von Altenburg appeared to be troubled by his cloth-covered wound, persistently touching it with his hand. Then he suddenly dropped to his knees, reached forward and held her tightly to him, with his face buried in her dress, sobbing uncontrollably. Hellalyle was momentarily taken aback by the soldier's show of feeling, and held his head firmly into the folds of her garment, looking down at him in desperation. She felt helpless to end his mental suffering. Von Altenburg, suddenly realising he had laid his hands on the king's daughter, withdrew and crouched over with head turned to the floor, mortified at his indiscretion.

Hellalyle, muttering soothing words, helped the unfortunate man back to his seat and stayed with him for a while until she thought he had recovered his composure. Feeling now significantly strengthened, using hand signs he apologised for his lapse of self-control and indicated his thanks for her kindness. As Hellalyle left, he motioned to kiss her hand.

Making her way back to the royal chambers, she pondered on the vulnerability of the great warrior and his seemingly precarious mental state. On entering her rooms, the lady-in-waiting attended to the princess, removing her cloak and day dress. As Runa, did so, she noticed staining on the front of the garment. Enquiring of Hellalyle, she said, "My lady, what is this soiling of your beautiful apparel?"

The princess was startled and took it from her, looking in bewilderment at the marks.

"Well, I am at a loss," Hellalyle exclaimed.

She then sat down in her underclothes as her hair was unbraided and combed. Deep in thought, and still holding the spoiled material, the answer finally dawned on her, and it came as a shock. It caused her to utter in a determined voice, hardly audible, as if addressing the stricken knight that was standing before her, "Why did you not reveal to me your wound has not healed – heaven knows what you must be enduring. How ridiculous to suffer in silence like a dumb animal while your lesion suppurates, commanding attention."

The next day, about the same time as before, Hellalyle set off to the stables to see the Teutonic Knight. Following her was Ethla, carrying medicines which the princess believed would assist the healing of the knight's laceration.

With her innocent, irrational fear of von Altenburg, the simple girl stayed close and tried to hide behind her mistress as they both entered and crept past the lines of horses. Hellalyle felt a combination of relief and unease when she saw the knight sitting there, seemingly engrossed in whittling a piece of birch wood. He looked up at her, wondering why she had returned.

The princess spoke a greeting. Von Altenburg jumped to his feet and bowed, and to the delight of his visitor, exhibited a display of gestures to show how pleased he was to see her. Going over to the same two barrels against the wall, he flicked them with a cloth, and with courtesy, motioned for her to sit.

Hellalyle commanded Ethla, who was in hiding, "Stop being silly and come out at once."

The knight, utterly unaware of the princess's intentions, looked on with his one eye in great curiosity as the girl placed the ointments in the straw as close as she dared, then retreated to somewhere safer. The princess shook her head in exasperation at Ethla's antics.

"Will you now leave us, young lady, and return to the kitchens. I am sure chores are awaiting you."

The girl obeyed gratefully, turning around and running out as fast as she could go, but her inquisitiveness got the better of her, and she returned to the stables to conceal herself in the shadows and watch her mistress.

Hellalyle did nothing with the medicines at first, but instead, talked readily to the Teutonic Knight to ensure he was entirely at ease with her presence. Feeling the right moment had arrived, she took his hand. Then, with a little apprehension, aware that his response to what she would say next could be fierce, she explained what it was she had come to do.

"My Deutsche protector, your wound requires immediate attention. I have brought ointments that I believe will sooth and speed its healing. Abbot Jurian with his grasp of the sciences has helped and guided me in the production of medicines, the raw materials of which nature has provided. Do not be afraid of what I am about to do next. Trust me to effect a cure, and your relief will be timeless."

Immediately the knight tensed, but, with Hellalyle appearing to hold some hidden power over him, the princess stood fast, and he surrendered to her.

"I am now going to remove your face cover," she explained.

Von Altenburg jerked his head away in fear, but the princess's soft, reassuring voice had a calming effect.

"Now, turn your head back towards me."

He obeyed, and slowly brought it around, so he was now looking upwards at her. She slowly removed the ensanguined mask of cloth. The sight that confronted her would repel most, but she was determined to keep her bodyguard at ease, showing no reaction. Only a barely slight narrowing of her eyes gave any sign of her feelings, as she tried to imagine the violent hand-to-hand clash that resulted in this man's unprecedented injury.

Gently holding his head still with the fingertips of her left hand to the temple, she proceeded to clean and then treat the ghastly wound that was once his face. With his one eye, he stared at Hellalyle with a feeling of spirituality coursing through him. This mighty warrior had now become like an obedient child in the presence of its mother.

Unknown to both, a second figure in the shadows was watching them; it was Hildebrand, come to see his comrade, stumbling on a scene of extreme privacy and sensitivity for this Teutonic Knight. He silently withdrew, taking with him a realisation that the bodyguard was escorting a woman like no other.

16

Ethla, ephemeral princess

When Ethla came up against any obstacles to communication, she summoned up her limited willpower and struggled to overcome them, with facial expressions, the use of gestures, and anomalous words and phrases. In the habit of speaking too rapidly, she would stammer, and with the faculty of hearing defective in one ear, it compounded her infirmities. These deficiencies were compensated by her skill in dealing with visual impressions, and Princess Hellalyle's patience and sensitivity to the child in making clear any gesture, mime, and nuance of intonation. However, her handicap sometimes caused problems…

From time to time, Hellalyle's bodyguard would hand to Runa bouquets of flowers for the princess – a token of thanks for her kindness and their innocent infatuation with Hellalyle's aesthetic quality. They preferred to channel them through the lady-in-waiting rather than directly to the king's daughter, to keep it on a platonic level. (It was sad to see that von Altenburg never took part, as he believed no woman would ever appreciate his affection.) The Teutonic Knight, Nienhault von Streitz, however, instead of giving his posies to the lady-in-waiting, thought he would distinguish himself from his comrades by using the little servant girl Ethla, as the go-between, as she was considered by many to be under the guardianship of the princess.

Hellalyle never forgot to thank each knight in person for their delightful offering, except von Streitz, who began to think their charge held him in disfavour, for she never once expressed her gratitude to him, and he became downhearted, but his sense of pride precluded mentioning it to his comrades.

There was a simple explanation for the princess's apparent indifference, and it was the fault of the knight. For he had not fully understood Ethla's difficulty in comprehending the simplest words if spoken at normal speed, and the girl had wrongly assumed von Streitz's flowers were for her.

With delight in her heart, believing that a man found her appearance pleasing, not troubling, she had taken the blooms to an unused, tiny storeroom she had discovered. The girl would go absent at frequent intervals, shutting herself away in this place, fondly nurturing the plants, talking to herself in a make-believe world, where she imagined Nienhault von Streitz loved her. She conjured in her mind how the knight had fallen under her spell, just as she sensed Hildebrand was in Hellalyle's enchant, and it set her wondering what gift she must reciprocate to the Teutonic Knight. She decided to seek the advice of Princess Hellalyle.

Seeing the noblewoman walking by, Ethla waylaid her, and in a state of abashment, twirling fingers in her hair, she asked coyly, in her indistinct syllables, "What should a woman gift a lover?"

The princess, decoding the girl's inarticulate language – although it was improving under the princess's tutelage – was puzzled and surprised by the question. Thinking Ethla was referring to her mistress, she indignantly replied, "Young lady, what business is it of yours?"

However, Ethla became tongue-tied and ran off giggling to escape the awkward situation.

Hellalyle, with a baffled expression, shrugged her shoulders and proceeded on her way.

By chance, the girl witnessed one of the garrison's soldiers – the depleted force left behind by the king – take from his wife a leather bag containing food. Ethla stood next them, straining to hear what they were saying. The woman suddenly noticed the features of an ill-formed, little face looking up at them, smiling inanely, and barked, "Go away, stupid girl!" causing Ethla to beat a hasty retreat, but not before she had managed to glean the essentials of their conversation, and it set her thinking she should do the same.

Next morning, in showers of rain, the mounted knights assembled in the courtyard waiting to escort the princess. The horses were startled, some rearing when the small figure of Ethla emerged from a doorway and darted amongst them to hand a package to von Streitz. The soldier, still feeling aggrieved, as the only bodyguard whose posy gifts to Hellalyle she had never personally acknowledged, thought it a joke as it came from the idiot girl, and with his comrades laughing, he erroneously believed they were mocking him. Feeling the butt of some orchestrated prank, he threw Ethla's parcel to the ground, the horse's hooves trampling it into the mud. The unfortunate girl watched from within the shadow of the doorway and, convinced she was publicly spurned and ridiculed, suffered near catatonic shock, imagining the reality of her ugliness had revisited in the cruellest of ways, causing Ethla to retreat to her little room, crying uncontrollably amongst her secret cache of flowers.

Ignorant of the grief he had innocently caused, von Streitz waited for the right moment to catch Runa alone. Seeing she was the only one present in the corridor outside the royal chambers, he caught her attention.

"Madam, can you afford me a few moments of your time? It is imperative I talk to you." Intensely curious of what the soldier wanted of her, she gestured with her hands an invitation to speak. Swallowing nervously, he exclaimed, "Do you know of any impediment that has caused me to offend the princess?"

Taken aback, the lady replied, "Nonsense, nothing at all! What brings you to ask such a question?"

The knight furtively looked about him, making sure there was no one within earshot and said, "Like my comrades, I have on occasion sent flowers to Her Highness as a show of innocent appreciation."

"Yes, yes, I'm sure it was," Runa replied with a mischievous grin.

To which von Streitz, in indignant tones, spluttered, "I know you do not believe me, but it is true. But what I really want to say is this: after handing many bouquets to Ethla – hoping she would pass them to the princess – the king's daughter has never once thanked me. What have I done wrong for Princess Hellalyle to snub me?"

Runa retorted, "Did you speak slowly to Ethla, in carefully chosen words, what you intended?"

"No, not really, I thought it would be obvious," the knight replied.

Runa, deep in thought, walked over to a window and with a sigh said, "I think I know what has happened. Leave it to me, and somebody will get back to you."

With relief, von Streitz departed.

However, it seemed the girl had disappeared. A thorough search carried out discovered her hiding in the storeroom in a state of distress. A request was sent out to Hellalyle to come quickly as Ethla refused to come out, throwing screaming tantrums when attempts were made to remove her, refusing to face the outside world. The princess duly arrived on the scene, and briefed on the situation, she entered Ethla's refuge and closed the door behind her, leaving her alone with the backward girl…

Nobody knew what Hellalyle said to placate Ethla, but sure enough, eventually, they both emerged, and much to everyone's relief, Ethla seemed her old self once again.

The unfortunate event prompted Hellalyle, with Runa in attendance, to visit her bodyguard.

"Gentlemen, may I have your attention," she exclaimed.

"No doubt you have heard all about the goings on concerning the little kitchen maid, Ethla, and her unhappy experience. I am aware you have many important tasks, namely the defence of the realm and myself within it, and what I am about to say will seem inconsequential in comparison. Nevertheless, I would like to ask you to be very careful in what you say to the girl. Her comprehension and articulation of language are limited, and with her defective hearing and sight, misunderstandings can arise. I am personally schooling her to improve the girl's verbal communication. A more desirable condition is ongoing, but, for the time being, please refrain from giving any messages to her."

Before she departed, the princess took von Streitz aside, to offer her heartfelt thanks for his floral gifts that had gone astray. But, now the truth had come out, the subdued soldier held his head in shame as he mentioned to Hellalyle his guilt in throwing Ethla's parcel to the ground. However, Hellalyle persuaded him to let sleeping dogs lie, offering her thoughts that Ethla was incapable of malice or forethought, bearing grudges was not in her nature, and all would soon be forgotten. For once, Hellalyle was proved wrong in part in this assumption, for Ethla had not forgotten as the princess was soon to learn...

Runa, the lady-in-waiting, was leaving the kitchens and crossing the courtyard after another heavy shower when she observed Ethla bearing a long stick in her hand, standing near a large puddle. The girl seemed to be staring at an object in the water. Suddenly, Ethla struck the surface of the pool with the rod, before running off in a fit of tears. Scurrying out of sight, she ran blindly into the stables, where she collided with a boorish, burly bumpkin who had just dumped a load of fodder. He was a Russian Tsygan, from near Novgorod Velikij, reputed to have been a horse-stealer, and now handicapped by drink. Reacting impulsively, the contemptuous fellow savagely kicked the witless girl.

"Get out of my way, you idiot!" he growled, as Ethla pitched forward onto the earthen, mucky straw-strewn floor.

Hellalyle – chancing to reach the back of the outbuilding at the same time – witnessed the confrontation, with Hildebrand and two other knights, Frederick Schtauffen and Uggi Bergfalk, stood behind her, their figures obscured in the dimness. The princess's usually equable manner turned to outrage as she raised her voice.

"Hey! Stop that at once you brute – what do you think you are doing!"

The bodyguard, Bergfalk, prepared to draw his sword, believing her to be in danger, and incensed a fellow countryman had disgraced his homeland, but Hildebrand, apparently unconcerned, restrained him, and under his breath, said, "Hold it, let's wait a moment; see what the princess does."

The coarse, unsophisticated man, visibly shaken at being caught in the act by the princess, blurted excuses. "Your Highness, please pardon me. I am only a poor peasant!"

But her steely-blue eyes flashing with anger transfixed his conscience like an excruciating sword thrust. His sturdy frame buckled, he groaned and keeled forward. Grovelling awkwardly, humiliated and in extreme pain, it was as if his unprovoked violence had incurred the wrath of some all-seeing goddess meting out justice, who, glaring down at a cowering bully, rebuked him sharply.

"My man, never let me see you do that again. Under my guidance, this castle should be a refuge from such brutality, but your action has besmirched its reputation. Be very thankful it is I, that caught you out. If it had been a certain bodyguard of mine, your life would have surely ended. Now go on your way and let this be a warning."

Little Ethla, still trembling as she knelt on the ground observing this remarkable castigation, gazed up in wonder at the vision of a person with extraordinary powers. Hellalyle gently eased the bruised and shaken waif to her feet and summoned help. Runa took the girl away, comforting her as they went, and at the princess's chambers Ethla received treatment for her injuries.

When Hellalyle was alone once more, her countenance returned to usual, displaying her innate nature of infinite kindness and compassion. It was in this tranquil pose that the three knights caught sight of her bodily outline (her eyes still pursuing the miscreant, as he took to his heels) silhouetted in the brilliant sunshine streaming through the stable door, and within its penumbra she resembled an inscrutable guiding light, gazing through the portal of an impenetrable world.

Later, Runa related the peculiar circumstance of Ethla gawking at the puddle, to which Hellalyle replied, "This is baffling, for

I observed the same, equally curious incident with the girl standing by a water trough. What on earth can it be that has given rise to her obsessive preoccupation? I have asked the girl about it, but she refuses to speak, and if you press her, a flood of tears comes on. It is most upsetting. Let us hope we stumble on the answer one day, and end Ethla's torment."

As if divine providence intervened, the puzzle resolved itself next morning, when Hellalyle, returning to her castle chamber and discovering the door ajar, overheard the voice of a child gabbling to itself. Edging forward quietly, she peeped through the opening and beheld the intriguing spectacle of Ethla seated at the princess's dressing table, trying to comb her dishevelled hair. All childish innocence, Ethla carelessly clutched a cherished, polished bronze mirror in her chubby hand.

This exquisite antique artefact – crafted in the Han dynasty – had been sent as a gift to Hellalyle by an admirer, a chieftain from a remote region of the Urals. The area had been the home to the extinct Potchevash people, who had once traded in such precious objects – Hellalyle's legendary name, spreading far and wide, had reached some of the remotest parts of the known world.

Chattering away, Ethla studied her reflection. Speaking in indistinct syllables, finding it difficult to articulate, the naïve girl was comparing her ill-formed features with the enchanting face of her mistress. Fortunately, Hellalyle could interpret what the girl was saying…

"I am an ugly girl. Never be pretty like the princess. She is the most beautiful lady of all." The hapless girl was doing her utmost to straighten her unkempt hair but to no avail. Her frustration reduced her to tears as she strove to blot out, trying to wave away, the deformed expression cast back by the inexorable reflector.

Deeply affected by what she had seen, Hellalyle moved silently away, down the steps and into the shade of the castle walls where she paused, lost in thought, hardly aware of her surroundings now she realised that what had so perturbed the witless servant girl had been the sight of her reflection in the water.

When her lady-in-waiting caught up with the princess, aware of her absorption, she enquired, "Your Highness, what troubles you so?"

Hellalyle's concentration disturbed, without so much as turning around, she said to Runa, "I have discovered the reason for the strange behaviour of Ethla, we both witnessed, when she was looking at the water. It appears she was repelled by her image in the reflection, comparing her unfortunate features with that of another woman." Pondering, for a moment, the princess went on to say, "We take for granted the normality of what we are. Yet, it seems only good fortune determines that it should be so. For there are some – shall we call them unfortunates – who, at birth, are unaccountably robbed of sound body and mind, condemning them to a life of humiliation and early death. This experience is a salutary lesson in humility we must never forget."

She effusively bade Runa summon her seamstress and several other assistants. She declared, "It is my sincere intention to completely transform Ethla's physical appearance from that of a plain, unappealing girl to a striking figure of regal bearing. She is to be beautified and decked in eye-catching apparel, and become a princess, if only for one day!"

Runa may have been intrigued by this unusual requirement, but was quick to respond. Soon, the disabled little miss, rubbing her eyes as if experiencing a dream, was ushered into Hellalyle's chamber to be bathed and perfumed, her face cleansed with unguents and powdered, her cheeks touched with safflower, her dishevelled hair professionally groomed.

Ethla marvelled at her mistress's extensive wardrobe. A bright yellow garment of rich brocade was carefully selected and painstakingly measured for adjustment to the girl's figure. This dress was put together with a delicate, gold-threaded veil to partially hide the face, a wimple of honey-coloured silk strung with pearls, and precious jewels to complement the ensemble. Hellalyle decided Ethla should wear a headdress like a Kokosh, the forerunner of the Kokoshnik, in tribute to the Slavic peoples that her father ruled over

and the Russian traders who frequented the town below the castle.

Hours later, after much expert preparation, and with close attention to detail, Ethla had to pinch herself – captivated, if extremely self-conscious – as into the Han mirror, held by Hellalyle, she gazed in wonder at the miraculous alteration to her appearance. Such was the skill of Hellalyle's retainers, the girl resembled a diminutive Byzantine Empress. The princess looked proudly at her innocent protégée, delighted with the result, and drew the girl's attention. With Ethla now standing before her with an animated expression and open-mouthed, the princess as plainly and kind-heartedly as possible said, "You are now about to perform the role of a princess!"

Before Hellalyle could say more, Ethla, overcome with excitement, jumped for joy, skipping around the room, while onlookers, including Hellalyle, laughed with expressions of delight.

Runa calmed the situation, and as soon as Ethla had regained her composure, she presented herself again before the princess, and listened attentively as best she could, as Hellalyle proceeded to offer the girl some elementary instruction in court etiquette, reassuring her she would be at hand if she lost her nerve.

Princess Hellalyle requested the attendance of Hildebrand, the castle sheriff, and the head of the household, as she had an important statement to make. These essential officials gathered before her, expecting an earth shattering announcement, were taken aback when she said, "I have already sanctioned this with Queen Gudrun, but now I request you inform everyone in the castle, that for one day only, I will be accompanied by another princess. She is to be afforded the same deference befitting one of noble birth, and there must be no show of mockery or ridicule of any kind, or I shall be much displeased. Do I make myself clear?"

As rumour spread concerning the real identity of this royal personage, incredulity gave way to unquestioning obedience to Hellalyle's wishes; in their eyes the king's daughter could do no wrong, her faultless judgements inspiring zealous allegiance.

Accompanied by her redoubtable mistress, Ethla, imitating her royal model, developed grace and an air of dignified reserve so that people would bow respectfully, without a trace of derision, even though it was humorous to observe.

In due course, Hellalyle formally presented the changed Ethla to the princess's bodyguards.

"Gentlemen," she announced, "May I present the Princess of the Hinterland." It was a title Hellalyle thought most appropriate, aware of Ethla's origins. The knights were on their best behaviour, dutifully presenting arms to this unfamiliar dignitary, their impeccable civility boosting the girl's self-confidence. It was Hildebrand, of course, who with characteristic bravado stepped forward.

"Princess, may I say what an honour it is for my comrades and I to be presented to such an appealing lady."

In a spontaneously romantic gesture he raised the girl's hand as if to kiss it. Hellalyle, watching the proceedings with reserved satisfaction, masked her natural amusement by subtly concealing her smile, while Ethla, instinctively aware of the knight's genuine fondness for her mistress, became coy and uncomfortable on becoming a momentary object of the knight's affection.

At nightfall, little Ethla, exhausted after all the exertion and excitement, rubbed her eyelids as the kindly Runa helped her undress. Once divested of her magnificent garments and adornments, bone-tired but utterly contented, she lay back on a makeshift bed the lady-in-waiting had prepared for her and fell sound asleep.

Next day, Hellalyle understood she must change the nature of Ethla's menial duties at the castle from mere functionary – or scullery maid – to a more significant role. She would now minister to the princess's needs, performing specific personal requirements within the range of her capability. Such an arrangement would also serve to shield the girl from ridicule or disrespect. Thenceforward, Thorstein's matchless daughter, and Runa, her devoted lady-in-waiting, would be followed on most occasions by a cheerful, simple-hearted, guileless girl, who now unmistakably exuded both more self-esteem and more significant joy in life.

The time came when the princess introduced Ethla to Christianity, but without influence, by showing her around the chapel at the castle, and the monastery at Thorbjorg. At the imposing, religious house, she set out the significance of the mediaeval sanctuary, the buildings orientation east-to-west. Once inside, Hellalyle attempted to describe the relevance of the images and symbols contained within.

"This building, like the chapel in the fortress, represents God's house on earth. Here in the windows, we can see images that represent the important figures from the Holy Bible, our book of guidance, for without it there would be chaos in the world."

Ethla stood watching and listening, her head slightly cocked to one side, with a finger to her chin, not giving away whether she understood or not. Hellalyle paused, as they both stood to watch a nun in front of the altar prostrate herself in confirmation – the princess whispering a commentary, explaining to girl the unfolded scene.

Pressing on with her discourse, she said, "Once again, here on the east side we have more scenes depicted in the glass... This area is what we call the chancel..."

Hellalyle then broke off and looked intently at Ethla, still with a finger to the chin, who now bore a distinctly vacant look, as if trying to understand it all. The princess, sadly and reluctantly, concluded that theology was beyond the comprehension of the simple girl.

Riding back to Preben castle, Hellalyle hardly spoke to her knights, preoccupied, tussling with what seemed, on the face of it, an intractable problem; does she arrange the baptism of Ethla into the Christian faith, an insincere gesture to the almighty, as the girl has no real understanding of spiritual movements? Or, leave things be, for the princess believed Ethla was an offspring of the pagan people, whose beliefs were the personification of nature, something she greatly admired. It was a conundrum she had trouble solving, so she consulted the learned Abbot Jurian, in his private quarters at the Abbey of Sunniva.

With both seated, Jurian, expressionless, with hands clasped, bare-headed with his mitre on a table at the side, listened to what the princess had to say. When the princess finished talking, she felt awkward in the long silence as the cleric pondered his reply. Finally, emitting a faint grunt, he said, "Your Highness, I have given this careful thought, and have concluded that the girl you found in the hinterland, because she possesses infirmity of body and mind, we could consider her to be an innocent child with nothing to cleanse from her soul – but my church will still require Ethla to be baptised into the Christian faith."

The princess, with an audible sigh, exclaimed, "My dear abbot, you cannot appreciate how much your learned judgement affects me. Please forgive my indecision of this important matter. I shall need more time to consider your prudence."

She then knelt before the abbot for his blessing, he responded, tracing out the sign of the cross over her, while murmuring words of Latin scripture. As he assisted her to rise, his deep voice spoke in a fatherly tone, "I hope my Hellalyle will now sleep on what I have said."

The princess, in response, stood on tiptoes and kissed him on the cheek, and he responded with a satisfied smile. She said her goodbyes and returned to the castle accompanied by her bodyguard.

But Princess Hellalyle never came to a decision – the first, and only, time a protracted puzzle defeated the eminent lady. Thorstein's daughter was not to know her subconscious, under the influence of the spiritual forces of the wild, was resisting the urge to transform their minion Ethla, from an innocent, empty vessel, to one of enlightenment. For there was a future perilous task they had mapped out for the little unfortunate, requiring a mind devoid of preconception.

17

A dancing lesson in the great hall of the castle

One bright, sunlit morning, a procession comprising Princess Hellalyle, her lady-in-waiting Runa, Ethla, and four attendant soldiers of her bodyguard, approached the great hall. On reaching the portal, Hellalyle dismissed her escorts, saying, "When I pass through this door my protectors cannot come with me. Although I appreciate the role you must play in defending my person, this auditorium is one of the most secure parts of the fortress, a place where I now need privacy, so it is with regret I only require one knight to be on guard outside. Would you decide amongst yourselves who it is to be?"

Hildebrand, nonplussed at the princess's casual attitude to matters of security, acquiesced to her demand rather than have another argument. The knights decided their leader should remain, for if anything went awry, he would take the ultimate responsibility; and so it was, the Prince of England guarded the entrance.

Standing alone, taking stock of his surroundings, the Englishman was eager to learn what the princess was up to. Peeping through a chink in a broken panel of a half-curtained door, he was surprised to see the king's daughter endeavouring to teach Ethla the elementary steps of dancing, energetically treading a reigen with Runa, while patiently stopping at intervals to engage the attention of the clumsy, unschooled child.

Hildebrand resumed his guard for a while, but then, unable to contain his curiosity any longer, watched the princess more closely. She was the woman with the gracious manner he had come to know, bearing all the hallmarks of royal upbringing, with her eyes fixed, no twisting of her head or stretching her neck to the object of attention, always controlling her body in dignified, harmonious motion. He now observed how the king's daughter had discarded her heavy dress of rich brocade and undergarments, leaving her wearing just a delicate, see-through petticoat. In the safety of the closed-off hall of the castle, its entrance guarded by the leader of her knights, the princess believed she was safe from the prying eyes of the outside world, so she had shed away her modesty. Hellalyle then put on lightweight shoes, unlike anything witnessed before. They were fastened with ribbons of silk over the top of the foot, around the rear of her shapely leg – above the ankle – and to the front again overlapping one another, completed with a finely executed bow above the heel, the silk band on the inside passing underneath the arch of the foot. The ends of the bow tucked tidily away out of sight. The lady then attended to her hair – securing the braids which glittered like gold with pins and a decorous strip of linen; accomplished in such a skilful way her "crown" of glorious locks remained absolute. These altogether, adjustments to the noble woman's attire, allowed her to move gracefully and with precision. She astounded Runa and Ethla with her adroit ability to mime with the supreme power of interpretation, the phrasing of arms, hand movements, gesticulating to heaven, even leaping, and performing pirouettes of remarkable agility and verve, while standing on the very point of her toes – illustrating the extreme strength in Hellalyle's perfectly sculptured feet. The beautiful lines of the arabesques, the expressive eyes – her ability knew no limits. It was such, the gallery was witnessing a dance in the classical and romantic style – a ballet, hundreds of years before its authentic appearance. The princess exhibited such artistic skill, the choreography expressed by the danseuse was pure poetry in motion.

Hellalyle's Ballet in the Great Hall

As she glided across the floor of the hall, Hildebrand was astonished and entranced to notice Hellalyle's exquisite figure silhouetted in shafts of sunlight from a high window, which shone through the diaphanous gauze of her silken undergarment. What he observed confirmed the rumours that were never openly spoken: the princess possessed such an appealing physical form that other women envied her; she was the desire of all men, but the ultimate untouchable. A legendary outline, worthy of veneration in moon-white marble.

How Princess Hellalyle learned her mastery of such dance art form was a secret that she withheld from even her closest friends. This excellence was thanks to the benevolent spirits of the wild, for she had lobbied them many times, requesting they teach her the dextrous motions, exquisite delicacy of the graceful crane, and the choreography of bird murmuration. They finally relented to the princess, descending on her chamber while she in a state of prolonged solitude, whisking her away to the farthest corners of creation, to learn the rhythmic structure of the cranes' movement and posture. These visitations went on, seemingly without end, until the princess had absorbed the elegance, beauty of form, of the gracious birds. Only then would she be taught the notation behind the shape-shifting patterns of the Sturnidae – the passerine, above Lake Eydis.

To improve her studies further, by adaptation of wardrobe, and footwear invention, she developed apparel specific to the ballet's aesthetic principles, enabling Hellalyle to reach pinnacles of accomplishment never equalled since, constructing solo ballets, one of which she devoted to the tutors of her craft. Via this medium, she would tell stories, and it fascinated, riveting the attention of the captivated onlooker. They were artistic gems which, when viewed through the telescope of history, were waiting for matrimony with altogether special music, composed to stimulate the mind and evoke visual dreams images consensual with her dance form.

When Hellalyle had finished her entertainment, Runa and Ethla clapped enthusiastically, with abandoned glee. The princess, now out of breath, curtseyed to acknowledge their appreciation before Runa demanded an encore.

"More, more," she said, and Hellalyle duly obliged.

The knight was tickled to observe this happy trio, relishing brief respite from the constraining etiquette of a royal court. Hildebrand, who had never seen such a powerful and imaginative rendition, said unto himself, "No longer am I surprised the princess had far outpaced me through the woods on the rescue of Ethla from that distant village. What an extraordinary and desirable woman, the original beauty, the like I will never see again."

The warrior, hypnotised by the compelling impression Hellalyle had made on him, was unaware of the Abbess, Princess Amora, accompanied by a nun, standing in the shadows observing the soldier. When she coughed, to make her presence known, he jumped out of his skin, like an unseemly youth caught in a mischievous act.

"Princess, I hope you did not hear my words, for I was thinking out loud. I did not mean anything by it, only idle talk," he said, standing to attention and saluting her with his sword, as he returned to his watch.

As she walked forward, there came no reply, only a faint expression of amusement on her face – for she had overheard him. Then, through the corner of his eye, he could see the abbess stood on tiptoes, squinting through the very slit in the door he had utilised to pry on Hellalyle, only then to glance at him with a playful smile, and say, "Young man, you must keep your ardour in check!"

On entering the hall, Amora closed the door, leaving the knight apprehensive as to what she might divulge to her niece – little knowing how astute and intelligent the king's sister was, au fait with the conventions of royal betrothals and marriages, while at the same time enlightened about affairs of the heart. Amora had already intuitively discerned an undeclared mutual attraction between the knight and Hellalyle and was ready to be entertained by the idiosyncrasies of Hildebrand's winning character.

When the abbess departed, it seemed to Hildebrand that she and the nun were trying to repress their laughter as they moved along the passageway. Hellalyle, Runa and Ethla left a few minutes later, the princess deliberately concealing her blushes beneath the hood of her mantle. As they proceeded, the knight at the rear, Runa persistently teased the princess.

Ethla was at a loss to gauge the meaning of the situation, until, unexpectedly catching the gist, she began to titter irrepressibly. In the end, Hellalyle lost patience, raising a finger and stamping her foot as she tried to put a stop to their playful antics.

On reaching her chamber, Hellalyle, in a hushed voice, asked Runa to instruct Hildebrand (the princess being too tongue-tied to address him in person) to arrange for some of her bodyguards to assist her aunt, in preparation for the arduous journey to the Monastery of Thorbjorg.

Late in the day, the princess solicited a private meeting with the Englishman. Entering her room, Hildebrand kept a respectful distance, while Hellalyle, with an inscrutable air, her head covered, contemplated the prospect from the window. In due course, she addressed him quietly, without turning around.

"Swear on your word of honour, as a Christian knight, that you will never divulge the intimate scenes you witnessed today."

To which Hildebrand replied, "Although I acted out of simple curiosity, I deplore my unwarranted inquisitiveness, even if it would be hard to imagine anyone betraying the confidence of one held in such high regard as you are. My lips are sealed, and I remain steadfast in my loyalty to King Thorstein's daughter."

He swallowed, and suddenly, in an uncontrolled outburst of emotion, blurted, "Still, I could not help being captivated by your dazzling and thrilling performance, especially bewitched by your physical beauty!"

Although he could not see it, his involuntary idolisation seemed to intimate that he had indeed seen the outline of her near-naked body. Hellalyle smiled reticently, as if, touched by his fondness for her, to excuse his outpouring. Then, with her back still presented to him, she let the matter rest and said, "You may go," dismissing the knight.

As he turned to go, Hildebrand cast the silent, inscrutable figure a quick look, with a dreaded feeling she had irretrievably turned away from him, and with pursed lips and shaking of the head, he left the room, regretting his stupidity.

Subsequently, for a short time, the chemistry between them became remote and inhibited, the princess looking self-conscious when their eyes met. On returning to the great hall, Hildebrand noticed that a carpenter had repaired the splintered panel in the door.

The warrior prince often recalled the day on which Hellalyle had danced so alluringly, with supreme artistry and brilliance, raising the question whether any woman could be more attractive and accomplished. Little did he know this theatrical spectacle was the princess's dramatisation of a tale of chivalry being recorded in the leaves of an illuminated manuscript, inscribed by the hand of this nonpareil daughter of an absent king.

Hellalyle had felt impelled to document – for posterity – a memoir of her life with the twelve knights, revealing not only a better understanding of her guardians but her passionate conviction that these brave soldiers, save Hildebrand, were transcendental beings. Their appearance at the castle had not been mere happenstance but held more profound significance – which she was still trying to summarise.

Also, there was the notable role of that English prince who had come to occupy such a prominent place in the narrative...

Frequently the princess would return to the manuscript, set on purple parchment, with its exquisite illustrations. Decorated with gold and brilliant colours, some pages depicted delightful, lifelike images of the animals and birds she held close to her heart. When light struck its surface, it glowed, displaying such sharpness of detail it could generate the power to affect even the minds of uneducated people, and reveal the very voice and vision of Hellalyle. However, in the hands of unbelievers, the script would become unintelligible, its image blurred; so, infidels were forced to abandon it, bewildered and frustrated. Only then would it return to its original state.

Residents at the castle became aware of the existence of Hellalyle's working Chronicle, but mystery still surrounded it. How had she devoted time and found inspiration to create a chef-d'oeuvre, which would have been a lifetime's work for a monastic scribe? The riddle was resolved one afternoon when Ethla, exhibiting her uncontrollable trait of falling asleep in unusual places – now slumbering unnoticed in a shadowy corner of Hellalyle's chamber – suddenly awoke to spot the princess, quill in hand, applying ink to vellum laid on a lectern by a window. Blinking in disbelief, Ethla focused her attention on the arresting sight of her mistress being instructed in her craft by strange phantom figures – tonsured polymaths, their heads clean-shaven from ear-to-ear in the Celtic tradition, were each dressed in the monastic garb of the time. In front of her very eyes were gathered the reawakened spirits of those remarkable Ionian confrères of the scriptoria, disseminating God's word to the pagans of the far north of Britain: the dissenters of the Synod of Whitby. Their very presence, in association with the enigmatic Hellalyle, helped to give authenticity to the legend that this religious fellowship was sympathetic to the participation of women, more connected to nature, and related to the princess's interpretation of the Holy Scriptures – if at odds with the Roman papacy.

The outlines of their figures were indistinct as they worked with remarkable skill, and at superhuman speed; dyeing parchment, marking grid patterns, applying gold, and preparing inks and glues. Mesmerised, Ethla watched one oblate standing close to Hellalyle, speaking softly in a foreign tongue. He was guiding her hand, her fingers moving nimbly and with such dexterity that Ethla thought the princess was possessed of magical powers – mainly when, at that very moment, an exquisite illustration of a knight in armour sprang to life on the page.

At the sound of a knock at the door, the apparitions would vanish abruptly, only to reappear when the visitor had gone away.

Ethla, now hiding behind a stone pillar, spellbound in wonderment, continued in her gawky innocence watching this astonishing scenario. She was unaware that the ethereal beings observed her presence, accepting the girl because her disability had rendered her incapable of malice or sin...for the benevolent spirits of the wild had chosen well. For they knew difficult times lay ahead for the Princess of Eydis and Orn. There would be events that required the presence of a seemingly insignificant, but innocent, child, incorruptible and unfettered by her physical body, to confuse the dark forces.

When the princess had finished her handiwork, and the ghostly tutors had disappeared, her manuscript was placed for safety in an ornate chest beautifully painted with woodland scenes. As Hellalyle was leaving she caught sight of Ethla, who looked apprehensive, fearful of the princess's reaction at discovering her, unwittingly an eyewitness to a manifestation beyond her wildest dreams. Deep in thought, she gave Ethla a penetrating look, unsettling the diminutive innocent, who stammered incoherently, "I did not mean to fall asleep. I have not seen anything. Please, let me go..."

She was increasingly tongue-tied as her fear mounted.

Hellalyle's expression, soon retrieving its empathy and warmth, broke into a radiant, reassuring smile, putting the girl at ease.

"Come, come with me, do not be frightened," said the princess, as she took Ethla by the hand, leading her from the room.

Hellalyle knew instinctively that any stray gossip Ethla might let out would bear little credibility, and in any case, this pure soul would never betray her obedience and trust.

18

Encounter on the turret stair

Hellalyle, followed by the young Ethla, crossed the castle courtyard to a concealed doorway, where they started to climb the winding stair of a turret leading to the princess's apartment and the fortifications above. On their ascent, they halted by a small window, overhearing voices below. Peering through the opening, they spotted a group of her bodyguards, returned from surveying the outer defences of the fortress.

Their leader, assigned to inspect the battlements in his line of duty, was about to enter the hidden doorway to the spiral staircase the princess and her maid had used, unaware the woman he loved was within. Catching sight of Hildebrand at the foot of the tower, Hellalyle, apprehensive their paths might cross, hastened up the next flight. Ethla poked fun at her mistress's predicament, and, finding this turn of events amusing, she impulsively chased after Hellalyle with hair-brained glee. The princess, shouting breathlessly over her shoulder, rebuked the girl's witless behaviour.

As the echo of the knight's footsteps grew louder, the princess was eager to reach the privacy of her room, but high-spirited Ethla had other ideas. Mischievously overtaking Hellalyle, she was the first to enter the room, and slammed the door, sliding the bolt, leaving her luckless mistress stranded on the landing.

The unsuspecting Hildebrand drawing ever closer, the panic-

Meeting on the Turret Stairs

stricken princess implored Ethla to come to her senses and unlock the latch, but the impudent girl refused, treating the precarious scene as a childish prank. The Englishman finally reached their level and stood spellbound by this unexpected vision of the princess. Convinced fate had brought them together, he pressed forward heedlessly to embrace her, but Hellalyle – timorous and abashed – took upward flight once more, gaining but half-a-dozen steps before Hildebrand caught up with her. Hellalyle's back turned, her left hand braced against the wall to support her slender figure, she bowed her head until it nudged the rough stone surface of the staircase outer wall. The ardent warrior, his chainmail-gloved hands gripping the right arm she had surrendered, buried his enraptured face in the smooth folds of her sleeve.

Besotted Hildebrand, his back pressed firmly to the newel, kept hold of her arm passionately and raised her delicate hand to his lips; Hellalyle swooned.

With trembling voice, the knight declared she was, in truth, the fairest woman he had ever beheld, far excelling his runaway dreams. He begged her to ride out with him to Lake Eydis, whose enchanting waters seemed to reflect her transcendental beauty.

Overwhelmed by conflicting emotions, the princess felt her heart about to break; wretched, apprehensive, she burst into tears. She knew it would be her father, the arbiter of her suitors, who would ultimately control her destiny. Mortified by her reaction, Hildebrand felt unnerved that he had crudely misjudged her nature. Hellalyle cast a momentary glance at him as she fled to her chamber, which Ethla had wilfully left open so she would be able to eavesdrop on the proceedings.

One peek at the despondent prince sufficed for Ethla to dart forward and embrace him with little inhibition, before skipping back into the room and gauchely elbowing the door to with a bang. The knight, stifling a nervous chuckle, wistfully reflected that he might have found an unusual ally in his struggle to win Hellalyle's heart.

Confused and downhearted, Hildebrand tried to compose

himself, counting aloud the uneven steps as he climbed to the ramparts where he was to finish his tour of duty that day.

Later, after an hour had passed, he descended, passing the princess's apartment. He noticed as the door suddenly swung ajar to reveal Ethla, beaming inanely, frantically waving a silk scarf belonging to her mistress. Impulsively, the girl ran up to Hildebrand and pressed the garment into his hand, then scurried back, tittering mindlessly. Stupefied, holding the kerchief to his face, he looked up and made out the figure of Hellalyle, poised in the shadows at the far end of her chamber. The exquisite features of her pretty face were just visible beneath her hood, with both hands holding her cloak together at the throat. In the intriguing image, although blurred in the ghostly light, her penetrating eyes could be seen intently focused, following him, before she slowly turned away, motioning Ethla to close the chamber door.

At nightfall, people flocked outside the castle to watch the awe-inspiring spectacle of a celestial body in the heavens. For it was a comet, which had suddenly appeared without warning, its dazzling tail on closer observation, just for an instant, appeared like the menacingly

The unheralded appearance of the Comet

shaped handle of a brandished mace; its spiked head glowed with ultimate white, like a cauldron of fire. Fearful, in disbelief, the mood of the crowd was uneasy, as they muttered amongst themselves, speculating superstitiously, about what strange portent it foretold.

19

The meeting in the garden

One afternoon the princess dispatched a message to Hildebrand, saying she would like to take a walk in the castle grounds, with the prospect of a bright, clear night in store. She explained that as she would be on her own, a bodyguard should be at hand, keeping a discreet distance to afford her privacy. Secretly though, Hellalyle hoped it would be Hildebrand in person who would undertake the assignment.

Wearing warm clothes to ward off the cooler elements, the princess stealthily descended the torch-lit turret steps to emerge in the fresh, evening air, and followed a pathway in the direction of the walled garden. Picking her way through the shadows beneath the high walls of the fortress, she put on an air of dignity and self-control, to disguise her heightened expectation of meeting the warrior who had secretly conquered her heart. By a rustic archway in the lunar brightness, she felt the presence of someone standing nearby and crept forward tentatively. The vague outline of a knight came into view, who was gazing up at the firmament, waiting patiently.

Ever closer she came, now glimpsing his surcoat, blazoned with three lions passant and an axe motif; he had a sheathed sword and dagger at his waist, a heraldic shield strapped to his shoulder, and a helm with a visor which he carried under his left arm. The soldier stood to attention, and after bowing formally to the princess, straightened himself, revealing the distinct features of Hildebrand.

At first, the princess showed just a glimmer of recognition in her smile. Then she acknowledged him with such inclination of the head that the pendant pearl earrings she had chosen to wear for this chance meeting began to dance and shimmer with their lustrous sheen, in the bluish radiance of a full moon.

Once again, the princess had been unaware that the benevolent forces of the natural world had worked their magic, seeping into her chamber to swirl invisibly around her. How subtly they had induced her to wear those droplet jewels on her clandestine assignation with Hildebrand, as if the very pearls reflected Hellalyle's true nature, one of innocence and purity – a quality mystically linked to that celestial body shining above. These gems, astral signs of Gemini, foretold a dramatic cosmic spectacle in time to come, a portent of this constellation. It was something beyond their comprehension now, but it would trigger unexpected events, bringing to fulfilment a heroic and romantic mediaeval legend.

Hellalyle stood there a short time, looking at Hildebrand, who complimented the princess, "Your Highness, are you aware of how the moonlight highlights your beauty?"

Hellalyle blushed, never had the princess been in a position of such disguised intimacy with a man, and was coy, unable to respond in a coquettish way, and slipped quietly through an archway into the garden, as if to escape the occasion. Hildebrand followed her at a discreet distance, but all the while inescapably drawn to the woman that aroused his deepest desire.

At a leisurely pace, Hellalyle thoughtfully strolled past beds of flowers and clipped hedges, pausing to pick an individual bloom exceptionally fragrant at nightfall. Holding the flower to sniff its appealing scent, she softly said, "I had sensed, intuitively, that it would be you who chose to accompany me, unwilling to place the responsibility on your comrades so late in the day," only to be surprised by his unexpected reply.

"I have not approached the others, for if I had mentioned it, they would have vied with each other, I dare say, a virtual fight could have ensued, for the once in a lifetime opportunity to chaperone the princess on such a beautiful evening."

Hellalyle seemed bashful, lowering her voice to express how much she owed to them, delighted her guard should think so well of her. On reflection, she motioned him to walk alongside, to discuss matters on her mind, so, Hildebrand and the princess, still bearing the flower in her hand, sauntered as a couple through the moonlit garden.

She asked many questions: concerning his family, his homeland, and how he came to be a knight adventurer. She wanted to learn about the lives and fortunes of the other soldiers – particularly von Altenburg – but Hildebrand discreetly refrained from divulging information about his comrades, so Hellalyle let it pass, moving on to other things.

She related to Hildebrand what Ethla had told her about Karl von Altenburg, how she gave him the nickname "the knight with no face" after secretly observing him in his quarters, consuming the bowl of soup specially prepared for him. Hellalyle reproved the impudent servant girl's insensitive remark, her ridicule of this unfortunate man with such a cruel and sinister epithet. The princess learned that Ethla had concealed herself in the corner of von Altenburg's room, watching him remove his bandage and recoiling in horror at the appalling spectacle of one eye flashing from the bloody mass of a festering facial wound. In sheer fright, she gave herself away, and the soldier, furious that she had caught sight of him without his face cover, flew into a rage. He hurled the dish of food onto the stone floor, bellowing strange noises as she fled.

"After this unnerving episode, the girl remained terrified – like many others in the castle – of encountering this wild and volatile figure," said Hellalyle.

The very drama of the tale induced Hildebrand to reveal more:

"This I can say: the knight will not return to his homeland, not wishing his friends to see his physical deformity. Also, he bears a heavy burden of guilt, having failed to save the life of his general, Barbarossa, as he drowned in the river Selaph at Cilicia. Von Altenburg remains convinced that the evil water sprite had been responsible for the Emperor's death, vowing retribution on this malevolent fiend of the underworld. Lust for vengeance has consumed him ever since."

Hellalyle was unnerved by his disclosure, but Hildebrand, now unstoppable in his narrative, went on to say, "As the Teuton's closest friend I have seen a marked change of mood when he returns from his stint of duty guarding the princess. It was as if he had found peace of mind, greater self-confidence – feelings, which in turn, even affected your other bodyguards."

Hellalyle listened intently, replying in her modest way, "You have moved my heart to its very depths by what you have just recounted. However, you must try to understand that I am a mere mortal woman, committed as a trustee of God's kingdom to do my best to ensure that all living things, man or beast, flourished, and came to no harm. I suggest that if my presence has brought comfort to those around me, it has only sprung from my inner being, not by divine guidance."

Hildebrand, moved by her sincerity, lightened his conscience, saying, "I would like to offer my sincere apologies for compromising you through my unchivalrous behaviour when I made advances to you on the turret steps."

The princess, with an affectionate smile, lifted her hand to touch his troubled brow.

"If the brave English knight still wished, then we will ride together to Lake Eydis."

Overjoyed, at her acclimation, and responding to Hellalyle's first caress, he gently raised his hand, holding her fingers to his face, but in this moment of bliss, he was unaware that their close association was observed, furtively, by a woman who had been sent to spy on them – under the orders of the princess's stepmother, Queen Gudrun.

The queen had been alert to Hildebrand's infatuation, but at first dismissed it as a simple matter, knowing full well that all men would be attracted to Hellalyle – who in return seemed oblivious to such attention. Gudrun had always been under the impression that the princess would be more committed to her duties to the kingdom, and would never compromise her father, who, as sovereign, had the right to determine her future. However, a rumour was now rife that the knight's increasing warmth of affection towards the young woman was now reciprocated. This new state of play had forced Queen Gudrun to keep an eye on her stepdaughter, and if substantial evidence of a liaison were proven, the queen would act to stifle it; should the princess refuse to yield, the seriousness of the situation would dictate an urgent message to inform her father.

20

Events at Lake Eydis

The Prince of England's consuming liaison with Hellalyle was cause for disquiet, not only within the royal household but amongst the soldiers appointed to protect the princess, who had persisted in criticising their leader's indiscretions. Their disapproval was aggravated further when Hildebrand instructed the eleven knights to remain on duty at the castle while he travelled, unescorted, to Lake Eydis with the princess, who, suggestively on this occasion, chose to wear a bright green dress as an expression of her love.

When they reached the lake (its expanse so broad that even on the clearest of days the far shore was barely visible), they crossed an extended isthmus to another water front, where they rode at a slow pace, side by side, skirting the water's edge. Absorbed in each other's company, they failed to notice being observed by a strange woman, swimming noiselessly, shiftily, a short distance out into the lake. Her lithe body was almost submerged beneath the surface – an ominous reappearance of the sinister figure that had tried to lure Hildebrand once before.

What had been a cloudless, azure sky became speckled with billowing cumulous, dove-feather grey and downy white, altering their shape propelled from one horizon to the other. Banks of reeds along the shoreline bent and swayed in the windy gusts as Hildebrand and Hellalyle passed by, while incoming waves curled and then broke, with a timeless, undying sound. High above, geese could be seen winging in their symmetric v formation, bound for a destination seemingly recognisable only to the birds themselves. Occasionally, the devoted couple would pull up to savour the nuances of these diverting scenes.

Further along the edge of the inland sea, Hildebrand suggested they dismount.

"Let me help you down, my distinguished young lady, and we will savour this wonderful day together. Over yonder, I perceive the very place for us, and not a finer location, with Lake Eydis to the front, and the mountains of Orn beyond. How amazing it is, that I share this locality with a woman who occupies my dreams to the expense of all others, and bears the title: The Princess of Eydis and Orn!"

Overcome by Hildebrand's romantic feelings of expression, she exclaimed, "Hildebrand, sometimes you say most wonderful things. I hope, I am the only woman that is drawn to you?"

Hildebrand smiled, as she placed her hand in his, and with her heart quickening with the intimacy she knew was coming, both headed to a smooth patch of turf beneath the trees. As the warrior led her across a meadow, the princess in a state of nirvana, she trailed out her free hand like a ballerina, her fingers kissing the tops of the waist-high grass that rippled in the wind, like the waves of the sea. Very soon they were lying down together embracing passionately, surrendering to the inevitability of their union, with their horses at ease, grazing contentedly nearby, seemingly innocent of the affairs of the heart.

However, silently, unobtrusively, the mysterious woman had waded out of the lake. Now, partly concealed behind some bushes, peeping out, she slyly observed the couple, spying on their intimate moments with an envious, vindictive look. Frighteningly, her expression suddenly changed into a mask of devilish possession, hissing and spitting venomously through her bared teeth.

All at once, at the exact moment of the couple's joining, the sky darkened threateningly, and the malevolent creature, raising her arms in terror as if to ward off some impending disaster, ran off, slipping back into the watery camouflage of the lake.

The gathering storm prompted Hildebrand to deliver Hellalyle to a secure place as soon as possible. "Come," he said, "We must urgently make tracks for home," and quickly drew the horses forward.

With the princess placing her foot into his cupped hands, she ably sprang up onto her saddle, and they hurriedly set off in the direction of Preben castle. Overhead, there was the sound of the frantic beating of wings as birds took flight, scattering in disarray.

With the knight in the lead, they followed the shoreline to the neck of the isthmus. They could not avoid re-crossing. Riding across this narrow strip of land, they experienced a disquieting change of atmosphere as an unnatural gloom descended. Now, menacing clouds appeared to plummet earthward, swirling in great vortices; and, further provoked, the squally wind howled and wailed with such force it buffeted and spun in a raging tempest. The surface of Lake Eydis was dramatically transformed, whipped into mountainous waves of water gyrating and colliding with each other, their foaming heads shorn off in gigantic sheets by the violence of the storm. The soldier feared for their lives as the maelstrom triggered flashing sabres of lightning and mighty reverberations of thunder. The horses reared in fright, almost unseating the riders, but suddenly the storm abated, as quickly as it had risen. The waters grew calm, casting an eerie silence.

The stunned couple stared at each other, bewildered by what they had witnessed. But before the two could utter a word, a terrifying detonation shattered the quiet, with ear-splitting impact. A horrid, smothering pall of black clouds split apart in the heavens, and out of its bright, lurid glare there loomed, at breakneck speed, a large and menacing troupe of phantasmal huntsmen. Some were mounted, some on foot, shrilly blasting their horns, with packs of yelping hounds streaking across the sky in manic pursuit.

As it thundered overhead, the sight struck horror in the princess.

"It is the *Wild Jagd!*" she cried out, familiar with its legendary prophecy of imminent catastrophe, of the sure death of those who witnessed it; she saw all too clearly, the ominous manifestation. The spectral trail hurtled onwards, before vanishing over the horizon.

"Hildebrand, please stop, I cannot go on."

Impulsively, the princess tried to dismount but slid to the ground in a state of shock. If Hildebrand was troubled by this inexplicable phantasmagoria, he concealed his reaction by trying to put her mind at rest as he helped her to her feet. It moved him that her ordinarily unruffled nature had exposed chinks of vulnerability.

"My prince, will you excuse my emotional behaviour," she said.

Eventually, they continued their journey, but in silence, as Hellalyle wrestled with the grave intimations of what the future might hold.

At the far end of the isthmus, where the tumultuous scene of the hunt had dissolved, Hildebrand began to make out a couple of horsemen advancing in their direction. Even at that distance the soldier, sensing danger, decided to hold his ground on the narrow strip and confront the riders. With tactical purpose, he instructed Hellalyle, "Now, princess, for once do as I say, and remain two horse lengths behind me, keep your head covered, do not look them in the eye, and above all, stay calm."

As the horsemen approached, Hildebrand was dismayed, surmising them to be warriors from one of the pagan tribes inhabiting the region – possibly a renegade force, ruthless and rebellious.

Now that a clash seemed inevitable, Hildebrand blamed himself for his bull-headed action, his unbridled passion. He'd put the safety of the king's daughter in jeopardy, shamed his fellow knights. If he were to lose this fight, Hellalyle would fetch an enormous ransom, but equally, she could disappear without a trace, or even be butchered to death at this spot.

As the rugged horsemen – now identified as Prussens – abruptly and belligerently pulled up, the first, wielding an axe, called out to the couple in a foreign tongue. He bawled again, even louder, while Hildebrand remained mute, stock-still on his steed. Hellalyle, rashly defying the knight's instruction and pulling down the hood of her cloak, edged forward, trying to communicate with the warrior, trying several languages but to no avail. Suddenly the other combatant, who had remained silent, observing the woman intently, spontaneously pointed his spear at her. He shouted hysterically at the top of his voice, "Look, it is Hellalyle, the Princess Hellalyle!"

The Wild Hunt

Her legendary fame had been enough to spark a dramatic recognition, but even as he blurted the revelation, his comrade crashed headlong from his mount. A lance, launched at lightning speed and with deadly accuracy by Hildebrand's reflex action, had pierced his chest. With his shield raised, the knight deftly deflected the heavy weapon hurled at him by the other horseman. Now, Hildebrand spurred his charger – which, as it had been trained to do, reared up, striking out with its forelegs at his opponent's mount, causing it to buck and throw the rider. With the Prussen spread-eagled on the ground, the knight dealt the finishing blow with his sword.

Shaken up by the speedy dispatch of the two warriors, Hellalyle looked petrified, locked in her saddle. Hildebrand dispensed with the niceties of formal address to shout out, "Princess, we must get out of here, fast! Do you hear me?"

But Hellalyle remained paralysed with fear, deaf to the knight's commands.

"Damn you, Hellalyle, hand me the reins!" Hildebrand said aggressively, and taking control of the situation, he seized the bridle of her horse, steering its course as they galloped off at speed, fearful there might be other raiders in the vicinity.

The fleeing riders quickly traversed the isthmus and left the shores of Lake Eydis behind them. At a break in the wooded tract, the knight pulled the horses up, and Hildebrand quickly swung down from his mount, going to the assistance of the princess who was weeping in the saddle.

"Your Highness," he said, pausing out of breath. "Please excuse my intemperate language, but the urgency of the situation dictated we both had to flee. Who knows what danger we were in if we had lingered."

Hellalyle reached out for the knight to assist her down. As soon as she alighted from her steed, the tearful princess buried her head on the broad chest of the soldier.

"Oh Hildebrand, what came over me – I was terrified, but now I am ashamed, for my inaction placed us in great peril."

As the Englishman put his arms around Hellalyle in a comforting embrace, the menagerie of the forest, unnoticed, peeped out, observing with satisfaction the princess and the soldier, attentive once more, like two devoted doves.

By the time they reached the shelter of the fortress, Hellalyle had gradually become more responsive to the heroic character and stature of the Prince of England, who had saved them from mortal danger. She became convinced that his bold action had nullified the prophecy that resulted from witnessing the *Wild Jagd*. By equal measure, her passion for this outstanding soldier had intensified, and grown stronger in its significance.

21

Hellalyle saunters alone in the Wildwood

The bodyguard of the princess had grown accustomed to her idiosyncrasies. However, there was one aspect of her behaviour that still perplexed: how, on occasion, for no apparent reason, she would impulsively express a fancy to ride into the Wildwood. After travelling a short distance into the Greenwood, she would always call a halt, instructing her knights to wait in a clearing until she returned – thus allowing her to venture by herself into the very depths of the forest.

Hildebrand confronted the princess about her risky escapades.

"My lady, I must lodge your bodyguard's strong protest on the danger of such ventures, and ask you to desist from it. Will you tell me, what on earth is the motivating force that is propelling you to engage in these absurd activities?"

To which Hellalyle promptly replied, "Please, Hildebrand, do not talk down to me in that manner. I take exception to it. Never once have I failed to return safely from the wilderness. Is that not so?"

The Englishman, now getting exasperated, raised his voice, shouting, "But, Your Highness, this is preposterous. You do not seem to understand, that if you were to come to any harm, the monarch would hold your minders responsible – surely you can see that, for heaven's sake!"

His outburst was heard by some of the other bodyguards in

an adjoining passageway, causing them to look at one another in astonishment. However, his pleas fell on deaf ears; Hellalyle quite calmly shook her head, tut-tutting at his outburst.

"The leader of my knights can shout all he likes, but you will not browbeat me. I appreciate your concern, however, but will you please accept my assurances that there is nothing to fear when I venture alone into the forest. Now, let that be the end of the matter."

However, Hildebrand did not let it drop, lobbying the princess from time to time, but she remained obstinate and inflexible, ignoring his advice and entreaties.

The knight commander inquired if anyone could shed light on Hellalyle's eccentric eremitic rambles, but no one could offer an explanation. He paid a visit to the castle sheriff, who said, "It is baffling, I must say. Her family have many times voiced their concern for the princess on her solo expeditions, but on this one subject, they have admitted defeat in trying to persuade her to do otherwise. As far as I know, even they have no knowledge or explanation for her strange behaviour. They, like everybody else, think it odd that she always manages to return unscathed from these unexplored primaeval forests, considered inhabited by vagabonds, dangerous predators and mysterious creatures that roam the day and the night."

Hildebrand listened intently, and said to the sheriff, "As leader of her bodyguard I am directly responsible for her safety, and that is an overriding reason for me to solve this enigma, and I will not rest until I do!"

The official gave him a withering look, saying, "Englishman, I would advise you not to pursue the affair, for there have been those who have taken it upon themselves to follow her, and they have never been seen or heard of again." Hildebrand thanked him, saying he would heed his advice, and marched off, but secretly, he was still determined to solve the riddle.

Hildebrand related to the other bodyguards of what he had been able to discover, and they gathered together by a small lake, down

Hildebrand watches Hellalyle set out on her lone sojourn into the wilderness

below the castle ramparts. As a pair of swans glided over the surface of the still water, the twelve knights held a conference, debating what strategy to take, should Hellalyle once again relinquish their protection in the wilderness. Unable to contain their curiosity any longer, they concurred that when she embarked on another solitary jaunt, their leader would follow undercover. Unknown to them, the Arthurian scene below was being observed by Runa, the lady-

in-waiting, from a window in the apartments.

"What I would give, to know what your guard is discussing," Runa whispered aloud.

"No doubt some nefarious scheme being cooked up by Hildebrand," came Hellalyle's voice from the other side of the chamber where she sat contemplating the start of a new embroidery.

One week later, Hellalyle drew once more to her remote and sylvan isolation, and, as on previous occasions, she brought her companions suddenly to a halt in a break in the wooded tract. This time, the commander of the knights shadowed the princess as she rode, side-saddle, assuredly and imperturbably, into uncharted territory.

As Hildebrand anxiously followed her, it crossed his mind that some unseen force must be guiding her through this awe-inspiring Arcadian habitat, little changed since the end of the last ice age. Umbrageous trees of great age towered above the forest floor, forming aisles as in a cathedral, while the sun's rays shone through chinks in their high canopies to illuminate in shafts of golden light the perfect loveliness of this solitary and silently moving figure.

In the enveloping quietness, the Beings who ruled this domain appeared to recognise the princess, and her presence seemed to suspend the dangerous, hostile and unpredictable world of nature, to protect her from injury or misfortune. Hildebrand, concerned that the alarming cries of any wildlife he might disturb would frighten the companionless rider, kept his distance as he cautiously and skilfully tracked her.

Hellalyle, in due course, reached a spot where she slowed to listen attentively to any noises around her, before coming to a halt. Tying her horse to a bough and slipping her bag over her shoulder, she stealthily tiptoed through the undergrowth, entering a natural gladeway running east to west that opened into the floodplain of an unnamed river. It was one of several which fed the distant lake of Eydis, a Terr aqueous region rich in alder, poplar, and willows; lush meadows teemed with bird life and provided a natural terrain for beavers.

Hildebrand, concealing himself in dense thickets, looked on, hoping to unravel this mystery. He imagined that he heard Hellalyle's voice calling softly to some invisible listener. Then, through a gap in the shrubbery, he watched as a giant elk emerged from the shallow water.

It was a bull with magnificent antlers, and a vicious injury was visible between its shoulder blades: an arrow still embedded in the flesh. Hellalyle showed no fear when the wounded animal drew close. To the knight's astonishment, she raised her hands to tenderly stroke its neck, acutely compassionate in its palpable distress. Hildebrand imagined he could hear Hellalyle talking to it in an obscure speak, quite unlike a human language, of that he was sure. After examining the wound, she took from her bag various ointments blended from herbs in the castle garden, and an instrument resembling tongs. With both hands, she used this to compress the barb, a task generally beyond the power of a woman; her facilities were momentarily strengthened by a divine spirit. She extracted the arrowhead before treating the laceration with a salve she had made of barley, honey, and turpentine. The calming effect she had demonstrated when she addressed von Altenburg's injury, she now exercised over this injured beast. In the presence of such mystical charm, the creature never uttered a sound, nor flinched from the unbearable pain.

Hildebrand had witnessed yet another example of the princess's extraordinary comprehension of the symbiosis of nature's forms with the human body. He was only to be further confounded by another incident involving a smaller elk that appeared just then – a female with a newborn offspring who looked exceedingly vulnerable in this wild terrain. Entranced by the unexpected appearance of this defenceless calf, Hellalyle bent down to nurse the little fellow, and with careful handling, she examined its delicate condition with her penetrating gaze. It was as if the proud mother, aware of the princess's unstinting kindness and understanding, had brought her youngster here for that very purpose. The king's daughter briefly attended to them before they vanished into the wilderness.

The Prince of England, anxious not to reveal himself, had intended to return before Hellalyle. Yet, from the moment Hildebrand began to track the princess, many a pair of piercing eyes had scanned his passage.

Still some way off from his comrades, he turned his horse to await the princess, who eventually appeared, riding slowly through the bracken. Hellalyle, startled at seeing the knight alone so far into the forest, restrained her usual radiant smile. She faltered in her path to cogitate, then raised herself in the saddle and looked carefully around while listening intently. Only when the princess assured herself that all was well did she continue and catch up with the soldier.

Once she was at his side, she admonished and berated the knight for disobeying her.

"How dare you disobey me! I gave you explicit orders to remain in the camp until I returned. Instead, I find you lurking about in the trees. I thought I could trust the Prince of England, but it seems my belief is misplaced."

Hildebrand was at first in two minds whether to admit culpability and then, like an excitable child unable to restrain himself, blurted out her secret.

"Your Highness, following your arresting image through the sunlit glades and bearing witness to your compassion to a dumb animal, has revealed to me a secret kingdom of the Creator, a most humbling experience."

He regretted it immediately when her look of dismay made him realise that he had broken faith; the princess had come to scorn him, in a manner entirely alien to her nature. In a fit of anger, she dismounted from her horse and scolded the knight, before bursting into tears and turning her back on him in disgust. Hildebrand, mortified at causing her such anguish, alighted from his mount and knelt before her to beg forgiveness.

She stood unmoved, absorbed in thought, before wiping away her tears. Then, she looked down at the knight and gently lay her hand upon his head, in the manner of a mother preparing to explain to her child the mysteries of life. After a few moments contemplation, she said to Hildebrand, "Because of what you have witnessed today, I feel disposed to reveal something to you – but only on the understanding that it is for your ears only, and if you were ever to mention this matter to others, I would surely learn of it. Then an unbridgeable chasm would open between us."

Unnoticed at that moment, a sudden gust of wind disturbed the treetops, as if to demonstrate displeasure at what the princess was on the point of disclosing, before the air became still again.

Hellalyle took a deep breath.

"You may well have compromised my particular relationship with the creatures of the wild. For they made it known to me many years ago, that I had been chosen by them to offer support to their lame and to help their unfortunates in moments of need. Tragically, most often caused by the cruelty of man. These commitments have inspired joy and given me a profound understanding of another sphere, which I have sworn not to describe to my fellow beings.

"You've caused me all this difficulty…nevertheless, I feel that your motives have been well-intentioned. However, my bodyguards are obliged to accept that I will come to no harm on those occasions when I choose to wander by myself in the forest. Nobody knows that I am under the protection of its wild inhabitants, girded by the Black Wolves of Europa. By trailing me, you put yourself in grave danger. Although you would not have known it, Lupus will have been shadowing, stalking you, to shield me from harm. Let us thank God they did not attack you."

The princess, keeping it to herself, remained perplexed though, as to why the predators had allowed Hildebrand to follow her. Unable to fathom it out she brushed it off and continued, "Be aware that even at this very moment my animal guardians will be watching, shielding me from peril, but they must be accepting your presence now that I am returning home. If I do not cry for help, you will be safe. The concern of nature's spirits for my welfare is all-embracing, for if the mountains called me, my escorts would be the bears and the eagles."

Hildebrand was stunned, being an eyewitness to the princess's preternatural faculties, and appealed to her to reveal more, but she placed a finger to her lips, unforthcoming.

In time, the princess forgave Hildebrand, and the knight, true to his word, never divulged the extraordinary things he had witnessed.

That evening, under a brightly shining moon, Hellalyle lay awake as she pondered the day's events, trying to work out why the wolves had refrained from attacking the knight. An owl hooted loudly. She rose from her bed and ventured to the window, where she listened intently to the bird's screeching refrain as it mysteriously conveyed an important message to her. Soundlessly, the owl flew away, and Hellalyle watched its winged silhouette crossing the lunar face, till lost from sight beyond the battlements.

At first light, having alerted Hildebrand, she hurriedly set out into the hinterland, leaving her bodyguards at a place just inside the woods. This time she wandered all day, frustrated in her efforts to contact the creatures of the wild, who were upset the princess had divulged secrets that might enable strangers to glimpse their world – prohibited to ordinary mortals.

Before dusk, the princess alighted in a remote clearing, and as a last resort (regretting her indiscretion) she shouted aloud, pleading to the creatures to show themselves, her voice echoing through the glades. The creatures, moved by hearing Hellalyle's despairing cries, emerged one by one from the wilderness, congregating in a circle where they decided to pass judgement. The princess repented, solemnly bowing her head to them, and they, the creatures of the three elements, pardoned her, out of respect for one of pure spirit, and assured that Hildebrand would keep the secret hidden forever.

Later, as they guided her back through inhospitable terrain to a place close to where the knights were anxiously waiting, Hellalyle seized the chance to ask them why the wolves had held back from savaging Hildebrand. But they declined to answer, for how could they harm the English knight, chosen by them to be her consort?

This meeting in the forest would also bring about a more portentous revelation, for the creatures travelling in proximity to the princess, with their heightened senses, were aware that Hildebrand's embryo had begun to germinate in the fount of Hellalyle's being. The knight and the princess were now as one. Nevertheless, they were mindful to keep secret these wondrous tidings, for she would learn of it in God's good time.

22

The princess and Mountain Everlasting

One sunlit day in early June, twelve knights ensconced in wooded uplands anxiously awaited while Hellalyle returned from the mountain.

The king's daughter, having fulfilled a mission of mercy, descended from the cloud-enveloped peak by way of a rocky escarpment. Below, she had to traverse the moorland to meet her knights at the edge of the forest. Accompanying her was a giant male bear. This powerful *Ursus* was her protector, and entirely dwarfed the slim and comely figure of the princess. Overhead soared a pair of wide-winged eagles, her watchful aerial defenders. One of these mighty predatory birds would alight near their charge to survey the terrain, the other remaining aloft. The sharp-eyed raptor on the crag above would dart its keen glances, only to take off again once her passage was considered safe.

Princess Hellalyle, wearing thick mittens and a weighty cloak to ward off the cold, a bag over her shoulder, leaned on her wooden staff. A sudden flurry of snow whistled across the alpine landscape, conditions not uncommon at this altitude in early summer. She hurriedly took refuge in the lee of a giant boulder, the bear's massive body shielding her from the hostility of the weather, preventing the hard-driven flakes from blanching the exposed face of this intrepid and graceful wayfarer.

When the squall had passed, the sun reappeared, its dazzling light exposing the icy white mantel of the landscape. The two figures then set off as the snowfall thawed rapidly, revealing a colourful eiderdown of wildflowers. As they traversed this floral tapestry, the princess identified some of the plants as *Mountain Everlasting*. Moved by this delightful discovery, she resolved to mention it to her bodyguards on her return.

When they reached the treeline, she stopped to bid farewell to her towering grizzly defender, and to that pair of winged sentinels circling high above. Running her hands through the bear's shaggy coat, she uttered soothing words of gratitude in the coded language she had learned, and then, craning her neck, waved goodbye to the soaring eagles. They responded to her with their shrill cries before wheeling out of vision. Sad to see them leave, and in sympathy with her thick-furred mammal in all his solitude, she stood with one hand shielding her eyes to watch the bear cross the escarpment and vanish into the distance, a mere speck devoured by the dense forest uplands.

When Hellalyle set foot in the knights' encampment, they gathered round, euphorically saluting her on her safe return. She had been away for two days and nights, yet amazingly, her vigour was undiminished. The bodyguards, with gladness in their hearts at her safe deliverance, each, in turn, lifted the hand of the princess and kissed it reverently. However, this time to her utter surprise, Phillip Guiscard abandoned such formalities and put his arms around the princess and embraced her, pulling her nearly off her feet and patted her on the back – like a loving brother greeting the reappearance of a sister lost, saying, "We are so relieved you have come back to us."

Hellalyle stepped away, flustered, and for a moment struggled to speak. An embarrassing silence ensued. It was Andre Grenier who broke the awkwardness, audaciously saying, "I assume all of us can now cherish you, my lady?"

She quickly realised, through her second sight, the significance of what had just happened: a man's platonic way of showing how much she meant to him. Suddenly, her expression of sheer surprise changed to that of an enchanting smile, and she exclaimed, "Oh, my boys, I did not expect such a greeting, for your loyalty to me is without question, and I am indebted to you all. Whatever will I do when my knights depart the kingdom, for you are such devoted friends. To such a degree, that noble thoughts within me, I can express to my bodyguards, which I could never say to my kith and kin, but that is the way of the world and is right that it should be so." To the joy of the soldiers, Princess Hellalyle then embraced each knight in turn.

Hildebrand looked particularly pleased, he alone aware of the true nature of her mysterious rambles; but he could only guess at the remarkable things she had encountered beyond the veil of the mountain.

While she had been away from the camp, the soldiers, who by this time were so captivated by this pretty young woman, had debated amongst themselves, if any one of them would dare cordially embrace the princess on her return. They drew straws to decide, the short one pulled by Phillip Guiscard. (Hildebrand observed it all in unrestrained amusement.)

Once back at the castle, the Prince of England unexpectedly went missing, causing Hellalyle some anxiety. She spent the afternoon on her own, engaged in embroidery at a window seat in her chamber, wondering where Hildebrand was. (Her work hampered by the presence of an impish kitten on her lap, playfully pulling the silk filaments of the floss.)

After some time, she was disturbed by rapid knocking, to which Hellalyle, reluctant to rise and disturb her work, called out, "Enter."

The door opened, to reveal, much to her surprise and relief, the figure of Hildebrand. In his hand, the knight was carrying an appealing posy – created from the very blooms that had so delighted the princess on her visit to the snow-clad eminence. The Englishman, noting the pleasure she had derived from them, had made a pilgrimage to that distant snow-capped peak to search its niveous slopes.

Kneeling at the feet of his fair lady, he presented his enchanting nosegay, and remarked, "Your Highness, the very name of the flower seemed to adequately express my adoration for you," adding, "This attractive plant from the highlands is also called *Immortelle* – a fitting description for a woman of undying spiritual power."

Hellalyle's reaction to his gift from the mountain brought a tear to her eyes which in her embarrassment she tried to mask, but she could not hide it from Hildebrand, inducing in the warrior knight a profound sense of achievement.

After a few moments of contemplation, he was drawn to add, "There is something else. While I was gathering the blooms on the hillside, I had the uncanny feeling, the strongest sensation, of being watched from the edge of the treeline. While overhead, two giant eagles, the largest I have ever seen, circled, as if they had marked me out. One even alighting on a rocky crag, so close, I could make out its piercing eyes staring at me. What was scanning my presence from the woods I shall never know, but it was large, for one could hear the breaking and splintering of saplings as it moved through the treescape. Such an eerie experience would instil fear in most, but to me, it was never a threat, more like spiritually uplifting. People can say whatever they like, even that I am mad, but nobody will convince me otherwise, that I sensed the wilderness itself was watching over me. On the journey home I pondered these events, over and over in my mind, only to recall Your Highness revealing to me, that in any sojourn you might make to the mountains, the eagles and the bear would be your protectors. My lady, were these the same creatures I saw on the upland slopes?"

Hellalyle returned the knight a knowing look, but was unforthcoming.

"I see," said Hildebrand. "I will interpret confirmation in your silence, Your Highness. I sense you are holding something back, and it installs in me the strongest conviction, that the flowers in your hand must hold an anagogic significance, which I pray, in time to come, will be revealed. However, until then, this day of mystery will live with me forever."

Their eyes met. Hellalyle lovingly searched his face, while suppressing a desire to divulge, once again, another of nature's secrets.

The princess attempted to break his questioning stare by gushingly exclaiming, "Hildebrand, whatever possessed you to go all the way back to the mountain on my account – but these blooms are beautiful – your gift means so much to me! From what you have just recounted, I will place them in the chapel, a no worthier place than God's house."

Before she could say any more, he placed a finger to her lips, saying, "My lady, do not speak further. The way your face lit up when I entered the room means more to me than anything else in the world."

Quickly kissing her hand, he hurried from the room, as if conscious that the delicate nature of their affection was already the subject of rumour and disquiet at court. In his haste, he did not even feel the tugging on his arm as the princess tried to restrain him.

Hellalyle, in a near state of lachrymose, considered Hildebrand's remarkable ability: not only to perceive her actual feelings but also to appreciate the beauties of nature that surrounded him. She focused her vision on the distant summit where he had gathered her favourite flowers. She began to surmise the supernatural events that Hildebrand had just described, and the time of the wolves, their inexplicable tolerance of him when following her in the Wildwood. Were these signs the benign spirits of the hinterland were singling him out as someone special? She could only wonder.

However, there was one thing she was certain of: her admiration for this valorous and sympathetic warrior had been powerfully transformed into an ardent passion, which now consumed her whole being.

In this state of ecstasy, she had lost sight of the mischievous feline companion on her knee. The young cat was now more diverted by pawing the petals of the posy in her hand than pulling the bright threads of her needlecraft!

23

Gudrun confronts Hellalyle

On an exceptional gloomy and gusty day, black-edged clouds scudding over the towers of Castle Preben, the queen requested the presence of Hellalyle. She wished to discuss a pressing problem which had been preying on her mind. The princess, apprehensive at first, foreseeing what was likely to be debated, finally plucked up the courage to visit her. She sauntered towards the queen's apartments, and once outside paused, taking in a deep breath before pulling herself together and knocking on the stout timber door. Gudrun's ladies-in-waiting, welcoming the princess, curtsied to her and left the room.

Queen Gudrun raised the troublesome matter of her step-daughter's dalliance with Hildebrand.

"Hellalyle, I must demand that you put an end to it at once. If you are not prepared to curb your infatuation, then your father should be informed. An obvious solution would be to banish Hildebrand from the court, but it would require the authorisation of the king, given that the knight was commander of your bodyguard."

Gudrun challenged her, "How could Hellalyle, the picture of good judgement and self-restraint, undermine her reputation by consorting with this soldier, and succumbing to a frivolous flirtation with him? More disturbingly, the subject has now become common knowledge, breeding malicious rumours – which could only serve to subvert the jurisdiction of the Crown."

Tears welled in Hellalyle's eyes as she stood by the window, trying to shut her ears to Gudrun's stern reproof. She felt helpless, endeavouring to express the irrepressible and passionate attraction she harboured for the Prince of England. The powerful and persuasive influence of the spirits of the Wildwood had affected her to such a degree that she had become unconsciously incapable of resisting the deliberate alchemy forged between herself and Hildebrand, which had evolved into a genuine, human emotion.

The queen, mindful of Thorstein's predictable reaction to his daughter's compromising behaviour, and in a marked change of mood, appeared more conciliatory; she was sympathetic to the young woman's predicament. The princess stood in front of her, speechless and distressed, and the anxious Gudrun, staring at the stone floor, contemplated her stepdaughter's plight. She rose, and standing behind the princess, gently laid a hand on Hellalyle's shoulders.

"My dear, I cannot bear to see you so unhappy – rest assured, I will do my utmost to sway the king's judgement into giving his blessing to the relationship. Until then, you must explain to Hildebrand the delicacy of the situation, and restrict any open emotional displays."

That night, the troubled princess experienced a curious dream. It contained a series of strange images which flashed through her mind. First, a bright-winged angel of the forest appeared, and with heavenly powers, breached the castle walls. Through this the princess was led to a spectacular prospect of Lake Eydis, its waters shimmering in the light of an ample moon. Next, a rapturous voice could be heard, summoning the nine Muses of Ancient Greece. They were bidden to take their place on a rocky promontory of the inland sea as if drawn to the mountain slopes of their hallowed domain on Helicon. Terpsichore at their head, the goddesses graciously invited Hellalyle to take the role of a principal dancer in a company of enchanting nymphs, skilfully tripping the aqueous surface to a choreography she had performed to such effect in the great hall at Preben. To celestial strains, the princess and her troupe of beautiful maidens moved elegantly and expressively over the delicate crests of the waves, radiating their presence to inspire the inhabitants in the farthest regions of a secret world.

As these luminous figures glowed on the water, sister muse Urania used her astronomical influence to ensure their reflection sparkled as brightly as her necklaces of stars – bright streams of light from *Aurora Borealis.* The vision faded, and the princess fell into a deeper sleep, unaware the angel had remained to watch over her as the benevolent guardian of her vulnerability. At daybreak, she awoke, refreshed and contented, but with a singular sensation of having been on a great adventure.

In the coming centuries, on certain nights, of certain days, till the end of time, a unique display of *Aurora Borealis* will appear, awe-inspiring as to be without parallel in all the histories of the heavenly vault. A visual jewel, shimmering and twisting in a rhythmic motion of rare beauty, supremely majestic as to be unforgettable, an image indelibly printed on the mind. Those fortunate to behold this spectacle should make a concession to their thoughts and never assume it is the solar wind. Instead, contemplate awhile, for the possibility exists you are witnessing the eternal spirit of Hellalyle, performing with ethereal grace her celestial ballet amongst the realm of the stars.

24

Abbot Jurian counsels the knight Hildebrand

Abbot Jurian considered it his duty to raise the embarrassing question of Hildebrand's involvement with the king's daughter. An opportune moment miraculously presented itself when the abbot chanced to discover the knight alone in prayer, before the altar of the Abbey of Sunniva. The lovelorn soldier had journeyed there in pilgrimage.

Standing silently, concealed in the shadows of the deserted abbey, Jurian overheard the subdued tones of the knight's tremulous voice praying to God for forgiveness and guidance, as he confessed his infatuation for the Princess Hellalyle. Even the imperturbable monk was taken by surprise, as he listened in on the outpouring of a troubled soul. He became conscious of how insensible he had been in his appraisal of the Englishman's character.

When the abbot felt it right to make his presence known, Hildebrand, startled by his sudden appearance, abruptly broke off his earnest invocation as if to flee the holy place. Jurian, unruffled, calmly prevailed on him to stay behind and unburden his afflictions.

"My son, have trust in me, let me hear what troubles thy soul."

At first, the knight hesitated, then appeared relieved; he was grateful for the opportunity to share his problems with a spiritual man of such eminence and profound judgement.

With dignity and patience, the abbot drew Hildebrand into

an adjacent chapel. In that peaceful sanctuary, the gallant knight felt able to open his heart and confide his problems, while in the distance, all the brothers of the religious house quietly gathered for prayers in the precinct of the abbey, and a monk began to read aloud from a Book of Hours.

The abbot was a spiritual leader of great learning and vision, who had tutored the young Hellalyle. He listened attentively to the knight's divulgences: his account of the extraordinary events that had impacted on their lives, so keenly affecting him and the princess. Heatedly, Hildebrand recounted the incident of the persistent, inexplicable attentions of a tiny songbird; the ominous spectacle of a mysterious comet, setting the firmament ablaze; the apocalyptic manifestation of the *Wild Hunt*, skyborn, looming over Lake Eydis… and beyond these visitations, an eerie perception of a more potent, supernatural manipulator at work.

"I have this suspicion that there is some agency, all-knowing, that is intruding and influencing the sacred space that lies between a man and a woman, that of myself and the Princess Hellalyle.

"Some say I am a proud individual, which is why I feel angry and intimidated at being unable to unburden affairs of my heart to fellow soldiers. They had, after all, cautioned me to distance myself from the princess, and abandon a liaison that threatened to endanger my chivalric honour and my loyalty to the king."

A torrent of confused impressions betrayed the knight's fraught state of mind; tears welled in his eyes and streamed down his tortured face, breaching the dam of pent-up emotions. Moved by Hildebrand's effusions, the abbot, quick to support, drew close, and looking him in the eyes, endeavoured to calm and console him.

Placidly, beneficially, the monk enlightened the soldier.

"May I suggest that the universe and the animal kingdom within lay beyond man's comprehension. Your tribulations, Hildebrand, were not mere symptoms of human weakness, but hold some divine purpose. I believe Hellalyle possesses a remarkable insight into the secrets of the natural world, an affinity with the living creatures from this division of the Earth. Surely the mysterious influence and oracular guidance of their benevolent spirits were determining the pivotal roles you and the princess would play in this romance?"

As Abbot Jurian led Hildebrand to the great west door of the house, he promised to exercise his influence with the king, and attempt to persuade Thorstein to look more sympathetically on the knight's close association with his daughter.

Outside the walls of the abbey, Hildebrand knelt in front of the abbot, who gave him his blessing for the journey. As the warrior — now more self-assured — rode in the direction of Castle Preben, Jurian discerned, in the distance, what might have been figments of his imagination: insubstantial shapes of animals and wild birds enfolding the equestrian figure, swirling and spinning around him in shimmering ribbons of spectral light. They emitted mysterious sounds, inaudible to the human ear, a paean in tribute to the soldier as he trotted across fecund grasslands, the knight seemingly oblivious to their presence.

His trusty stallion Fortis, however, acutely sensitive to the atmosphere of this venerated terrain, snorted impulsively, nostrils flaring and ears pinned back. Hildebrand lightly pressed the rowels, spurring his charger onwards over the vast expanse of turf. The abbot, shaking his head in disbelief, was unaware his inborn spirituality had allowed him to witness an incomparable vision.

For the knight's prayers, offered up at Sunniva, had inspired nature's past generations to rise from their hallowed ground to offer praise and support to the Prince of England, peerless guardian of their Princess Hellalyle.

25

*The king receives news of his daughter's intimacy
with one of the bodyguard knights*

At the king's quarters in the lands to the east, a messenger arrived
with urgent news for His Majesty. Asking to see the monarch in
private, the bearer of the message delivered the stunning news that
his only daughter, Princess Hellalyle, was in an intimate relationship
with one of her bodyguards.

Deeply hurt that she had dishonoured her father, and angered
by the betrayal of a knight, Thorstein asked, "Why have I not been
informed of this earlier, to put a stop to it?"

The messenger replied, "Sire, messengers were sent twice. Unfortunately, it seems both had been intercepted by the lawless pagans."

"Who is this treacherous fiend?" Thorstein growled, his fury
simmering.

The messenger, now increasingly apprehensive, exclaimed, "It is
Hildebrand, the Prince of England."

The sovereign gasped in disbelief.

"What! Never, never, it cannot be! Are you claiming a royal
prince has betrayed the king?"

The messenger nodded, and then hung his head in embarrassment and fear.

"How can this have happened?" Thorstein exploded, "All of you
get out, go now, leave me, I need to be alone, to think."

His subjects considered him to be a calm and kindly man, and his outrage, indeed, subsided quickly, enabling him to weigh his options.

He was given little time before being harangued by his stepson, Prinz Paulus. The prinz bore down on the monarch.

"Sire, you must avenge the knight's insult and punish Hellalyle who has brought shame upon the family. If you do not act swiftly, you will be perceived as weak."

Bullied into action by the prinz, he instructed his minister to call an urgent meeting with his sons – including Paulus – to consider the appropriate action to take against the princess and her bodyguard.

Amongst the hastily arranged council, his seven sons assembled before him: Borr, the oldest, and then in descending age, Heidr, Dabrel, Ramung, Orendel, Lanthar, and the youngest, Ansilo, who was a mere teenager. Prinz Paulus stood prominently.

The convocation descended into a shouting match, Paulus's voice heard loudest of all. The king became aware he was losing control of the situation and appealed for a calm and rational discourse. He waited for a few moments, for quietness to descend, and when he felt he had their undivided attention he spoke. "It appears my dearly loved daughter, who has been an inspiration to all, has fallen for the attention of one of her bodyguards – a Prince of England. If true, his actions will have brought dishonour on the knightly order, humiliation to his comrades.

"However, I cannot believe that your sister, so loved and respected by the people of my kingdom, has freely entered this liaison without careful consideration. Never has Hellalyle, since birth, given a reason for admonishment, so faultless has been her existence. Now here we sit, expecting to pass judgement on her. We are not worthy of such a task, as she is unblemished. Therefore, I suggest we delay, for I am sure a sign will come…to show that this situation is not her fall from grace, but some eternal plan."

It was noticeable that Hellalyle's blood brothers were very like their father, with a gentle bearing and disposition, only knights because their father was king. They found it unpleasant to condemn their sister – unlike the stepbrother, with his violent nature, showing a jealous and vindictive attitude against the princess.

Paulus, with his dominating persona, began to wear everybody down. In sheer overbearance, he forced the others to give way, eventually persuading them to accept his opinion on the action to take. The benign king, against his better judgement, decided to dispatch his reluctant sons to arrest Hildebrand and execute him, and to confine the princess and await the monarch's decision on his return.

The champions received warning the princess's suitor would be a formidable adversary. As for the other bodyguards, the messenger reliably informed Thorstein that these knights were of one mind in rebuking their comrade for his indiscretion. They had scrupulously honoured the chivalric code. The message-bearer believed the knights would not defy the king's judgement.

Concerning his daughter, Thorstein urged them to exercise caution, commanding that no harm comes to her. Ushering his eldest son, Borr, to one side, he instructed him to keep an eye on Paulus, for during the year he had noticed an inexplicable change in the prinz's behaviour; his relationship with the princess had hardened, his manner becoming increasingly hostile.

The king dispatched his messenger to inform the princess's bodyguard of his strict orders: that his sons on arrival will instantly arrest their leader, and confine Hellalyle until her father's return, and they must not interfere. Soon after, the champions reluctantly set out on their mission to Castle Preben.

It appeared that the stratagem of those good spirits of the wild to keep the princess in their midst might have begun to unravel, with unfortunate consequences.

26

The king's champions arrive to arrest Hildebrand

In the great hall, Hellalyle, on hearing the news that her brothers were coming to arrest Hildebrand, pleaded with him to leave.

"Hildebrand, you must leave – my father has dispatched my brothers to seize you. Our relationship has set in motion a fait accompli, and now your life is in great danger."

However, Hildebrand, staring into the fire, was in no mood to listen to her pleading, saying, "Whatever the other knights decide to do, I cannot in all consciousness allow myself to abandon you to an uncertain fate, as I feel responsible for this dire situation."

Hellalyle, in desperation, pleaded, "Will you, please, be sensible! You cannot defeat eight armed men! Remember, these are my brothers, and at the end of the fight you will lie dead, and so will most of my brethren, and for what end? My family destroyed, and Prince Hildebrand ignominiously buried in a foreign field, which will be a tragedy for the English nation, and it will not end there, as I feel further calamity awaits those remaining at this fortress."

"Fate must run its course!" exclaimed the defiant knight, raising his voice. "If you think I will deliver you into the hands of Paulus, you gravely underestimate me. No greater evil walks the land, and he will surely die on the blade of my sword! As for my remains lying beneath the woodland floor, that holds no fear for me, as you have introduced this knight to the beauty of nature, and honour awaits if wild creatures should walk across my grave!"

The soldier's expose of his inner self prompted Hellalyle to gently grasp his forearm, in a gesture of empathy to his plight, with a pained expression etched on her face.

The other bodyguards met to decide on what action to take considering the king's command, knowing that they must not obstruct. All – save one – agreed that they should depart, convinced their contract with the monarch was severed by these unfortunate events. Von Altenburg, at first, declined to abandon his friend. He was fearful for the safety of the princess, but he eventually conceded, opting to join his comrades in arms.

News of their impending departure reached Hellalyle, who decided to visit them. In a fractured voice, she addressed the company.

"Honoured knights, whom I might almost regard as my brothers and such gallant men, warriors of the Christian church...my heart is about to break. I stand here now imploring you to persuade Hildebrand to leave at once with his fraternal fighters, for if he were to stay, I fear that some tragedy may befall him and my family."

Her impassioned speech prompted the knight von Streitz to say, "He appears to be deaf to our pleading, Your Highness! What more can we do to sway him?"

Hellalyle, almost in despair, raised her hands to her face and burst into tears. All eleven knights, embarrassed, kept their eyes fixed on the ground before stealing past her prostrate figure, anxious to avoid an uncomfortable situation.

As they rode from the castle, von Altenburg lingered to pay one last visit to Hellalyle and Hildebrand. Entering a chamber, he observed them by the window, Hildebrand pacing up and down, stabbing the floor with his sword, in apparent frustration, the princess standing in sombre contemplation of the densely wooded prospect below. They were all alone as she had sent her staff to the safety of the kitchens. As they turned to face him, von Altenburg became struck by their dramatically altered demeanour. The once-resolute Prince of England now despondent and downcast; and Hellalyle, her face once so radiant now shut down, her eyes that brightly sparkled now eclipsed. She appeared almost lifeless.

Bidding his comrade farewell, he hugged him like a bear, then, turning to the princess, knelt and bowed his head in deep sadness as he genuflected. Touchingly, she laid her hands upon him. With feelings of extreme guilt that he might be thought to be abandoning them, he struggled to regain his composure. Intensely moved by Hellalyle's benevolent spirit that helped to comfort and restore him, he rose to his feet and strode resolutely from the room without looking back. Meanwhile, the other ten guards of the princess were heading for Lake Eydis. On arrival, they set up camp to assess what the future held.

For Hellalyle and Hildebrand, three quiet days elapsed. On Sunday, eight horses burst onto the scene, their heavy hooves thundering across the courtyard of Castle Preben. Astride them were the king's champions, his seven sons and stepson. They quickly learned that Hildebrand was in the tower directly above them; equipped with accoutrements of battle, they surged forward impetuously, quickly mounting the stone steps. The English prince prepared himself for the fight. At his side, Princess Hellalyle, who had ignored his orders to conceal herself, was convinced that she could persuade her brothers to desist from engaging in this violent confrontation.

As the champions bore down on him, the cacophony of clanging armour and the rattling of spurs filled the air. The blood brothers of the princess were driven, en masse, through the archway, Paulus at the rear, while the princess tried to intervene, pleading for sanity.

"My dear brothers, think what you are doing and cease this recklessness, for Hildebrand means no harm to your sister. His devotion to me is all-encompassing, and so I in return. A brave and nobler man you will never meet, so please, I implore you, sheath your swords and do nothing, while we await my father's return!"

It was clear to her that her brothers had little inclination for this conflict, and that Prinz Paulus had goaded them into rash action.

Aware that Hellalyle's presence fuelled their caution, Paulus barked foul expletives, screaming for her to get out of his way.

"Blast you, Hellalyle, you obnoxious wench, cease your whining and remove yourself. Do you hear!"

The prinz was so enraged his nostrils flared, and saliva dripped from his open mouth. Blood vessels could be seen pounding across his temple, as his terrifying eyes bulged in their sockets. Hellalyle's brothers were now in fear of Paulus, as he was visibly changing to an uncontrolled monster.

Scared to death by this figure of bloody-minded hostility, Hellalyle retreated in terror as Paulus malevolently manoeuvred the youngest knight, Ansilo, into a head-to-head. In this brutal clash, Hildebrand quickly realised how swiftly he could dispatch his opponent. He wavered, shouting, "Ansilo, for your sister's sake, yield!"

The hysterical princess begged her brother to surrender, but lest he be accused of cowardice, the boy boldly persisted until the Englishman, in exasperation, aimed at his temple, a violent strike instantly killing his adversary.

In retaliation, Paulus inflamed the brothers of the dead man to set upon Hildebrand, bellowing vindictively, "Spare no quarter!"

Paulus cunningly held back, avoiding danger, as Hildebrand dextrously drew the fight into the narrow compass of the tower, to counter any numerical advantage his foes might have. Heroically, he began to overpower and slay his assailants. First collapsing dead on the stone steps was Dabrel, followed by Lanthar. Then, conscious of the effect these traumatic scenes were having on Hellalyle, the Englishman tried to restrain his natural aggression and withdrew to the chapel, believing that those left behind would not follow, ending the carnage. However, the vicious Paulus, who seemed to hold some diabolical influence over the king's unfortunate sons, provoked them to move forward, he appearing unwilling to cross the chapel threshold.

Roused to fury, the beleaguered Hildebrand dispatched two more of his opponents, Orendel and Borr, leaving their blood-soaked corpses on the stone floor of the holy place. Once again, the supreme knight skilfully manoeuvred the conflict away from the sanctuary, while the princess became increasingly overwrought at the sight of the dead bodies of her kinship. Fighting for his life with fortitude, he slaughtered the last brothers, Heidr and Ramung, until only Paulus remained, that perfidious individual, whom Hildebrand now cornered and quickly forced into submission.

With the prinz disarmed, Hildebrand's foot pressed firmly on his chest, the English prince wielded his sword to deliver the *coup de grâce*. Hellalyle screamed in distress, prostrating herself before Hildebrand, trying to shield her stepbrother and begging leniency.

"No, Hildebrand! For the love of God, spare him! There must be no more killing!" Heeding her entreaty, he lowered his weapon and stepped aside.

No sooner had he turned his back than Prinz Paulus rose, treacherously transfixing the English knight, brutally assailing him with his dagger.

Mortally wounded, Hildebrand staggered towards Hellalyle. In acute distress, she tried to support him as he slumped beneath the archway near the turret stairs. Kneeling at his side, the grief-stricken princess cradled his head in her arms, praying that he would survive.

Hildebrand, in excruciating torment, knew his end was near. He lifted his gaze to see for one last time the face of his beloved angel. Tears welled from her eyes and dripped on his cheeks as she looked down at him.

The courageous knight swallowed, his face ashen. He took a shuddering breath and managed to utter some last words before he expired.

"Your Highness, the Lord has blessed this world with your inimitable presence and granted me the greatest fortune to have loved you!"

Overcome with the most powerful emotions of despair, Hellalyle drew the now lifeless body of Hildebrand to her in the tightest embrace, inconsolable in her desolation.

Suddenly, the stepbrother seized her by the hair and wrenched her to her feet.

"Now I have you – the enemy of the underworld!" and he contemptuously stamped on Hildebrand's spread-eagled corpse.

At that very instant, the other ten knights, still camped on the banks of Lake Eydis, with daylight receding, were mesmerised to see, out over the water, the clear and unmistakable vision of Hildebrand, supernatural in its perception, walking towards them over the surface of the inland sea. As the aureole spectre neared, it appeared to be signalling a revelation, an urgent warning, only then for the apparition to be snatched from view as the fingers of a dark shadow swept over him, leaving the soldiers overwhelmed in their wonderment, perplexed at the meaning of the visitation.

In the depths of the night, the Holy Spirit came unto the sleeping men, a serene beam of light from heaven, immersing the warriors in its quiet serenity, and under its divine influence, the power of the slumbering warriors increased, preparing them for an impending confrontation with unholy forces.

The soldiers broke camp at dawn, and as they cantered along the coast of this inland sea, an almost Biblical scene unfolded. Offshore, a solitary fisherman casting a net from his boat in the morning mist made out these knights on horseback, only to be overcome with fear when the warriors reached the place, near to their first encounter with Hildebrand, now so long ago. The equestrians rose from the land, as they had originally arrived on earth, ascending an invisible causeway to the heavens. When they reached the base of the clouds, the soldiers' burnished armour caught the golden rays of the early sun, reflecting flashes of radiance like the fiery chariot of Helios. Suddenly, the cloudscape changed to an ominous, towering nimbus, as the shape of the anvil made its reappearance, for Satan's warrior army intercepted the valiant knights – the very same that had kept watch over Prinz Paulus's secondment into an evil netherworld, while in the foothills of the Riphean Mountains. A violent battle erupted, resulting in intercloud bursts of lurid light, followed by extreme fulminations

— thunderous crashes, reverberating throughout the high cloud mass. The ten peerless combatants of the princess's guard fought with distinction as they dispatched their enemies. Some of the vanquished fell from the sky in their death throes, momentarily becoming incandescent, before vanishing, like mysterious ball lightning seen from afar. Hellalyle's heroes conquered all who came at them without loss to themselves until none of the adversaries remained. The nature of the empyrean then changed dramatically, from the threating pawl of a storm to that of brilliant white cumuli, which parted, allowing the horsemen to resume their journey, riding ever upwards, becoming lost to view as they returned to the Maker.

This miraculous occurrence became part of folklore, that ball lighting was indeed demonic fighters falling from the vault of heaven, killed by Hellalyle's warriors in the continuing struggle against the destructive forces of hell. It gave lie to the consensus of future generations, that lightning flashes seen in thunderous clouds were always electrical in origin.

It was even said to have inspired the Renaissance artist, Raphael, who, three centuries later, on completing the commission of his masterpiece *The Miraculous Draught of Fishes*, took it upon himself to create another, illustrating this epic scene at Lake Eydis. Sadly, no record of this painting has ever come to light.

Runa, Ethla, and some of the servants who had left the kitchens to mingle at the bottom of the tower, listening, had been horrified by the noises of the violent conflict. But now came the terrible screams of the princess, and they could not block it out, as she was dragged, kicked and verbally abused by the evil Paulus, on the pretence of dishonouring the king and bringing shame on her family.

The labyrinths of the castle echoed to the hapless Hellalyle's stark cries. She was hauled to a garret at the top of a bower and then thrown to the floor, where she lay battered and bruised, to be locked away until the king's return.

With Hellalyle's bodyguard now gone and Hildebrand dead, Prinz Paulus bribed the skeleton force at the castle and coerced them into becoming his henchmen; of these, eight renounced their loyalty to the monarch and treacherously schemed to slaughter the sheriff and the remaining garrison.

With the return of the king and his army months away, and Princess Amora absent in Holy Orders at the Monastery of Thorbjorg, the maniacal prinz took control of the fortress. To deter unwanted visitors, he spread rumours of plague and pestilence within. Paulus placed a sentry outside the princess's rooms, one at the foot of the bower, and one outside the chambers of his mother, Queen Gudrun, others, securing the bastions. With his soldiers manning the castle entrances, no one could enter or leave without permission of the prinz.

The incarceration of Hellalyle caused most of the occupants to flee, panic-stricken, but a few were forcibly detained for domestic duties. When Hellalyle was confined, her personal belongings went with her, but her lady-in-waiting had been banished, leaving only Ethla to attend her mistress. This servant girl from the pagan world, of deficient faculties and unknown parentage, dearly loved the princess who had rescued her from destitution. It was a devotion so absolute she felt the king's daughter to be the mother she never knew. The prinz's callous attitude to his stepsister exemplified his loathing of her, and so frightened did Ethla become on his visits that she cowered away in the darkest corners of the prison. Whenever he departed, the simple girl was so affected to see Hellalyle sobbing that she held the princess tightly and wept with her.

The effect of Hellalyle's imprisonment generated unbelievable scenes of a pantheistic nature. Recurring flights of wild birds, including those vigilant eagles from the distant mountain, would alight at her window in unearthly greeting. At daybreak, a majestic stag, like some messenger from the wild, would lead a herd of tarpan out of the woods to meadows below the fortress, expressing rapturous adoration in homage to their princess trapped in the castle tower.

This remarkable and uplifting sight induced in the woeful princess such feelings of joy and renewed hopefulness she waved an enthusiastic response to their demonstration of support. The deer, in a statuesque pose with its imperial horn, roared a message of assurance from those ardent and devoted followers in the hinterland, who had not forgotten her. A hymnal of the forest, echoing a passage from the Book of Psalms:

"As a stag longs for flowing streams, so my soul longs for you, O Hellalyle!"

Overwhelmed with emotion, the princess watched as the regal hart and the wild horse changed course, and on thunderous hooves sped headlong back to the safety of the primaeval forest.

Observing this young woman standing at the window, one could see a marked change in her appearance; that which had once radiated such high appeal and warmth now held a profoundly sombre air. The lustrous strands of her golden hair, once stylishly platted in beautifully formed braids (formerly the focus of such admiration and attention), were now tarnished and split, gathered and swept back with the tangled tresses pulled over one shoulder. Her perfect blue eyes looked sunken and hollowed, strained and bloodshot from the shedding of tears, her blooming complexion etiolated. However, the deterioration of her natural beauty did not concern the princess. There were more important matters at stake, such as endeavouring to inspire her maidservant Ethla to keep up her spirits in adversity, while Hellalyle, as if at the behest of the Almighty, continued her work on the manuscript.

After those peaceful interludes, there followed violent confrontations with the fiendish Paulus; as soon as he departed, the ghostly polymaths would return to assist the dispirited but zealous princess in her composition. When Ethla observed the princess removing the Chronicle from the locked chest, she sensed that the apparitions would be returning soon, and felt compelled to watch them at close quarters. On this occasion, though, she was unaware that the scholars were now setting out the circumstances of her mistress's incarceration. As she caught sight of Hellalyle's hand sketching at lightning speed her depiction of the cruel Paulus bullying and intimidating his captive, the hypersensitive Ethla became extremely upset, burying her head in the folds of the princess's dress and sobbing desperately. She ran away, concealing herself in a hidden corner of the bower. Distressed by Ethla's extreme reaction, the princess insisted that in future the girl should absent herself from the scene.

On one occasion, the brutish Paulus physically forced the princess to reopen the painted trunk to pry into her memoir, bellowing, "Open it, deceitful jade, open it I say!" while grasping her neck, and holding a dagger to Hellalyle's throat.

However, when he scanned the pages, the apparently meaningless words and images defeated him. Scowling contemptuously, he flung the sheets to the floor, leaving the unhappy Hellalyle, once dignified and self-controlled, scrabbling on her hands and knees as she tried frantically to retrieve the scattered leaves.

A witness acuter than the unsophisticated girl might have asked herself why these mystical men of learning, with their superior faculties and understanding, had not come to the aid of the princess in her hour of need. However, the king's daughter was aware that as this epic story had unfolded, these figures were merely a part of the narrative, without cause or authority to intervene.

Prinz Paulus returned from one of his visits to the princess confined in the tower, and there waiting was his mother, Queen Gudrun, herself a virtual prisoner. Once again, the queen earnestly enquired of the wellbeing of her stepdaughter, acutely aware of her son's sinister mental state and the danger it posed; even his mother had become fearful of him. He curtly replied, "Will you desist in your obsession with this harlot I have locked away!" and stormed out.

27

Von Altenburg's vision

In the meantime, Karl von Altenburg's character had markedly altered, his bitterness assuaged. His insular attitude had broadened, thanks to the influence of that remarkable princess. No longer displaying an inclination to fight, he prepared himself for monastic life at a Cistercian Abbey in a distant land. The monastery was austere. The interior, with its plain windows, avoided ethereal depictions of any kind. There, with the help of the monks, he gradually adopted a condition of contemplation and peace, and his unsightly grievous wound went unnoticed by his spiritual brothers.

Months passed before an individual event triggered vivid memories. One day, when von Altenburg was at prayer, he suddenly noticed a portrait had appeared on a blank wall in front of him. The image bore a striking resemblance to the princess he remembered. He snatched a furtive glance at his companions, to see if they had noticed anything, but they appeared oblivious.

The unaccountable appearance of this mysterious mural perplexed him, but, fearing ridicule, he tried to conceal his astonishment – while at the same time comforted by his strange anamnesis.

Returning to worship on Easter Sunday, his attention became drawn to a cornice above him, on which the image of a woman so skilfully executed in stone might have been an exact copy of the figure in the wall painting. Disregarding what he had seen as some trick of the mind, von Altenburg went about his daily business, until another strange incident perturbed him. The images in the picture and on the stone carving had faded away, only to reappear in the great wheel window over the chancel. The window's plain grisaille was now boldly replaced with brightly coloured stained glass, each depiction within delicate tracery radiating into one substantial picture.

Von Altenburg was overwhelmed when he saw that the disturbing subject matter of the new window revealed the figure of a fair woman in shackles, and a waif with anamorphic features crouching fearfully at her feet. Remarkably, so startling was the impact of this unsettling scene, in all its vibrant hues, that when brilliant sunshine gleamed through the tinted panes to such powerful effect, even the gloomiest shadows in the nave of the abbey became bathed in heavenly light.

It began to dawn on the former warrior that this extraordinary scene might have been intended to convey to him a significant message. This notion strengthened with the association of the name *Catherine*, given to a circular fenestra commemorating the death of the Saint of Alexandria, executed on a spiked wheel.

For several days, the troubled man avoided looking at the stained-glass window. Finally, though, the temptation became irresistible, and, raising his eyes, he was relieved to find the image gone; the episodic visions had come to an end. His equanimity restored, he convinced himself that he must have been suffering from a severe delusion – even imagining hearing the peal of a great bell coming from afar.

The work that von Altenburg most enjoyed at the abbey was preparing the land for crops. The satisfaction he drew from his manual labour would persist, particularly after observing a young woman of seraphic beauty so engrossed in a scene of ploughing that she seemed to epitomise a profound communication with nature, engendering an unforgettable prospect of pastoral paradise. In a confident and cheerful mood, effortlessly guiding the oxen as he worked a straight furrow, he was about to turn the plough when an intense, blinding light flashed before him. (A similar event would be claimed by an infamous, Siberian strannik in future times.)

He held up his hands in terror. To his amazement, the beasts of burden remained quite still, showing no sign of panic. Dazzled, but aware of moving shapes in this incandescence, he stared at the spiritual vision of a woman assailed by a knight, and of a young girl cringing in distress, before the visitation faded away.

Anxiously, he hurriedly returned to the monastery, stumbling as he went. Past events revolved in his mind: the unique rainbow with its glittering chromatism that Princess Hellalyle and her knights had observed, the portent he experienced then, now reaffirmed by the symbolism of that colourful image in the wheel window of the abbey. In a fit of desperation, believing something momentous was imminent, he gestured to the monks the disturbing world he had seen and heard, but their reaction was one of bewilderment and disbelief.

Convinced that he alone, by some divination, had been summoned back to Castle Preben, realising that Princess Hellalyle must be in extreme danger, the knight solicited an audience with the abbot to ask if he might renounce his vows. He received sympathetic counsel, and with the Cistercians' considerable influence within the Teutonic order, they sought help in re-equipping him for battle.

Shortly afterwards, the abbot recalled him.

"I have excellent news for you, my brother," said the cleric, "The Vogt and Komtur have forwarded your request for assistance with the utmost urgency, and now I can happily report, they have found a wealthy burgher willing to provide you with the necessary funds."

On a late spring morning, Karl von Altenburg left the sanctuary of this religious house to embark on his long journey, strikingly attired on his warhorse and furnished with all the necessary accoutrements of battle; the knight's stasis was at an end.

The beginning of his quest took him through a stand of apple trees in full bloom – until something caused his horse to halt in its tracks; for there, perched on a blossom-laden branch, some force for good had dispatched its miniature emissary in the shape of that tiny bird, tugging the conscience and beckoning the heart as it serenaded them with its captivating song.

28

The birth of Prince Hagen

Time passed quickly, and despite her desolate existence, it heralded joyful expectation for Hellalyle. Seated by the window with Ethla kneeling by her, the princess, in an astonishing revelation, confided in the girl, saying, "I have wonderful news, Ethla. The Almighty has blessed me with the greatest fortune in all the world, for I am carrying Hildebrand's child. See!"

The princess placed Ethla's hand onto her protuberant abdomen through an opening in the folds of her outer garments.

"You can feel it moving, can't you?"

The girl nodded in surprise, hardly able to contain her excitement. However, Hellalyle then looked her firmly in the eye, with a finger to her lips, exclaiming, "Now I must impress upon you, little madam, of the need to keep this all a secret. It is of the utmost importance; do you understand me, Ethla?"

The smile slowly disappeared from the diminutive helper, as she started to realise the significance of Hellalyle's grave warning.

The princess, blessed with a gift of divine insight, was all too aware of the devilish intent of her evil captor, her stepbrother Paulus. Now with all her blood brothers slain and Hildebrand dead, the demonic prinz schemed to annihilate any legitimate heirs to Thorstein's throne, casting the realm into conflict and chaos. Queen Gudrun, Paulus's mother, who might have exercised a moderating influence on him, had not been seen for weeks. Hellalyle feared for her safety.

Conscious of the terrible danger she and her newborn infant would face, the princess conceived the idea of concealing the physical effects of her pregnancy by wearing heavier garments – ostensibly to ward off the unseasonal cold at the setting in of the early autumnal weather.

Little Ethla could come and go freely from the castle tower, the prison of the princess, avoiding suspicion of the guards – who regarded her as a harmless idiot. They merely shrugged their shoulders when they caught sight of her performing a make-believe errand, or innocently scurrying off to pilfer food to supplement meagre rations. If she encountered anyone, she would reduce her pace and gape at them with a dull-witted look before skipping off. Hellalyle never ceased to be amazed at the items Ethla managed to remove from the kitchens, often coming back with bread, cheese, fruit, or even a roasted chicken, tucked beneath her clothes. Her loyalty to the princess knew no bounds, for it would have been easy for her to try to escape – but she always faithfully returned.

As the time approached for Hellalyle to give birth, she felt it imperative to get in touch with Abbot Jurian. Standing at her turret window, the princess raised her hands in an attitude of prayer, and with her spirit in high concentration, she called on the Creatures of the Wild to come to her aid.

"Please hear my call, Holy Spirit of the Hinterland. Never once have you had reason to question my loyalty, for I have served you without question, assisting your subjects in their moments of distress. But I now request your help in return. If it is your pleasure, please send the mighty Aquila to assist me in my moment of peril."

The abbot, vaguely aware of the king issuing an edict for Hellalyle's detention, was ignorant of its full wording – the execution of Hildebrand – so Jurian had decided to wait until Thorstein's return, before lobbying him on the English knight's behalf. The unfortunate abbot was ignorant of the disastrous events that had unfolded at the Castle Preben. Soon, he would learn first-hand of its enormity.

Far away, in the garth of the Abbey of Sunniva, Abbot Jurian was engaged in animated conversation with three lay brothers when a dark shadow fell across them, obscuring the morning sunlight. Instinctively, the group ducked, holding up their arms as if to shield themselves. In disbelief, they watched a giant eagle swooping down, then hanging momentarily above, its powerful wings outstretched. The eagle released from its talons a piece of rolled-up parchment, which fell to the ground and landed at the feet of the abbot.

Stooping to pick it up, Jurian discovered a message from the captive Hellalyle, pleading with him to come at once. The abbot, gazing up at the magnificent bird circling overhead, surmised that under Hellalyle's influence the creature needed his assent. After nodding his head, with an understanding gesture to the airborne courier, the eagle flew away directly into the blinding sunlight, towards the castle of Preben.

As the monks watched it disappear into the distance, they made the sign of the cross, believing what they had witnessed to be the work of the Almighty.

The abbot, deeply affected by the miraculous communication and perceiving the urgency of Hellalyle's plea, prepared for travelling to Preben as soon as possible, accompanied by two able-bodied monks and a spare horse. After an arduous journey, he could hardly have anticipated the hostile reception he received on arrival at the castle. With the drawbridge closed, a guard bawled out from the battlements to the three clergies.

"I have my orders. You cannot see the Princess Hellalyle."

The abbot, in indignation, stormed, "What do you mean I cannot see Hellalyle? I am the Abbot of Sunniva! Do you hear me? I take my authority from canon law, even the king bows down before it!"

Jurian's bold remonstration frightened the guard who sent a message to Paulus. After a short interval, the chains creaked into action lowering the drawbridge, allowing Jurian and the two monks to cross the deep trench in the rock. However, the portcullis was not lifted, and standing on the inside, peering through, was Prinz Paulus. The abbot, not at all happy being forced to speak through the heavy grating, said in an irritated voice, "I insist on being allowed to see the princess. Has it come to this that men of the cloth, Christ's representatives, must grovel before an iron cage? It is outrageous! I insist you let us through, or by heaven and earth I will bring the wrath of King Thorstein down upon you!"

The offensive Paulus grudgingly conceded, as if still harbouring some superstitious apprehension of the power of the church.

"You, Abbot, can pass, but not your assistants, they will remain outside the fortress walls. If you don't approve, then turn around and leave. I am in charge here."

Jurian, supressing his temper, retorted, "The king shall know of your insolence! Now let me through, and be quick about it!"

The portcullis rose, and as the abbot passed underneath and out into bright daylight, he came face-to-face with Paulus, and was shocked at his changed appearance, malevolently glowering at him, entirely unlike the friendly Prinz of old.

With Jurian's companions forced to remain behind, one of the prinz's henchmen led Jurian to the turret room, Hellalyle's virtual prison. Greeting her warmly, he could barely conceal his amazement at discovering she was with child, and his absolute horror at the events that led to her incarceration. With voices lowered, they conferred about the extreme precariousness of her situation. He promised to support her in every way... The abbot then revealed, "Your Highness, a strange rumour circulates amongst the fellowship at the abbey, for one morning, a written message in Aramaic script was discovered, deposited on the eagle lectern. Where it has come from nobody knows. Eventually, it was deciphered by my brethren in the scriptorium, and it revealed a prophecy, foretelling that one of your bodyguards will return, the Teutonic Knight with the mutilated face, vowing to avenge Hildebrand's untimely death, and deliver you from harm. Now, amazingly, I receive a message from you, borne on the wing by an immense eagle. Princess, can you shed light on such wonders?"

However, as before when asked by Hildebrand to solve a similar mystery, she feigned ignorance, but the prophecy of von Altenburg coming back prompted Hellalyle to move to a window in contemplation. When she turned around, tears were rolling down her cheeks, and she said, "My dear abbot, ever since the arrival in this kingdom of my bodyguard, I alone sensed their very existence was not as it seemed, and now, I feel the time is right to tell all that I know."

The princess then revealed, to the incredulous cleric, the secret identities of ten of the knights.

"Yet," she said, "I am sure, but for reasons I cannot understand, the whole bodyguard were not chosen by my father, but instead by some entity beyond my comprehension, who somehow induced the king to recruit them. Now sadly, along with my brothers, they are all gone, while somewhere in the boundless forest lies Hildebrand's unmarked grave. However, you bring me news the Monastery of Sunniva has received, what could only be called, a divine message, forecasting Karl von Altenburg's return. It all seems to be a narrative unfolding on a scriptural scale. What can all this mean? It is as if I have been singled out for protection by an all-seeing spirit, but why me? For I have no importance, no more than a moth that rotates about a candle flame."

To which the abbot replied, "Princess, you cannot but know it, but I have long suspected that your presence here is an exalted one."

At these words, the emotional woman prostrated herself before Jurian and dabbed her tearful eyes on his vestments. Consoling her in a fatherly way, he continued, "What you have told me, Hellalyle, indicates that something is holding out its hand to shield you from evil, and the return of the Teutonic Knight can be no chance appearance."

Shortly afterwards, the queen received a visit from Abbot Jurian. Discreetly, he shared some significant news concerning the princess: Hellalyle was carrying Hildebrand's child. Her spirit was robust, with Ethla, the servant, attending to her needs as best as she could, the little maid company for her in moments of distress. However, the cleric did say, "Having had a chance to observe the princess in her bower, I find it ironic, dare I say, even slightly amusing, that their roles are virtually reversed, for Hellalyle fusses so much over the wellbeing of her little helper – motherly, it might be said – it has transposed her role into that of the servant!"

Abbot Jurian went on to explain to Gudrun that only he and the girl knew of the princess's development, and now the king's consort – and that was how it must remain.

The queen was amazed at first, but then displayed considerable concern at her stepdaughter's predicament.

Jurian, with trepidation, respectfully requested forgiveness for what he was about to say:

"Your Majesty, I consider the prinz is trying to erase all those of hereditary right to the throne. With all the king's sons dead, he thinks only Hellalyle remains, and it is highly probable she will not live to see her father's return. It distresses me to speak ill of a mother's son, but say it I must. Paulus, as I recall, was once an optimistic, friendly fellow, who would speak no ill of anyone, yet now harbours disdain for Hellalyle – for what reason, I cannot understand. It has intensified to an irrational loathing as a man possessed. Now she is incarcerated in the tower she is at his mercy, but what she is enduring now will soon be as nothing when he learns her secret. For if Hellalyle's child escapes the prison and lives, Paulus's plans will receive a fateful blow, and it means the princess and all who know of her situation are in mortal danger! Your Majesty, if you sympathise and have the influence to deflect him away from this abomination and release the princess, then I earnestly plead with you to act."

At the abbot's declaration, the queen sank slowly into a chair, shocked by his words.

The days moved on; the malevolent spirit that was now Paulus sensed the princess's unborn child. Realising his strategy to seize the throne could unravel, he became ever more callous to his stepsister. He verbally abused her, incessantly, screaming most foully – but as usual, he avoided looking directly at her face. Evil was, indeed, repelled by the righteous.

In due course, the princess gave the delivery of a child, a healthy boy. Ethla, fussing foolishly, was barely aware of the momentous nature of the occasion but smiled to herself as she clasped her mistress's outstretched hand, while just noticeable in the background, Abbot Jurian, discreetly trying to merge into the shadows, was the all-important witness in one of the most influential scenes in this mediaeval saga.

The supreme drama was worthy of depiction, paint on canvas, in the hand of the future Leonardo de Vinci, where the diminution of light and form in the darkest recesses the supreme genius would have captured in his mastery of *sfumato* – the exquisite blending of tones, ensuring obscure outlines and the shadows of living things had no borders or lines, replicating this vision in Hellalyle's prison.

Afterwards, the girl, in quixotic fashion, skipped and clumsily cavorted around the forlorn room in abandoned celebration, endeavouring to emulate the dance she had witnessed her mistress perform in the great hall. The princess, however, was oblivious to Ethla's antics, and so was the abbot, seated at a table by the window, engrossed in scribing out a document confirming the royal birth. Unable to smuggle out the all-important scroll, he surrendered it to the safe-keeping of the princess, who secreted it away in a most secure location within the chamber.

The eminent cleric, Jurian, present at the birth, paid dearly for his unswerving loyalty and administrations. He was never to be seen again, as one night, as he was sleeping in a temporary room at the castle, to be near the princess, two soldiers entered and smothered him to death – presumably on the orders of the monster Paulus.

Lying on her makeshift bed cradling her baby, Hellalyle looked momentarily radiant and joyful. She had chosen the name Hagen for the newly born child, who brought her great happiness and delighted Ethla.

However, the princess soon became increasingly fearful for her own life and that of her son. She drew Ethla aside and impressing on the tearful girl said, "I believe the time will shortly come when the newborn and his mother will be in mortal danger. When that moment arrives, you must flee the fortress with the infant. After that, you must never let him out of your care, or reveal the child's identity, and must never return. Then you must seek out the knight, Karl von Altenburg, for his protection. Now, I ask of you Ethla, to swear an oath to this effect. To search out 'the knight with no face'?!" The little miss shook her head, conscious in the enormity of fear she held for the disfigured German. The princess, in desperation and anguish, her hands gripping the little girl's shoulders, said, "Ethla, I implore of you not to be fearful of the soldier. If you love your mistress and the infant prince, you will carry out what I ask!"

Ethla, possessing the mental capacity of a young child, gradually began to understand the enormity of the crisis soon to unfold. Realising that she would soon have to part with the one person in the world she loved more than any other – the princess – she became overwhelmed with grief. Anxious to appease her mistress, she nodded and swore in a garbled fashion the oath asked of her, not yet fully understanding what it meant. She had no comprehension of the superhuman task the princess – with nobody else to turn to – had set for her.

That same moment, Queen Gudrun paced distractedly about her bower, wringing her hands in agitation. Her lady-in-waiting fretted, endeavouring to calm the queen's disquiet. She was anxious herself for Hellalyle, the queen, and anguished by the wretched conduct of her son Paulus. The queen could not bear to keep the secret of Hellalyle's pregnancy to herself (not aware it was now brought forth) and had felt the need to disclose the news to her confidante.

Violent hammer blows on the door to his mother's chambers preceded the explosive intrusion of Paulus, who had forced the bolt, bursting into the room. He yelled at the lady-in-waiting, "Get out."

But as she fled, loath to abandon her charge, she managed to slip unseen behind heavy drapes that concealed a secret closet. From there, she listened in horror as the demented prinz rounded on Gudrun, screaming obscenities, in his wild imaginings cursing his mother for aiding and abetting the fallen woman whom he had confined to an isolated part of the fortress. Horrified by her son's abuse and aggression, she stumbled back towards the window as Paulus pressed his livid and contorted face close to hers. With a courageous outburst she said, "I demand that you free Hellalyle. How can a son of mine be so cruel and barbaric? This treatment of the king's daughter carrying a child must cease at once. Do you hear me!"

Her brave invocation left him lost for words, glaring at her malevolently, for she had let slip Hellalyle's secret. It triggered such an outburst of hysterical rage that with a violent push he propelled his mother through the yawning casement, from which she plunged to her death.

Staring down at the corpse of his mother, spread-eagled on the flagstones far below, he became paranoid. Convinced her lady-in-waiting might also be privy to the princess's condition, he swore aloud he would track her down. Suddenly, he detected in the shadows a slight rippling movement in the curtain. Furiously wrenching the drapes apart, he revealed the woman he sought, cowering before him and shaking in terror.

"Don't, please, I am innocent of all this, I beg you, spare me!" She screamed, but to no avail. He remorselessly, savagely, gripped her by the throat and strangled her.

When her frail frame became limp in his grip, he casually dumped her lifeless body on the floor like the carcass of a hunted animal. His vengeful eyes aflame, he bolted at lightning speed from the homicidal scene.

29

*Von Altenburg heeds the prognostication
of a Hungarian soothsayer*

The Teutonic Knight headed north-eastwards, swiftly, on his return to Castle Preben, the seat of King Thorstein. Later in his journey, he arrived at a remote mountainous area containing a rocky gorge, where he heard a surge of fast flowing water coursing through a defile, out of sight. Glancing down, he stopped to survey the road where it twisted into the canyon. Convinced that it was safe to continue, coaxing his horse, he cautiously descended. Soon, he reached the bottom of the chasm, at the brink of a swollen river.

As he searched for a secure crossing, a surreal scene unfolded, suffused with spectral light, causing the roaring sound of the rapids to diminish to complete silence. He negotiated a trackway which clung to the steep side of the abyss, but a sudden fall of rock blocked his way, and as he turned, another landslip of boulders tumbled down right in front of him.

The desperate knight, trapped in an unstable gulley, was startled by the sudden appearance of a large ibex with impressive, curving horns. The creature had sprung from nowhere. With staring eyes, flaring nostrils, and swivelling its thickset neck, it looked as though it were enticing von Altenburg to follow. In great trepidation, with no other option to hand, the knight steered his mount in the tracks of this agile animal as it climbed effortlessly through a cleft in the defile he was sure had not been there before.

Unerringly, the goat-like mountain climber safely led rider and steed through terrain that miraculously the horse could navigate, and on through a narrow ravine until they emerged on the banks of the silent rapids.

Before him lay a picturesque bridge of small structure, set in a striking landscape some artist might have conceived to delight his fancy. A stranger sat on a stone parapet in profound contemplation, facing outwards, his feet dangling over the chasm. The knight thought it odd that this solitary had travelled to this isolated place, without so much as a horse or a knapsack; von Altenburg was still ignorant of the work of those powerful spirits which had engineered his journey to this desolate location.

As the warrior drew close, the mysterious figure sitting on the stone wall noticed the black cross on the knight's surcoat and addressed the horseman in the German tongue. Von Altenburg, unable to articulate, resorted to sign language.

As he dismounted, von Altenburg could hardly have been aware that this encounter, so compelling yet disquieting, would engender the dramatic recounting of two prophecies.

"I am Taltos, summoned to forewarn all I come across of the imminent danger which threatens to engulf Europa. A recurrence of the most disturbing dreams has compelled me to predict terrible destruction, escalating from the east. Populations uprooted, lands laid waste – and the overwhelming might of the invaders is sure to defeat any army ranged against it."

The stranger paused for a few moments.

"Although…it is curious that in my wanderings I have always sensed a malevolent entity opposing me, castigating my auguries of impending catastrophe – the aforesaid that has caused you to embark on your journey."

The speaker drew a breath. The knight listened in horror and disbelief, becoming even more alarmed by Taltos' second prediction.

"You are Karl von Altenburg, the Teutonic Knight, and privy I am to the nature of your quest to save Hellalyle. I judge that she represents the marked antithesis of the commander of those powerful forces from Asia. In different circumstances, had she survived, her body of knights would surely have resurrected their armies of old, and under the leadership of an English Prince, they would have vanquished those hostile hordes, in an Armageddon of unimaginable ferocity.

"Your task will not be easy, for our devilish adversary has already done away with Hildebrand – and is now hell-bent on destroying the princess and her progeny. However, your horrific and unsightly wound will serve as a hidden weapon, and with the help of a disadvantaged yet kind-hearted child, you will triumph, even if the outcome will not be as you might expect. Now, it is imperative you leave at once, for time is pressing!"

The luminary fell silent, absorbed in the inner world of his prophecy. Von Altenburg, troubled and frustrated, deprived of speech, could not press the Hungarian to explain one comment, "*had she*" – Hellalyle – "*survived*", so resignedly he remounted his charger and rode off, headed by the ibex. Glancing back from time to time, he noticed that Taltos never turned his head towards him, remaining rooted to the spot like some sentient monolith. Von Altenburg surmised that the outlandish diviner had somehow foreseen the knight's appearance at the bridge, and at that moment of realisation, the eerie hush lifted like a dark veil. The synthetic luminescence that had infused this wild and rocky scene was miraculously transmuted into natural light, as the eclipsed sun rose again.

They reached a place where the original road revealed itself, at which point the mythical goat impetuously scurried away. It began to scale dextrously a near-vertical arête; perilously ever upwards it climbed, eventually appearing on the brink of a knife-edged mountain ridge, and there it remained – the symbol of determination, imperiously posing as it watched the equestrian figure of the Teutonic Knight far below, receding into the distance, in search of his destiny.

As he rode on, the warrior was unaware that a magical world of nature was guiding and protecting him on his journey. After he had rested, a sharp-eyed crow would gently peck him as he slumbered, to wake him. If any brigands were lying in ambush, wildlife would gather, emitting raucous noises to alert the lone horseman. Bears and wolves kept their distance, respecting his patch of ground, invisible, watching over the soldier through the darkest hours. The knight's horse, knowing nature's protectors posed no danger, was pacified. His safe passage was aided by other beasts, aurochs, bison and deer, which would send pathfinders to lead him, unwittingly, by their secret trails through the untamed landscape.

30

Violence in the tower

The ill-fated day unleashed when the princess's stepbrother, the inimical Paulus, came back hell-bent on abducting the newborn Hagen. Hurtling up the turret steps as a man possessed, he burst into Hellalyle's chamber.

"Where is the child?" he bellowed, as he stalked the chamber, casting his eyes around the room. "Hand it over, I say. I know it is here – do not make a fool out of me!"

He was unaware of the terrified Ethla crouching nearby in the shadows, as she nursed the baby in her arms. The prinz, ever more with rage, uttered a chilling threat, "Princess, you will not live to see the end of this day if you do not comply!" and grabbed her by the neck in a vice-like grip, pulling her upwards as if she was a rag doll. He then viciously wrenched her delicate arms in a lock, before forcibly throwing her down, where she smashed her head with a thud on the rough stone floor.

Unnoticed, the petrified Ethla emerged out of her hiding place with the baby Hagen and nervously made her way to the open door, where she paused, to stare in horror at Paulus's monstrous act of brutality on the princess. Hellalyle, although in acute pain and bleeding profusely, managed to cry out, "Ethla, run, run for your life!"

Wheeling around, the maniacal Paulus managed to catch sight of the fluttering hem of Ethla's cloak as the girl fled, sobbing uncontrollably. Stung with rage at being outwitted, Paulus swivelled his attention back to the princess, her battered body face-down on the blood-soaked flags.

"You devious, skulking rat, you will pay for that!" he screamed, and with dagger drawn, he pulled up her limp frame by the hair and savagely plunged the blade downwards into her spine. Like a scene of torment drawn from the infernal pit, Hellalyle's cries of agony echoed along the labyrinthine passageways of Castle Preben.

Ethla, carefully bearing her precious bundle, took to her heels as fast as her stubby legs would allow, dodging past two guards confused by the anarchy, stumbled breathlessly to the last doorway at the foot of the tower, and, there, she abruptly came to a halt, for someone was blocking her way. In the bright light of the open door stood the dark silhouette of the tall figure of Karl von Altenburg, wielding a bloody sword, towering above the corpse of a sentry he had just dispatched; the brave warrior was on a mission to save Hellalyle and wreak revenge on Hildebrand's killers.

Ethla felt trapped, cowering uneasily, doing her best to shroud the swaddled baby Hagen in the folds of her garment. The knight bent forward, fixing his single eye on the badly frightened girl, trying to understand what was going on. Then more spine-chilling screams rang out. He jerked his head, glancing up at the top of the fortress. Ethla, paralysed with fear, unable to utter a sound, pointed with a trembling hand in the direction of the harrowing sounds, her eyes desperately pleading with the soldier to aid her wounded mistress.

Von Altenburg, incensed by the horror of what was taking place, bellowed aloud as a wild beast provoked; the power imbued in the mighty Samson, as recorded in the Bible, was now in him. With blades at the ready, he sprinted up the turret stairs, impaling two of the prinz's hired thugs blocking his way. Rallying all reserves of strength in his muscular body, von Altenburg hurled himself at the door to Hellalyle's chamber, splintering the massive timber with the weight of his charge.

What he saw inside sickened even the hardened soldier in him: Paulus, devil incarnate, his bloodshot eyes burning in their sockets, looming menacingly over the crumpled body of the princess, on the point of stabbing her again with his dripping weapon. Suddenly becoming aware of von Altenburg's vengeful presence, Paulus tried to defend himself, but one swift strike of the knight's sword severed his raised arm.

Von Altenburg seized Paulus by the throat – intent on throttling him – but the princess, lying on her side as her life ebbed away, whispered inaudibly to spare him. A last act of compassion. Oblivious to her plea, the knight forced Paulus to his knees, and in the struggle the cloth masking his unsightly features slipped to the ground. The knight, furious his identity had been revealed, hoisted Paulus's body high above his shoulders before hurling it violently against the wall – bones cracked and splintered on impact.

Racked with excruciating pain, Paulus, twisting his fractured body as he tried to raise himself, stared in horror at von Altenburg's grotesquely mutilated countenance, glowering down at him like an inexorable agent of Nemesis. The knight, wielding his steel like an executioner, brought down his sword with one, well-aimed heavy blow, shearing edgewise to disfigure the prinz's evil face, splitting his skull.

Not even his death would exorcise the iniquitous influence of this detestable tyrant. His corpse seemed to effuse a noxious emanation, soon to be transformed into the shape of a hideous demon, leering over Hellalyle in contemptuous triumph. The evil being, turning menacingly, fixed his glaring eyes on von Altenburg to intimidate the Teutonic Knight with his inimical stare, and take possession of his soul. Yet, as Beelzebub tried to analyse the knight's inner self, he became aware that this soldier's heart and mind was steely and unflinching, an impermeable barrier. It had been moulded and hardened by terrible experiences, further compounded by the truth that the one human being on God's earth who rekindled his deepest emotions now lay dying at his feet.

Thwarted, the devil in defeat made to depart but wavered in his course. Von Altenburg brandished his blade with a look of such heroic defiance that the evil creature, venting high-pitched shrieks like some infernal chimaera, leapt onto the stone ledge of the window. Turning ominously on its claws, it cast one last malevolent glare at the knight before pitching headlong into the void. Lightning flashed, and thunder clattered as the warrior watched the beast fall to the earth far below, swallowed by the ground, restoring the devil to the hot magma flowing through the underworld. Thus, in times to come, the Gargoyles' stubborn faces would carve their place in legend, recalling the vanquishing of Satan by a brave Teutonic Knight.

In a state of shock at this sinister confrontation, the knight pulled himself together as best he could. After retrieving the protective cloth from the floor and holding it to his face, he dropped to his knees, tenderly cradling Hellalyle with his other arm.

Although desperately weak, the princess managed to raise one hand, gently brushing away the material held by him and ran her delicate fingers, ever so gently, across his mutilated features, imparting a soothing caress (confounding her father's prediction that no woman could ever bring herself to touch the decimated visage of the Teutonic warrior). Then, with the sweetest smile, her voice but a whisper, she spoke unto him, *"Mîn tiuscher helt, ir ensult daz antlütze mir niht vor verbergen."* (My German hero, do not hide your face from me.) "Your redeeming presence is no accident. The spirits of the natural world will now have their revenge, channelling their powers through you, and around you, and under the guidance of the Almighty will save this kingdom from the horrors of chaos and conflict, denying Satan his victory."

Von Altenburg was overwhelmed by her heartfelt words, bringing great comfort and inner strength to him, having endured the trauma of his terrible wound for so long. A tear rolled down his cheek, moistening the lesions on his face like a healing balm.

Following her impassioned utterance, Hellalyle looked utterly drained. To the knight, cradling the frail princess, her physical shape felt insubstantial, almost weightless, as if she had already departed this life. Suddenly, a Celestial Being appeared at the side of the princess, invisible to the knight. Its presence briefly reignited her dying spirit, like some almost-extinguished flame rekindled from the ashes, enabling her to recount to von Altenburg the catastrophe that had befallen the castle.

Spellbound, he listened to her narrative, her irrevocable entreaties, how Hellalyle had given Hildebrand a son, in the presence of one Abbot Jurian, how the child who had been named Hagen bore a distinctive mark behind his left ear. Von Altenburg flinched in horror as Hellalyle revealed how the devoted monk, the sole witness to the royal birth, was smothered to death as he slept in his cell, on the orders of Prinz Paulus. Fearful for her son's life, the princess had entrusted the child to the only person she could turn to, into the care of a pure soul, her loyal servant Ethla. The necessary attestation of Hagen's birth, bearing the abbot's seal, Hellalyle had carefully concealed in a secret niche within the walls of her chamber, and her record of events, the manuscript, locked in a chest, which now drew his attention. The knight realised the abbot's scroll and Hellalyle's Chronicle he must guard at all costs.

Hellalyle pleaded with him to urgently seek out Ethla and under his protection guide her and Hagen to the Monastery of Thorbjorg, where the abbess, the king's sister, Princess Amora will give them sanctuary.

The king's daughter was relieved her father was out of danger, now the prinz's evil spirit had been dispatched back to hell, but with all her beloved brothers slain, she insisted her son Hagen – sole heir – receive preparation for his role as future monarch, both for his safety and the stability of the kingdom.

With her eyelids closed, the legendary princess passed away, her fragile figure resting in von Altenburg's powerful arms.

At that instant, the seraph departed.

Her untimely death precipitated an eruption of disturbing, unnatural occurrences; in the surrounding countryside, peasants toiling in the fields, unaware of the horrendous scenes at the castle, were startled out of their senses. Hundreds of panic-stricken birds burst out of woodland canopies, flying haphazardly to join other agitated flocks, wheeling and diving high above the fluvial waters of Lake Eydis. Throughout the forest, on the mountain slopes, the creatures of the wild became restless in their natural habitat, and the plaintive howling of wolves echoed across the untamed wilderness, onwards throughout Terra Incognito.

In Hellalyle's chamber, von Altenburg distractedly cast his eyes about the room in search of the hidden document. At first, the princess's mirror on the wall made no impression on him – until, stooping to examine part of the stonework below, he recoiled in horror, catching the distressing image of his terrible maiming trapped in its reflection. Compelled to look again, the soldier shuddered, seeing Hellalyle's corpse prostrate on the floor behind. Mysteriously, though, he now heard her talking clearly, yet from afar, speaking across the great divide. "Warrior from Germania, the agony of your countenance lost is near its end. Your unfortunate physical appearance has struck terror, defeating the very Prinz of Darkness. By the same means, you will vanquish one more disciple of the devil, before eventually, the curse of your intolerable affliction shall be lifted. This covenant, I swear will come to pass..." The voice's soft melodious tones then trailed away into the nothingness, and an eerie silence reigned.

Regaining his composure, he continued his search for the hidden scroll. He was astonished to see an aumbry magically open before him in what had been a featureless, solid wall. His hand trembled as he reached over to remove the document from the stone recess.

With the certificate and Chronicle in his possession, he gently lifted the princess's body, bearing it with the utmost care from bower to chapel. Inexplicably, from a cavernous veil of clouds overhead, the solemn chimes of a colossal bell tolled, its sombre tones resounding dolefully like deadened rolls of distant thunder, its final majestic peal humming interminably.

Entering the shrine, the lifeless Hellalyle in his arms, he came unexpectedly upon servants who had taken refuge in the holy place. At the sight of the corpse of their revered princess, women wailed in anguish, terrified faces peered from the shadows. As the knight laid the ashen cadaver at the altar, he made a sign of the cross, then fell to his knees in homage. The imperishable blooms of *Mountain Everlasting* Hellalyle had placed in the chapel now inexplicably withered before their eyes. The castle itself was weeping.

Drawing himself to full height, von Altenburg turned to the distressed gathering, urgently gesticulating for information of Ethla's whereabouts. Most shook their heads until one woman cried out, "I saw Hellalyle's young servant girl running across the courtyard towards the main gate, awkwardly cradling what appeared to be a bundle of rags. Whether she fled from the castle, I cannot be sure!"

Impetuously, the knight strode quickly across the courtyard to the gatehouse to confront the one guard he had left alive, who pointed frantically towards the surrounding forest.

In great urgency, von Altenburg made preparation for his journey, saddled his destrier and rode off in search of Ethla and the infant prince. Close to the portcullis, he reined to a halt and skilfully turned his steed to face that haunting tower where Hellalyle had met her tragic end. With his war horse impatiently stomping, he brandished his sword aloft, saluting the imitable princess, bidding her a sad farewell as her ghostly last words of exhortation resounded in his ears.

31

Ethla's first night alone

Terrified, with her heart beating fast, the little girl bearing the infant prince in her arms hurried through this ancient land in which the verdure of the fields separated castle from the forest. With little idea of where to go, she entered the sylvan tract and then stumbled with difficulty through dense and gloomy woodland. Breathlessly, she slumped to the ground by the moss-clad trunk of a dead tree, and the baby started to cry. Pulling a bag from her shoulder and remembering Hellalyle's advice, she took a cow's teat and udder and filled it with milk from a goat's bladder. Then she held it to her body to warm, and thankfully, the baby suckled from it. This young woman, so prone to fits of panic, would have her mettle tested to the full during the coming days. As the infant contentedly drew in nourishment, the pressures of the day abated, and the exhausted Ethla fell into a slumber, clutching the Crown Prince, the boy whose survival was so vital to the future stability of the kingdom.

She woke in the early hours, to the mournful stirring of the wind that had started to increase in strength as she slumbered. It was a night with heavy clouds covering the land, with the result that an intense darkness prevailed beneath the dense treescape. She wrapped the infant in swaddling clothes and drew him close to her breast, bringing warmth to his tiny frame. With her eyes wide open in terror, she steeled herself to face the advancing dawn, unaware that those dark Cerberean wolves who had once shielded Hellalyle in the wild had now returned to protect her son and his diminutive minder. The daunting, spectral figures of the black lupines circled silently and watchfully, ready to defend these children from the impending danger of a sinister underworld.

The wind got up, and the gale rocked the trees, moonlight intermittently penetrating the swaying foliage. Under the restless canopy, this helpless but plucky girl suddenly detected the eerie – yet seductive – cries of a woman who reiterated her name with spine-chilling magnetism.

*Ethla...Ethla...Ethla...*and so on, until the high wind subsided, and quietness returned, occasionally interrupted by the distant calls of wild nocturnal creatures.

After what seemed an eternity, the subdued light of dawn now infiltrated the forest, enabling the girl to make out the shapes of individual trees. Ethla, relieved that this nightmare had nearly come to an end, checked the condition of the baby boy she embraced. Under the impression all was well, she set out. Coming upon a clearing with a rivulet, she stopped to bathe the infant, who burst into tears at the shock of the cold immersion. A sip of milk and a change of clothing from her bag eased his distress. Recalling her mistress's careful instruction, keeping an eye on the child now asleep in the ferns, she freshened herself and then immersed the infant's garments in the brook.

Unknown to the little girl, great danger lurked near the flowing water, but protected by the unseen phalanx of wolves, she was safe.

With the heat of the autumn sunlight in the air the clothing eventually dried, and she left the woods. Aware that her disability of mind and body could cause the removal of the baby from her care, and the milk now all but consumed, she resolved as best she could to keep her promise and seek the help of the fearsome knight, Karl von Altenburg, but with little idea of where to go.

Hugging her precious bundle, she reluctantly followed a track that led in the direction of a distant village. Innocently unaware that the princess was dead, Ethla convinced herself that the assistance of the German warrior would enable her to meet Hellalyle once more, and proudly restore the child to its rightful mother.

32

Karl von Altenburg rescues Ethla

After walking some distance, Ethla was famished, her arms and feet aching from exhaustion. There was no milk left for the infant. She reached a junction of the track where a little-used cart-way veered to the right. At this point, she caught sight of a single thatched dwelling, with smoke rising from a gap in the roof, and the girl decided to seek help. Cautiously and silently she moved towards the building, following the edge of the woods. Approaching the house, she stopped, remaining hidden, and kept watch, frightened to continue, but the child in her arms had grown restless from hunger.

Plucking up her courage, Ethla crept forward hesitantly and in apprehension knocked lightly at the door, and when no one answered, rapped the panel harder until the catch rose, causing the little girl to step back in fright. A middle-aged woman dressed in coarsely woven garments stooped under the low doorway, staring in astonishment at the sight of the idiot girl in her dirty clothes, bearing a bundle in her arms.

A simple plea for help was all Ethla could utter, "help me, help me," before bursting into fits of tears. The peasant lady bent forward to unfold the parcel Ethla was carrying and exposed the tiny face of a baby boy. She held out her hands in surprise at the appearance of a vulnerable child.

"My, my, what have we here?" she said, before regaining her composure and ushering her mysterious visitors into the sanctuary of her simple dwelling.

At that very moment, those menacing lupine guardians who had been keeping watch at the edge of the woods dropped their guard and disappeared into the forest.

The pine log cabin was small but cosy, and with winter still months away, the livestock were kept outside. The woman, out of natural concern for the child, offered to nurse it, saying, "Little girl, don't you think you ought to let me look at the infant?"

Although Ethla was reluctant at first to surrender her charge, the woman smiled and gently persuaded her to release the baby.

"Come, come, I mean no harm," she said and took hold of him, unwrapping the soiled swaddling clothes.

"What is your name?" she said to the little minder.

"Ethla," came the reply.

The lady cocked her head, unsure if she heard correctly. "Ethla," repeated the girl, trying hard to form the word.

"Well, Ethla, bring me some fresh linen, and warm water from the pot by the fire," she asked the girl, pointing to the other side of the room.

After observing the woman as she began to wash the infant, Ethla intervened, trying to honour her promise not to relinquish the baby from her care until under the protection of Princess Amora. However, touchingly, Ethla was also exhibiting motherly instinct, which, for someone of her affliction, they would never experience, but fate had dealt her a miracle.

Standing aside, the woman asked, "How has the infant, with these costly garments" – suggesting a person of high rank – "come into your care?"

Ethla, averting her eyes, tried to conceal the truth, fabricating some story of how she had found it.

"Baby in ditch."

It was the only thing she could think to say, mumbling with her limited vocabulary. To which the onlooker frowned, hardly able to believe what she was hearing.

The peasant woman went outside to get fresh milk from her cow which had just calved, and when she returned she requested of the girl, "Ethla, I want you to show me how you have been feeding the infant."

Anxious to prove her skill, Ethla went on to demonstrate her newly acquired skills, chattering away with a speech that the listener sometimes struggled to understand. The youngster removed the cow horn and udder from the bag, to rinse it in hot water before filling with milk of a suitable temperature to feed the baby. That this innocent simpleton could take care of a child in this way led the woman to believe that there might be much more to this story than met the eye.

After a meal, Ethla slept, until she was disturbed by the voices of the woman's husband and son, who on their return were told the story of these mysterious visitors. The girl, resting in the corner of the room, could see them glancing in her direction. Even though she was mentally deficient, she felt an instinctive fear of being misunderstood and ostracised, just as she usually was, resulting in Prince Hagen taken from her.

What she feared came to pass.

Ethla became the virtual prisoner of the husband and his son, and was in a desperate state, longing to flee, but they took her and the child to a neighbouring village. Here, they locked Ethla in a cramped wooden cage in the square, where she became the object of curiosity and mockery, while the infant prince was secretly abducted by a couple residing at a local inn.

For many days, she endured her captivity, with its privation and humiliation; the world where she lived with Princess Hellalyle was now but a poignant memory. It pained her that she had failed her mistress. Then, one morning, while watching the people, she noticed a young woman leaving the inn with a baby concealed in a shawl. Convinced that it was Prince Hagen, she shouted incoherently at the woman, "Thief, thief!" The woman cursed her in return.

"You miserable little clown!" said the female, and inciting passers-by to ridicule the girl's behaviour, she shouted, "Look, the fugitive from the ship of fools shouts her fantasy. See how you like this, you imbecile," and threw a sod at the captive in the cage.

Ethla became a figure of fun, poked with sticks and pelted with rubbish.

When she could endure her torment no longer, a disturbance occurred, causing the crowd to scatter.

"Take cover! A soldier is running amok – he will kill us all!" The voice of a woman screamed.

The fearsome figure of Karl von Altenburg had appeared, leaving dead and injured people in his wake, those who had deliberately impeded him as he strode towards Ethla in her little prison. At last, he had found her; his search was at an end. Then, two violent, drunken men foolishly called out, "Come on, we can take him. He may be a giant, but he has only one eye – what are you all frightened of?"

Within seconds of attacking the soldier, both lay slaughtered at the German's feet. The knight looked about him in a defiant stance, ready for the next assailant, but the village had emptied, the inhabitants running away, disappearing into the alleyways and dwellings, like cockroaches that scurry off into the crooks and crannies, when their darkness is interrupted by light.

On breaking open the cage and releasing Ethla, he motioned to her as to the whereabouts of the infant. She led him to the inn, where, finding the door suddenly barred, he shattered it into a thousand pieces, to reveal himself standing there, glaring down like a primordial, giant cyclops, on the terrified people inside, with little Ethla, scared witless, hiding behind him; it was as if he had been raised from the dark pit of Tartarus – a terrible place, as far beneath the earth as heaven above it – to kill everyone, to wreak vengeance on the child abductors and Ethla's tormentors. He pulled the girl in front and signalled to her to search for the baby boy. She soon found him: concealed behind the woman who had mocked her when imprisoned in the village square. The knight, wielding his sword, threatened to strike unless she surrendered the infant. The petrified woman handed the prince over to Ethla, but von Altenburg lingered, staring murderously at the kidnapper, his sword still raised as if contemplating whether to deliver the fatal blow. She raised her hands, fearing the worst, but the soldier thought better of it and turned away, sparing her.

Von Altenburg then plundered the kitchen of the inn for provisions. Once he adjudged the supplies were enough, unforgiving, he glared in contempt at the miserable wretches huddled in a frightened mass, and in rancorous spite laid waste the hostelry, but, conscious the innocent Ethla was watching, he mercifully refrained from spilling the blood of anyone within. As they left the tavern, Ethla paused to stick her tongue out in derision at the still cowering throng, causing the knight to gesticulate impatiently for the girl to hurry. As she scampered after him, carrying the little prince, she bore a triumphant expression.

The soldier commandeered a horse and cart, and, with his war steed attached, the three of them headed for the forest and the Monastery of Thorbjorg beyond. As they entered the woodland, von Altenburg was ignorant that the black wolves were once again waiting, camouflaged in the treescape, to assist in the guarding of the fugitive children through a land where a malevolent entity might make one last attempt to destroy them.

That first night was spent deep in the wilderness around a campfire, near a river. The knight stared into the flames as he pondered the calamity that had struck this land. The death of his friend, Hildebrand, he found hard to bear, even as a hardened soldier; but the death of Hellalyle, a virtuous woman without equal, was an insupportable loss. He looked across the camp at Ethla, and decided, for now, not to let the girl learn of the princess's demise.

Ethla, attending to Prince Hagen on the other side of the fire, could but sense the deep sadness that had enveloped the knight. No longer afraid, she tried to cheer him by preparing his meal of liquid food before leaving him alone to consume it.

As the night advanced and the embers died, Ethla suddenly

awoke to hear the wailing of a woman's voice calling from the direction of the river:

Ethla…Ethla…Ethla…

Before the calling died away – the very same sounds she had heard before – she looked across at von Altenburg who was fast asleep and moved closer to him, in a state of terror. Twice more she made out the strange summoning, but the girl remained close to the Teutonic Knight and did not respond.

Thankfully, the dawn broke, giving her an excuse to wake the soldier. She gainfully attempted to describe what she kept hearing.

"A voice, a voice…" Ethla repeated many times, pointing at the forest to signify its origin, but he waved dismissively, as if he believed the girl to be not of sound mind, and this was some figment of her imagination.

After eating, he motioned to her to prepare to leave with the infant. Von Altenburg judged that one more night in the woods would be sufficient to achieve their goal of sanctuary at the monastery, with Princess Amora.

At the end of this final day, a suitable site presented itself near a pool of clear spring water. In the early evening, the knight was troubled by irritation and pain from his facial trauma, causing him to bury his head in his hands. Aware of his extreme discomfort, Ethla looked for the medicines that Princess Hellalyle had given to von Altenburg, and cautiously prepared to experiment with the treatment of his wound. Copying her mistress, recalling the day she witnessed her at the castle stables, the girl nervously signalled to the knight what she intended and stood firm in her purpose. The very spirit of Hellalyle seemed to emanate from the girl's expression as she looked down at him, resting at the foot of a fallen tree. He removed his bandage to enable Ethla to cleanse the wound and apply an unguent. She then looked away as he replaced the mask dressing.

This unlikely bond was forged by circumstance, and an understanding of the burden of one another's disabilities: he of facial deformation, she mentally and physically compromised. It confirmed how two very different human beings could coexist, even without the concourse of speech.

In the early hours, the knight sound asleep and the girl hiding beneath a blanket, the haunting female voice called once again. From afar, thrice it cried, and then as before, it ceased. Too scared to peep from hiding, Ethla remained rigid, waiting for first light. Slowly, to the relief of the frightened girl, the eastern sky started to brighten, and unable to sleep, she set about her chores early, even though it was still difficult to see in the first blush of dawn.

Careful not to disturb von Altenburg, she picked up the infant to attend to its needs and headed for the pool through the trees. With the sun near to breaching the horizon on this last day in the wilderness, and Thorbjorg now very near – its outline visible in the middle distance – the wolves vanished; so, seeing the knight was inattentive in his slumbering, a devious, maleficent force decided to make its move.

As Ethla knelt by the water's edge, she became aware of a pair of eyes – just breaking the surface – staring at her. Petrified by the strange, intensive gaze, she tried to avert their hypnotic hold, springing up to race back to the camp.

As she ran, the figure of a woman rose from the pool and was suddenly transformed into a black cloud, changing shape as it whirled along cutting off Ethla's escape route. The voice she heard in the night now came from this dark apparition, bearing a chilling message.

"I saw the mighty Hildebrand first, by the inland sea, and there I marked him to be the father of my child. For Satan promised then that I too might become mortal, but the fateful beauty embodied in the princess took him from me, and for that reason, my helpless wanderings in the underworld are destined to continue. Because of this, I shall not allow the child of Hellalyle to live. Give him to me. Now!"

Brave Ethla shrieked in horror, as she held Prince Hagen tightly, unwilling to lose him.

Now the awful spectre altered its appearance to a grotesque figure with a human form and advanced menacingly towards the girl, who was desperate to avoid it as it closed in. Just as it was about to overwhelm and destroy them, von Altenburg appeared, alerted by Ethla's cries for help. Bellowing aloud, he brandished his sword and aware of the demon's fatal weakness, he ripped his cloth mask away, causing the monster to face head-on the terrifying countenance of the warrior. The water spirit, held in the stare of his single eye, witnessed his grim disfigurement. It had long waited for some handsome stranger to make it mortal but was utterly repelled by the presence of this Teutonic Knight. Emitting a shrill cry of defeat, it collapsed, slithering back to the pool like some infernal serpent, and slid into the water. Its surface convulsed, and the crystal pond instantly drained away into the earth, taking the phantom to destruction with it.

Knowing the creature had gone forever, this seemingly cold, insular man knelt and clasped Ethla close to his bosom to calm and comfort her. While holding the girl, he looked on victoriously at where the water had been, for he had, at last, avenged the death of Barbarossa.

33

The return of the king

With the persistent exigencies of a protracted winter now but an external memory, Thorstein marched home to his stronghold at Castle Preben. Spring was far advanced, the weather agreeably warm, as a column of soldiers crossed far-flung boundaries to enter established territory. Yet, for all the seasonal sunshine and showers, even these hardened troopers were taken aback seeing the dearth of vegetation – the dun meadows parched, the buds not so much disinclined to open as clenched in an iron grip. There was also a noticeable absence of birdsong. The peasants, looking grim and downhearted in arid fields, nonetheless waved deferentially, duty bound to honour the return of their long-absent monarch.

A functionary close to the king called out to a serf, "What ails the crops? His Majesty demands an explanation for this disquieting alteration in nature."

The old man looked distressed, when, in a confused and disjointed way – his simplicity of speech paralysed, his voice choked with sorrow – he replied, "There is a pervasive atmosphere of despondency, sire, even of ill omen, that has infected the countryside following that insurmountable tragedy at the fortress. Ever since the sudden appearance of a comet a short time before, a fiery giant that dominated the heavens. It reminded everyone who saw it of a window in the Abbey of Sunniva. An image of a comet depicted in the coloured glass, illustrating Jeremiah's prophecy, who, when seeing such a visitor from the cosmos, predicted: *An evil shall break forth upon all the inhabitants of the land.* Your Majesty, it appears that prophecy has once again come to pass."

The bare-headed peasant, unable to say more, looked down at the floor in embarrassment, holding his bonnet, twisting and crumpling it, knowing a devastating discovery awaited his monarch when he entered the fortress of Preben. While above him, the mounted Thorstein was filled with apprehension, his face ashen-hued, his upright frame transfixed in the saddle like a leaden statue.

On reaching the courtyard of the castle, the captain at the head of the guard suddenly stopped in his tracks when he beheld a scene of utter desolation, draped in eerie silence. Gritting his teeth, he turned back to report what he had seen to the king, prompting Thorstein to move forward with a detachment of soldiers.

The monarch had been entirely ignorant of the tragedy at Preben, for it had been the treacherous Paulus's evil intention to keep the king in the dark concerning the terrible events that had unfolded there. After crossing the drawbridge, entering the confines of the fortress, they drew close to the principal entrance, where a group comprising Runa (the lady-in-waiting), servants, and a priest intercepted them, looking fearful and distraught. Dismounting, Thorstein's prime concern was to ask about his family. The women immediately burst into fits of tears, and the monk prostrated himself, breaking the shattering news.

"Sire, it befalls on me to reveal an appalling thing has happened. Queen Gudrun, your only daughter Hellalyle, together with all your sons, have been mercilessly slaughtered."

In extreme shock, Thorstein felt his legs buckle beneath him, and, supported by his aides, he listened in horror to an account of the bloody fight that had ensued when the king's champions came to arrest Hildebrand.

Later, the king was taken to the crypt of the nearby Abbey of Sunniva and shown the resting places of his line, their effigies awaiting his approval before being crafted in stone. Overcome with indescribable grief, Thorstein knelt at the tomb of his beloved daughter Hellalyle. He appeared to incoherently mumble as he offered prayers, before breaking down with emotion, only able to raise himself with the help of his attendants.

Convinced by a portent that he would have no heir to succeed him, the king, fearful for the stability of his kingdom in the event of his death, became a broken man – at first introspective, and then irascible and schizophrenic.

What aggravated his unstable temperament, even more, were disturbing reports of vengeful spirits, which irregularly patrolled the fractured battlements and labyrinthine passages of an abandoned tower of the fortress, repelling unwelcome intruders with their supernatural fastness.

Their influence was so powerful, few dared approach – let alone set foot in that forbidding structure.

Not long after his return, Thorstein was wrenched from his slumber at dead of night, by the piercing shrieks of a woman in extreme distress. Donning a cloak, he stole into the corridor to try to identify the source of the terrifying outburst, but, by now, the panic-stricken cries had become barely audible, now grim murmurings percolating the fortress. Determined to pursue the matter, accompanied by a pair of petrified guards and a small group of frightened servants – unceremoniously roused from their beds – he picked his way through the gloomy interior of the castle. Once again, the blood-curdling screams of a tormented female splintered the nocturnal silence, followed by a fierce clashing of blades, bellows and obscenities of fighting men, cursing and shouting agonising cries to the death.

As the unnerving clamour subsided, Thorstein, rooted to the spot, stared blankly into the void, unwilling to move forward and his attendants reluctant to follow. The abnormal and unsettling sounds had appeared to erupt from a lofty, dilapidated tower of the stronghold. However, the cacophony did not recur that night.

Alone in his chamber, incapable of rest, the king was forced to reflect on the series of tragic events which had so adversely affected his troubled reign. He realised for the first time that all these ill-fated incidents were somehow inextricably linked with the macabre antics of the restless spirits haunting Castle Preben, a conclusion too uncomfortable to contemplate. His brow furrowed deeply.

For some time, rumour had been circulating amongst the ordinary people concerning the identity of the woman whose harrowing cries had disturbed normal life at the castle, but they dared not voice their suspicions, fearful of its effect on the king.

One day, without warning, Thorstein summoned his court to make an announcement, and profound was its message.

"I have decided to make the critical and far-reaching decision of razing Preben to the ground. The evacuation of the entire building and its destruction by fire!"

His soldiers and officials listened in disbelief, horrified by the king's rash and catastrophic judgement.

"Your Majesty," said one of his confidants, "Please see reason. This castle is the main focal point for your rule. Destroy it, and it will send out a message the monarch is in retreat. Preben fortress was built on the sweat of many, toiling away year after year, lives lost in the dangers of its construction. How many soldiers killed? Too numerous to mention, protecting the fortress from the constant harassment of your enemies. It shelters us from an uncertain world, and all this will be in vain if we cannot persuade you to reconsider. Some say ghosts are transient, my sovereign, I respectfully request you wait a while, in the hope they will soon depart."

"No, absolutely not!" retaliated Thorstein, "My decision is irrevocable. Only such extreme action can assuage my torment and exorcise the malevolent spirits!"

A man at siege with himself, the grief-stricken ruler barked a volley of peremptory commands to his men. They were to vacate the site, and, by any means whatsoever, set the accursed fortress ablaze. When pandemonium broke loose, the king's soldiers took control of the situation, determined to fulfil Thorstein's orders to the letter, working all day incessantly at fever-pitch. Faggots were stacked against doors, and anything else that would combust, such as the massive support timbers, was liberally daubed with tar. By dusk, when everyone had abandoned the fortress – the king and his followers had set up camp at a safe distance, intending to travel to Yrian on the morrow – the monarch's guard set light to the castle.

As the fire took hold, an unexpected gale blew up, fanning the flames into an unstoppable inferno which illuminated the darkening skies with an unnatural blue and violet incandescence. The shrill whine of the howling wind seemed to bear the wail of a woman's spine-chilling voice, on its fierce trail of annihilation.

At break of day the following morning, on Thorstein's instruction, brazen trumpet blasts and the rattle of kettledrums and tabors distracted the few that had managed to rest that night. Soon, journeying northwards in the direction of Castle Yrian, an extended caravan could be seen, the royal entourage at the head of the army with a straggling crowd of refugees following behind. From this funerary procession, resembling some lost crusade, those who steeled themselves to look back wept as they caught sight of their former stronghold. It was like the spent cauldron of an old world, the empty hearth of a lost horizon. Even the great wooden church and the now vacant houses of the community burnt to cinders. Not even a deluge, drawn from a reservoir of their fallen tears, could have extinguished the terrible holocaust that had reduced the fortress of Preben and its surroundings to a smouldering ruin.

In truth, Thorstein, traumatised by the apocalyptic outcome of his drastic actions, had become a broken man, an ineffectual leader, no longer optimistic about his power to control his kingdom from his new headquarters at Yrian.

34

The knight and Ethla reach sanctuary

Von Altenburg, keeping a watchful eye on Ethla – who was nursing Prince Hagen, rang the convent bell. After a short while, they heard a latch, and a small wicket in the door opened, revealing the face of a nun who looked surprised to see these refugees in distress.

"What is the nature of your business?" she demanded.

The mute knight presented to the nun Princess Hellalyle's attestation, and after briefly inspecting the document, she returned it and said, "Wait here."

Eventually, the party was ushered through the stout wooden barrier, to be received by three of the sisters which included the abbess. After a brief silence, the Superior addressed them.

"I am Princess Amora, Abbess of this Holy Order, and I recognise the knight before me to be the bodyguard of my deceased niece, and the hapless girl at his side her former servant; but who is this child she cradles, and what do you require of us?" On reflection, she continued, "Your name, I recall, is von Altenburg – the man unable to communicate – and you bear a document that might help to enlighten me."

The Teutonic warrior submitted Hellalyle's Testament, and the princess motioned to the other nuns before leaving them to give her due attention and deliberation to the scroll. As the visitors waited patiently for her return, the knight could see her through the open doorway, reading alone in the privacy of the cloisters.

Astonished by the nature and content of the document, the abbess made the sign of the cross, and hurried back to authorise food and lodgings for the three visitors; distinct responsibility was given to the care of the infant, whom Amora now removed from Ethla's arms and fondly embraced. She was overcome with emotion to be clasping the infant son of Princess Hellalyle, her deceased niece.

As Hellalyle had predicted, her aunt afforded them sanctuary.

"Ethla and the infant housed in one of the dormitories," she instructed, "and the German soldier will have shelter in the guest house of our community."

Before they left for their lodgings, von Altenburg deposited Hellalyle's manuscript, which he had found difficult to construe at the time when he and Ethla had been journeying through the forest.

One late evening, seated by the fire, he had become more eager to learn what Hellalyle had recorded. When he turned the leaves, though, they appeared to be unintelligible, but the simple-minded girl, who was peering over his shoulder, had reacted vigorously, jabbing her finger at a striking image and bursting out excitedly, "Me, me…it is a picture of me!"

The knight had got the impression that Ethla must have lost her senses, for the "picture" appeared to him to be nothing but a baffling and meaningless daub.

As the abbess was perusing the folio, the knight, scrutinising her face for some reaction, was taken aback when, contrary to his expectation, she appeared intensely delighted by what she read. Compelled to discover more of its history, she removed the Chronicle to the scriptorium, where the nuns might have the opportunity to study it.

That evening, seated in his candlelit quarters, the Teutonic Knight was in a serious frame of mind as he stared at the shadows on the stone floor. He questioned himself as to why this Chronicle should refuse to reveal its message. With the heaviest heart pondering this conundrum, he concluded that in his function as a fighting man, some incidents in his military life now stood in the way of understanding a story penned by the woman he revered – and prevented him from knowing its message and the true nature of her feelings towards her knights.

The next morning, the abbess was urgently approached by the nun Bozhena.

"Abbess Amora, please come quickly to the scriptorium."

"Whatever has happened sister?" enquired Amora.

Bozhena could barely contain her excitement.

"A wondrous occurrence has taken place," she gasped, and the pair hurried along, nearly breaking into a run.

As they entered the room, another nun, Isengard, was standing at a table, where she drew Amora once more to the Chronicle laid out before them.

"During the night," Isengard said (leaning over and pointing diligently to certain areas of the parchment), "It seems in the most mysterious circumstances, additions have been made to the manuscript," causing the sisters to marvel at this miraculous visitation.

Then, the members of the order, out of respect, stood back, to allow the Abbess to read and digest the whole bewildering, inexplicable appendix, recounting her niece Hellalyle's tragic demise; Ethla's wanderings with the infant prince and their deliverance by the valorous von Altenburg; his slaying of the evil water spirit, and subsequent asylum at the monastery. Each episode, as before, was painstakingly embellished with vibrant illustrations. Captivated by the story, the Mother Superior was reduced to tears, moved by this tale of adventure, adversity, and human dedication.

The princess, applying her keen intelligence as she studied the text, then spoke, "Sisters, have you noticed how the writing style had altered subtly? In contrast to Hellalyle's account, she is now referred to in the third person?"

At first, the abbess looked perplexed, and the nuns watched the expressions on her face intently, hoping she might unravel this mystery. Amora, as if momentarily bestowed with divine inspiration, exclaimed, "Please listen carefully. This will sound unbelievable, but I have finally adjudged that the convent had indeed been visited at dead of night, by those spectral polymaths my niece had earlier reported. Those phantom scholars have phenomenally manifested themselves to carry on her handiwork."

As the sisters pored over what they thought was, ostensibly, the final entry, this curious and unaccountable request, a short script, unveiled itself before their eyes in the manner of the "Writing on the Wall" from the book of Daniel:

"Forbear the task of having these leaves bound, as this narrative remains unfinished."

Believing that this extraordinary revelation had been God's doing, the community assembled for prayer in the chapel.

Later in the afternoon, Princess Amora related this miraculous occurrence to von Altenburg and led him to the room where this sacred document was now enshrined. He showed reluctance to enter, aware that he might be considered a sinful person, unfit to cross the threshold or view the manuscript. Sensitive to the knight's feelings of self-doubt, Amora offered him words of encouragement, guiding the great soldier into this learned, holy place.

With the Chronicle at his front, he forced himself to look at the parchment, unable to envisage that the script, with its beautiful illustrations, had now become not only coherent but also a glorious sight to behold. The knight prostrated himself in prayer, awestruck. The abbess, standing at the rear of the chapel, brought her hand to her mouth, deeply moved by the intense emotion she witnessed.

After leaving the soldier to contemplate and worship, Amora later visited him in his quarters, where the German, using sign language and with quill and parchment to hand, made plain his inadequacy when first trying to interpret what had appeared to be an indecipherable manuscript. Without hesitation, she said unto to him, "It is my conviction that after you had destroyed the demonic Paulus, from the very moment you performed my niece's tasks and found refuge for Ethla and Prince Hagen, you were redeemed

– and, though unknown to you, your perception of Hellalyle's journal would have changed immediately."

In one of the rooms of the abbey, a nun, seated, gently rocked a cradle cosseting Hellalyle's baby son. The crib constructed quite skilfully by a passing craftsman, adapting a manger obtained from a nearby livestock barn – an object long associated with the divine.

By a remarkable coincidence, the artisan was the very person who had been chastised, rebuked by the late princess, for the brutal assault on Ethla in the castle stables – the Russian, Tsygan. It was as if he had undergone atonement for his wicked deed; a prisoner of his fate.

It was not long before Ethla pestered the sorority, innocently enquiring when she would be taken back to Preben to reunite with Hellalyle. With her faltering enunciation, she would repeatedly ask, "Princess Hellalyle, when shall I meet her again? When are we going to see Princess Hellalyle?" assuming the nuns understood her clamorous utterances.

The impaired adolescent, poignantly unaware of the passing of the king's daughter, possessed a character devoid of moral wrong, forever positive in her view of the world about her. Never a more cheerful little soul the nuns would ever meet. Her happy disposition and angelic nescience stymied the hand of the nuns in the religious order, for no one could bring themselves to be the bearer of such calamitous tidings: the disclosure of the princess's murder.

It finally fell to the abbess, who, resignedly, made the decision to reveal all to Ethla. She took her to the room where the nun attended the cradle, where lay the newborn. Placing her hands on the shoulders of the girl, she guided her over to the rocking crib, where both looked down on the sleeping child.

"Ethla," said Amora, "The time has come for you to learn the truth of your mistress, Princess Hellalyle. It will be sad for you to know that she is no longer with us, but in a much happier place, a destination where we cannot go." Before the abbess could say more, Ethla, surprisingly, knew the meaning, and burst into a flood of tears. Her sorrowful outpouring knew no end, for she cried and cried, the front of her garment damp from sobbing, at the realisation that the one person in all the world that she adored was gone. She would never see her again. The nun, attending the manger, overcome at the sight of the distressed Ethla, reached forward attempting to comfort the distraught figure. Princess Amora leaned over, closer to the one good ear of Ethla, and softly uttered in a soothing voice, "Do not despair, little lady, for the spirit of Hellalyle is all around us, endowed in every living creature, from the waters below, to the land and the sky above. A woman so rare, she need not ask of the Almighty to live her life again – put right wrongs committed – for the existence of the king's daughter was perfect in every way. Take comfort in the vision of the baby before us; it is the princess's own, and in her offspring, memories of his mother will endure. Recollections of Princess Hellalyle will never die; she will become a legend, and your name, Ethla, will be part."

The Abbess Amora could not be sure if the words she spoke were wholly understood, but both the nun and herself sensed the girl knew something, as an awareness came over Ethla, and she stopped crying, to tenderly hold the tiny hand of the baby; looking down at it in adoration, and then to a window with a faraway look in her eyes, self-absorbed as if she was one of the magi reincarnated from the stable at Bethlehem.

Ethla's transformation triggered a climatic change in the heavens above; the leaden skies suddenly changed to that of white billowing clouds, and through them, smiling, sweet-faced, chubby cherubs emerged, seemingly lighter than air, accompanied by the music of the empyrean, 'The Cherubic Hymn', sung by an unseen choir of a thousand voices. The beguiling winged angels carried baskets full to the brim with sunshine, the contents of which, they cast out in handfuls onto the land stretched out below; at its eye the religious house of Thorbjorg. The golden rays splashed upon the earth, illuminating the delight and delicacy of nature in all its thralls as no scene of a more exceptional loveliness could one behold. While in the abbey beneath, the expression on Ethla's face changed, her mouth agape in utter astonishment, attention caught by the speckled colours of light dancing against the glass windows and the sound of the Byzantine chant heard beyond – the girl's limited mind overwhelmed by the exposure to two enormous events, one of this world, the other beyond her wildest imagination. This seemingly lesser mortal, considered a changeling by the unenlightened, was unaware the choral and light spectacular were the product of the protectors of Eden – the unearthly spirits in the sky – the winged cherubims, their bodily appearance symbolic of the pudgy Ethla. The whole ensemble celebrating her extraordinary achievement, cementing her place in the pantheon of humankind. While in the room with her, the abbess and the nun, both of Catholic persuasion, genuflected in prayer before the holy acclaim of the Orthodox; demonstrating, albeit momentarily, a healing of the great schism of AD 1054.

In Princess Hellalyle's manuscript, there is a reference to the above event, inscribed in the hand of the mysterious polymaths. It describes how, many centuries later, under celestial influence, the musical genius Pyotr Ilyich Tchaikovsky wandered Europe and Russia, curiously shunning sociality, in search of the legendary lands of Princess Hellalyle – Lake Eydis and the Mountains of Orn. However, his search proved fruitless and he settled briefly in Prussia, the ancient lands of Ethla's people. While ensconced there, Tchaikovsky's creativity was stirred by inspiration on high, and in the year of our Lord 1878, he produced the ecstatic choral piece, 'Hymn of the Cherubim' – song of the angels.

His harmonious score, adopted by the Spirits of Heaven, was not confined by the laws of the fourth dimension, but was able to swing back and forth throughout the aeons, until a time portal – a gate – opened, allowing his masterpiece to regale the Abbey of Thorbjorg in that unique moment of the thirteenth century.

Having given her guests time to readjust and regain their strength, Amora summoned von Altenburg. The pair met in the cloisters, and it was there the abbess broached an important matter.

"Dear von Altenburg, we are all so grateful for the valorous deeds that you have accomplished at the behest of my deceased niece, Princess Hellalyle, and no one could ask more of you. However, there remains one more crucial undertaking. King Thorstein must know of the incredible news that he now has an heir, so arrangements have been made for Ethla and the infant prince to accompany me in the journey to Castle Yrian. Will this dauntless knight come with us? I must reassure you, that in my role as an abbess, and the sister of the king, you will come to no harm at the fortress."

Von Altenburg, without hesitation, signalled his acceptance, by nodding and saluting her with his arm across his chest. Amora, overcome by his act of loyalty, smiled and leaned her head on him affectionately, acutely aware of the sacrifice the soldier was making; the knight believed hostility awaited any former member of Hellalyle's bodyguard.

35

Amora informs the king that he has an heir in Hellalyle's son

King Thorstein had become a virtual recluse, avoiding other people and only forcing himself to leave his rooms when essential affairs of state necessitated it.

One day, he received a rare visit from his sister, Princess Amora, bearing important news for His Majesty. Grudgingly he consented to see her; he met with her in his private apartments, where the princess delivered her message:

"Brother of mine, I have startling news that will both stir your heart and may increase the grief that you have tried to suppress. Do you remember on your return from the East, being told of the simple servant girl Ethla, who your daughter rescued from poverty? What amounts to a miracle has occurred: Hellalyle, while held in captivity by Prinz Paulus, secretly gave birth to a baby boy. She named him Hagen; his father was the Prince of England – Hildebrand, the leader of your daughter's bodyguards. Everything is proven, for we have your daughter's attestation, witnessed by Abbot Jurian. This infant, your grandson and heir, owes his life to Ethla, who had been Hellalyle's only companion while in confinement. Hellalyle had no other option but to entrust her son to this girl to save him from Paulus. The girl then fled the castle with Hagen, and, as if under the guidance of the Almighty, managed to survive until the knight, von Altenburg, found her.

Then, honouring his promise to Hellalyle, he brought them both to me at the monastery. Is this not miraculous?"

On being told this incredible story, the king was at first ecstatic, but his joy was soon tempered by the revelation that the child's father was the very man whose obstinacy triggered the events that led to the slaughter of his family.

His sister reasoned with him, pointing out, "We all knew Hellalyle possessed innate wisdom and kindness – these qualities are now inherent in her offspring. Also, let us not forget that the father was of English royal blood, and had been renowned as the greatest knight in Christendom. Such was his ability as an invincible warrior and general, the name of Hildebrand holds mythical status throughout this continent. As a man, he exuded great charisma and was fearless in his protection of your daughter. These rare attributes invested in his son, Prince Hagen, will determine him a great ruler if you allow him to succeed you."

Amora continued, "Hildebrand's actions in this tragedy were in consequence of his love for your daughter, and her love for him, and he was not prepared to abandon her to what he thought was an uncertain fate. Most importantly, your grandson is innocent of all this, and one can be sure Hellalyle would want her father to cherish and love him."

The king, reflecting in silence at a window, listened to his sister's plea, and was filled with fresh hope in response to the rationality of her argument. Excitement once again took hold of him, and he turned and embraced his sister with a broad smile on his face, something people thought they would never see again.

"Where is my grandson?" he exclaimed.

"He is with his rescuers outside the great hall, awaiting you, but dear brother, please be patient with the girl Ethla. You will see she is of diminished faculties, and in these circumstances needs careful handling. It has taken all my persuasive powers to bring her before the king," Amora replied.

The monarch moved quickly, summoning his courtiers to the great hall while his sister went to reassure and prepare Ethla for the audience. The enormous double doors swung open, and a hushed silence reigned as four figures entered: Ethla, bearing the infant Prince Hagen; and in a supporting role, Princess Amora, with her hands on the girl's shoulders; followed by the imposing figure of Karl von Altenburg. As they approached the throne, King Thorstein knelt with his arms outstretched, and smilingly beckoned Ethla to come nearer.

The girl appeared apprehensive, looking back at Amora who responded with a reassuring smile, nodding to her to approach the king. Ethla stepped forward, offering Prince Hagen. The monarch stood for a moment, holding the infant, studying him, only to then lift the baby aloft, before all those in attendance and exclaim, "Behold, this is my heir, Prince Hagen!"

Looking at the representatives of the church, he instructed them to prepare the boy's baptism for the next day. He asked Ethla to come forward, and to the astonishment of everyone, he returned the infant, saying, "Little girl, I owe you an enormous debt. Your bravery has secured the future of this kingdom. It is no longer uncertain. In this little boy, my precious daughter is reborn. From this day, you shall take part in his care, under the supervision of persons nominated by Princess Amora."

Ethla appeared to understand on some intuitive level, without fully knowing what the king meant. Gleefully holding the baby, she re-joined the smiling Amora.

Thorstein summoned von Altenburg forward, and the knight presented himself, dropping to one knee. The king protested, and duly assisted him to rise, exclaiming to the assembled company, "If it were not for this man, the murderer of my daughter and Queen Gudrun would have remained unpunished, and the girl with Hellalyle's son might have disappeared forever."

To the bafflement of Thorstein and everyone assembled in the hall, the Teutonic Knight merely bowed and then backed away to stand alongside Amora. There he remained at attention, as solid as a statue, staring straight ahead. It was impossible to gauge his emotions, but those assembled experienced the strangest of sensations – that his consciousness was momentarily no longer amongst them.

They were not aware that his fellow bodyguards, who had risen, disappearing before the fisherman on Lake Eydis, were summoning him away. His task was complete. He was agonising, resisting the call, not feeling ready to depart.

Amora would later reveal to the king the existence of his daughter's extraordinary manuscript, detailing other remarkable events, so out-of-world as to be scarcely believable.

However, when the monarch later visited the abbey to view the book, like von Altenburg before him, he found it indecipherable, like a tarnished soul. Thorstein would often return to peruse the document, hoping against hope that something in his fortunes had changed, but it was never to be.

Being unable to decipher the stories it was said to contain caused the king anguish, but it was tempered, in the belief that the writings of his daughter were inspired by the Almighty.

36

Ethla reminisces

One day in autumn, a young girl could be seen ensconced on a seat in the delightful gardens of the castle of Yrian. Her unusually short legs were swinging freely below her, unable to touch the ground. It was Ethla, relaxing from her duties of care of the infant Prince Hagen. In this tranquil place, she felt close to the spirit of the departed Hellalyle, knowing that the late princess derived great pleasure from her horticulture, resulting in a display of superior plants and arboreal splendour. A story was often told that whenever the lone princess strolled along the enticing paths in the evening, an enchantment of nightingales from the south miraculously appeared, and gathered to serenade her with its corpus of a song.

This haven at the fortress evoked in Ethla sweet memories, such as the occasion when she discovered her mistress crouching to sift a patch of ground while a tiny bird fluttered, as if in communication with her. It had alighted intermittently on her braids of golden hair, causing her to gently brush away the little creature – only for it to perch once more on her shoulder. Such was the trust these feathered creatures held for this remarkable woman. Ethla, charmed by this curious occurrence, had approached stealthily, hoping to share this magical moment. To her disappointment, the bird had darted away when she drew near.

On this day, the atmosphere had changed dramatically, for there appeared to be no sign of life in the eerie quietness save the stirring of a bitterly cold wind. Dark clouds, flame-red at the edges, sat curiously motionless in the sky, giving the impression of some hostile and forbidding spectacle. The last petals dropped from summer blooms, and the dead leaves of fruit trees rustled, propelled by the mistral.

A repeated summons was heard, reminding Ethla of pressing duties. Preparing to return, she shivered uncontrollably, for this sombre scene induced deep melancholy, and her spirit ebbed.

Climbing the turret, she felt unwell but defiantly persisted, finally reaching the royal apartments, where she struggled to perform her daily tasks. That night she spent in fitful sleep, as the biting wind moaned, blowing through the window and beneath the door, causing the temperature of the room to plummet. Next morning, she had to be roused from her bed more sharply than usual. Once alert, she laboured in much discomfort, valiantly shrugging off the concern of other people, as she tended to her supervised care of Hellalyle's son. She yearned to revisit the garden, but, aware of her vulnerable state, the other servants tried to dissuade her from these obsessive missions. They were unaware, though, that invisible forces were influencing this girl to make one last sacrificial journey.

Undeterred by their criticism, Ethla departed, cautiously descending the narrow spiral stairs, hindered by her weak and stunted physique. In the courtyard below she felt faint. This plucky young girl, for all her desperate condition, persevered and entered the garden, where she stopped in utter dismay, observing a terrible transformation. It had become a landscape of desolation: blackened, withered, the cloudscapes almost indistinguishable from their first appearance – save that their fiery colours had become more intense. The scene was enveloped in a sinister stillness.

Now extremely frail, Ethla rested on a turf bench in a small pergola, where she fell away into a deathlike sleep, unaware that the Princess Amora was at her side holding her close. Amora placed Hellalyle's treasured sapphire necklace around Ethla's neck. The knight von Altenburg was also there, on one knee stooped before her, in mystical contemplation as her life waned to its quietus.

With the king's permission, Princess Amora dispatched an envoy to the leaders of the pagan tribes requesting a meeting at the castle, under truce, to discuss Hellalyle's devout wish to afford Ethla's mortal remains a marked burial appropriate to the beliefs of her people. For the late princess believed that Ethla was the abandoned offspring of a heathen.

Hellalyle had been a Christian, but deeply respected the religious customs of others, notably when they involved the powers of nature, which she valued. She had also been acutely aware that Ethla, destined for an early demise caused by her disorder, was regarded by the pagan tribes as a pariah, of little value. Her people would condemn the girl's malformed, puny body to be consumed by fire, leaving no monument to commemorate her ending. To prevent this eventuality, Hellalyle informed her aunt Amora that when this fateful day arose, the king's daughter would bequeath Ethla her precious sapphire necklace. She reasoned that this bestowal might help to ensure that the former waif possessed the wealth and status required by the heathens for a sacred sphere burial.

A delegation of pagan elders and their priest, escorted by six warriors, reached the castle, apprehensive at finding themselves in this colossal fortress so long regarded as a symbol of hostility and oppression. They were led under escort to the hall, for an audience with Princess Amora.

In this great chamber with its gloomy aisles, they gazed awestruck at its overpowering construction, combined with its impressive piers, soaring to support the massive timbers of an ornately carved and gilded ceiling. Below stood a profusion of carved stone figures and capital-topped pillars. The impressive outer walls and those above the arches of the arcades were painted with vibrant religious scenes in a single register, only broken by tapestries of unusual quality, woven with dramatic illustrations of Greek and Roman civilisation – save one, based on Dionysius's famed picture, *The Lone Lady in the Landscape*.

239

On one area of stonework, fixed rows of battle shields with crossed swords beneath were visible. Daylight shone through four large vertical windows with cushioned stone seats set at their base, where visitors could take advantage of the prospect. Stately wooden furniture of worktops and benches were arranged about the flagged floor, and many torches were inserted through iron supports to give extra light when required. The focus of the room's expanse was at one end: an imposing dais with a long table placed at its centre.

The guests regrouped in front of an enormous stone fireplace, save for one of their number curiously drawn to a specific tapestry. Here they waited uneasily, intimidated by their forbidding surroundings and the presence of armed guards strategically placed in the shadows. A door opened, and an abbess entered, Princess Amora, accompanied by a single escort, von Altenburg, walking two paces behind her. To the relief of the assembly, she signalled to the guards to leave.

Amora briefly surveyed this group of heathens, ten in number, studying their traits. All bearded, their features were hard-bitten and sunburnt. Three of them – designated their leaders and called "Princeps" – were elderly, their heads uncovered, their silver-grey hair in thin braids. Each dressed in loose garments of best animal skins, decorated with strips of coloured fur. Their breeches were made of soft but durable felt, their boots of leather, supple at the leg but reinforced at the sole; each Princep bore a hornbeam stave.

The six combatants looked like barbarians, such was their hostile, wild appearance. Far from being rigged out in skins, they were attired in coarse woollen clothes, rough fleeces around their shoulders and their legs felt-clad, feet shod with boots of tough hide, sturdy underfoot.

Crude steel basin helmets with nose guards protected some, for the remainder the armour covered the whole face except for eye slits. Each warrior was armed with a dagger, an axe for hurling and a sheathed sword which they grasped firmly by the hilt, prepared for any encounter. They carried cleft-marked wooden shields with dented bosses, and although they travelled on horseback, it was noticeable that they did not wear spurs.

Standing apart from all of them was an old man, tall and thin with shoulder-length locks, flowing beard and an amiable expression in his startlingly bright eyes. Wearing extended robes of golden damask, with long ornate chains about his neck, he carried a hornbeam staff, but unlike the others, it was carved with unknown religious symbols. He was their revered holy man, and his name was Kriwe.

The princess, on her entrance, noticed this individual standing in front of the *Lone Lady* tapestry, scrutinising it intently. He then turned away with a knowing expression, as if he understood the obscure meaning in the visual imagery of the picture.

Amora introduced herself, accompanied by the Teutonic Knight whose dominating presence was all too familiar to them, regarded with acute suspicion because of his former membership of the Sword Brethren – a brotherhood notorious for its cruelty and ruthlessness in the subjugation of the heathen tribes further to the north-east.

The princeps and the priest sat opposite Amora, von Altenburg standing behind the princess while the Prussen fighters waited in the background, their eyes fixed on the knight in concentrated hatred.

Before the abbess could speak, their spokesman offered his condolences for the distressing loss of Hellalyle, whose universally venerated reputation seemed to transcend all the different peoples of this land and continued to burn like an inextinguishable flame. Thanking him for such heartfelt sentiments, Amora explained the essential purpose of this gathering.

"It is with great sadness we relate to you the story of a young girl, called Ethla, an unfortunate, who might be described as deficient in mind and body. We believe she had her origins in your people, but we cannot be sure. The daughter of the king discovered her, living as a destitute, an outcast from society. The princess learned her name was Ethla, and taking pity, took the waif into care, allowing her to work in the royal household, a place she could call home. This urchin was blessed with an innocence unparalleled in

241

humankind, and her loyalty to Princess Hellalyle was steadfast; but Ethla is now dead, called away early to the afterworld, inevitable, as we knew she would.

"However, it was the late Hellalyle's devout wish concerning this young girl's remains, the reason we have asked you here today. It was the Princess's fervent desire, which when the time came of Ethla's passing, her obsequy should be undertaken by her people living in the hinterland.

"I implore you not to regard this once destitute creature as a traitor who had chosen to serve the daughter of their enemy. Only to fully appreciate that she had been a simple soul, a guiltless individual, utterly devoted to the woman who had given her such confidence and self-esteem."

Hearing her speech, one of the princeps replied, "Rest assured, the actions of this little unfortunate in helping Hellalyle in her hour of peril were a brave and fearless gesture to everyone. Most likely you will not know of this, but my people owe the king's daughter a great debt of gratitude. One remembers how the winter before last was particularly severe, and many of our people had perished through starvation. In sheer desperation, we decided to appeal to the one person who might assist us, the Princess Hellalyle. In answer to our prayers, the princess did indeed arrange that aid be given. Even to this day, I suspect that her father may still be ignorant of the support she gave us. It is almost incredible that her extraordinary powers of persuasion and political skill must have inspired the authorisation of this critical undertaking."

In a labyrinth beneath the fortress, they were shown the girl's body – the church would not permit a child of the pagans to lie in the chapel. On examination of the corpse, they were awestruck by the sight of a precious blue stone around her neck, and astonished to be informed that it had once belonged to the illustrious princess, who had, in turn, bestowed the jewel upon Ethla.

In the gloom of this vaulted underground chamber, the pagans stood to one side and took counsel before thanking Amora for the respect shown to their faith. After no more than a few minutes of earnest discussion, the conclave turned to the abbess, and announced the girl would receive an appropriate burial.

As the visitors prepared to leave with her remains, their priest Kriwe requested a talk in private with the princess and the knight. In a gentle and persuasive voice, he said, "What I will now disclose, you will find an unsettling revelation, and it is this: I believe Hellalyle's immortal essence to be still present. However, her spirit is in a state of torment, unable to leave this world because of the guilt and sorrow she had caused to so many, and the insurmountable loss of something close to her heart."

The priest made clear his admission, telling Amora, "Because Hellalyle had been such an exceptional and significant figure to everyone, at her death our gods had unleashed a white stallion to transport her to a happier existence surrounded by the souls of the righteous. But it had sped back companionless, the workings of her tormented being ordering it to return – and so conveyed the truth of her tragedy. Nonetheless, the steed that hastens unseen through the firmament will persevere with its mission until an individual event sanctions Hellalyle's surrender. The solution will lie in the hands of the young prince who now resides at this castle. As he grows older, that moment will surely arise; only then will she be obliged to choose the spirit world of nature, or to pursue her pilgrimage to the Christian afterlife. Until that time comes, the poor harvests that have blighted the land since her death will not cease."

Amora, visibly shaken by his words, clasped the knight's arm to steady her nerves. Von Altenburg gazed into the far distance, recalling that strange encounter with the Hungarian on the bridge over the ravine, and his mysterious prognostication. The abbess then confronted Kriwe, with one last question.

"Please tell me, holy man," she said, "Just now, on my entrance into this great room, I noticed you studying the scene in one of the tapestries, the one we call, *Lone Lady in the Landscape*. The expression I saw on your face indicated you might understand the mysterious meaning portrayed in the picture. It is of the greatest importance to all of us, especially the king, the father of Princess Hellalyle, that the riddle is solved. I beg of you to tell us what you know." Kriwe, leaning on his staff with both hands, considered the eyes of Amora, holding her stare for a few moments, and then straightened up to walk purposely over to the wall hanging, and with a flourishing sweep of his staff, he pointed to the figure in the panorama and said firmly, "Can you not see? She is waiting for someone!"

He then turned away, and the party of Prussens departed, leaving Princess Amora to wander over to the tapestry and gaze at it in a mood of increased curiosity.

"What did he mean, she is waiting for someone?" she voiced aloud to herself. "Who is she waiting for?" The abbess shook her head, for the solving of the riddle's imagery seemed as far away as ever.

A sacred burial ground was found for Ethla's remains at an isolated grove atop a forested hill, with a tree of unusual shape at its centre. At the foot of this eminence flowed a stream, running north and west. Here she was laid to rest, with a large granite stone placed nearby, and then she was all but forgotten.

37

Von Altenburg's exploits concluded

Princess Amora came back to the Monastery of Thorbjorg, attended by Karl von Altenburg, who had, in effect, created for himself the role of protector to the Mother Superior, escorting her occasional excursions from the convent.

As time went on, the abbess began to worry about the unconventional notion of a knight lodging within the walls of this religious community, but, sympathetic to the lot of a friendless man, could not bring herself to ask him to go, despite the strict rules of the order. Even the sisters seemed to find the presence of this lofty, leonine soldier, bearing the disfiguring scars of grievous wounds in battle, more reassuring than a threat to their everyday devotions.

About a week later, a frightening incident took place at dead of night, when one of the sisters on her rounds of the monastery precinct heard a disturbing noise near the knight's quarters. The nun, tiptoeing closer, a candle flame flickering in her trembling hand, pressed her ear to the stout door of the chamber. She could make out the distinct sound of an old woman's voice, speaking in a foreign tongue, which, unknown to the nun, was Aramaic, a language not unfamiliar to the German knight from his days as a crusader in the Holy Land. When the stranger's words were cut short, sepulchral silence enfolded the gloomy corridor. The anxious eavesdropper, fearful of being discovered, hurried away as fast as she could. She was too late to catch a glimpse of the wraith of a shrunken, ragged crone, materialising from the secure entrance to von Altenburg's room before passing ethereally through the solid masonry of the convent walls. Post-haste the nuns reported the matter to the Mother Superior. Amora was cool-headed, saying to the distressed sisters, "I suggest there will be a rational explanation to this. Bear with me, and I will approach von Altenburg for a possible explanation."

On confronting the knight, she asked of him, "There are reports that a strange voice has been heard emanating from your quarters. If it is true, can you enlighten me of the origin?"

However, von Altenburg was unforthcoming, signalling ignorance and evasiveness.

On successive nights, with increasing persistence, the sinister voice could be heard. The experience was unsettling for the sorority, and the knight's relationship with the abbess began to change subtly. Not that his unwavering respect for Princess Amora was in doubt, but his troubled state of mind suggested a division of loyalties.

The chain of strange occurrences broke on the night of a bright, full moon, when sisters Agnes and Isengard, apprehensive about going out alone, conducted their tour of inspection together. In trepidation, they walked the corridors, eventually reaching the area leading to von Altenburg's room.

"Look," said Sister Agnes in a hushed voice, pointing in the direction of the knight's quarters, "There is a bright light showing under his door."

The nuns were in two minds whether to quickly extricate themselves from the scene or pluck up courage and investigate; they chose the latter and advanced cautiously. Isengard, overcoming her fearfulness, knelt and braced herself, blinking as she squinted through the keyhole. Making the sign of the cross, she whispered, "I can see the soldier kneeling in front of a young woman."

"Who is it, tell me?" replied Agnes in a hushed voice, hardly able to contain her excitement.

"I do not know. The lady's features are incandescent, her face unrecognisable, such is the intensity of the light. You will not believe this, sister, but I can make out in the corner of the chamber, a misshapen hag crouching, undisguised, her form seems somehow insubstantial, as we would imagine a ghost... I cannot be certain in this, Agnes," Isengard whispered, "But I surmise von Altenburg is receiving instruction from the radiant figure of the lady...who is now laying her hands on the knight's head."

Then, Isengard's commentary suddenly halted, for, without warning, the searing light extinguished, and the nuns drew back before concealing themselves around the corner to see what would happen next.

For the first time, they momentarily picked out the flitting shadow of the shrivelled beldam, followed by discordant sounds of the tortured cries of a man in extreme distress. Suddenly, the door was flung open, and the knight staggered out, holding his head, groaning in agony. The terrified sisters fled and rang the bell to rouse the community, and shortly afterwards, bearing candles and torches, they joined an anxious but well-ordered flock led by Princess Amora. The crowd moved swiftly to von Altenburg's quarters – but they found the knight's lodgings deserted. The community stood way back from the entrance, too afraid to venture nearer. The abbess, demonstrating her leadership with dignity and composure, had no qualms about entering his unlit sombre chamber. Once inside, the flaming torch she held bathed her face in radiant light, while around her an empty darkness reigned. The Mother Superior reflected on what had happened with an air of omniscience and authority that appeared to calm the unease of the nervous spectators who had edged closer, looking through the entrance in trepidation and wonder, as if they were gazing in on Christ's empty tomb, after the doorway-blocking stone had inexplicably been rolled away in the night.

At dawn, the exhausted Mother Superior found a letter, unaccountably planted by her bedside while she fitfully slumbered. Standing before the light at her window, she realised it was written by von Altenburg, telling her that having fulfilled his mission, he intended leaving the next morning, never to return. No mention was made of the disturbing incidents in the night. Next morning another unexplainable episode transpired: while the knight's horse had remained in its stable, and seemed well cared for, of von Altenburg, there was no sign.

At sunrise, the final day of his promised departure, the nuns gathered outside the monastery, hoping to catch sight of the warrior and wish him well on his travels. To their surprise as they waited, an equestrian figure with a familiar black cross on shield and surcoat was suddenly spotted, leaving the rear of the monastery, galloping along a straight track towards cover of the woodland.

In a flash of the eye, the scenery changed in remarkable ways. Brightly coloured landscapes – the visionary invention of luminaries, through whose imagination and inspiration the road ahead had been rendered serpentine – wound dramatically towards a most spectacular horizon. When the knight set out on this singular highway, he could pick up distant voices of blessing and farewell on the wind. Inspirited by these salutations, he turned in his saddle to look back, then raised his sword aloft in homage to the religious order he had left behind.

When the nuns caught sight of the warrior, mounted high on his charger, they were astonished to observe how his severely injured features were physically transformed, the features restored to his once handsome face. Those who witnessed this miraculous transfiguration were spellbound.

A sequence of events was now unfolding, as in a dream, without a rational foundation. It was like a tapestry woven from the fabric of von Altenburg's life – his Spartan boyhood, the harsh military training, challenges of jousting, quests for adventure, and dedication to the chivalric code. There were scenes of battle, sieges that seemed everlasting, and striking silhouettes of castles and monasteries. It all culminated in a vision of the towers of Constantinople, rising from the Bosporus – its straits flowing with blood, reflecting the knight's horrendous injury, inflicted on him in the encirclement of that fabled city. In the last place, all those ghostly pilgrims roamed or rested by the side of a highway that was von Altenburg's Progress of Life.

The sisters, shielding their gaze, were riveted as they watched the figure of the knight gradually reduced to a speck of dust, before vanishing in a far country, beyond human comprehension. The inscrutable controller of the Cosmos chose that moment to return the scene instantly to its natural state.

Endeavouring to contain her confusion, after careful consideration the abbess spoke loudly, commanding the nuns, "Sisters, I request that nobody is to enter the scriptorium. It will be out of bounds for three days."

When Amora, with sisters Agnes, Isengard, and Bozhena, returned to inspect Hellalyle's manuscript, after careful examination they confirmed that the text bore addenda – as the princess had anticipated. The additions were inscribed in the hands of those spectral polymaths, throwing light on what had taken place.

Moved by this extraordinary revelation, the abbess resolved to make her findings known to the community, as soon as possible. The nuns assembled, barely able to restrain their excitement, as Amora prepared to address them. With the altered document in front of her, the abbess spoke loudly and clearly. "My sisters of the Monastery of Thorbjorg, let me describe what we have just learned from these recent additions made to the manuscript of my niece. It is this. We knew that Karl von Altenburg had doubts about leaving the monastery, the reason was not privy to us, but now, I can reveal all. For it appears this great warrior, along with the other eleven knights that constituted my niece's protectors, was chosen, by what we can only call the benign, phantom spirits of the wild – their reasons now revealed in this wonderful document. They considered the king's daughter their princess, bestowing on her the title: The Princess of Arcadia. After guiding von Altenburg to this realm, they were now calling him back, his assignment apparently completed. Yet in good faith, he mistakenly believed that I, Princess Amora, would still be under threat from other followers of the evil force that had destroyed Hellalyle and Hildebrand, and was loath to leave me, exposed to utmost danger."

Amora continued, "In the end, the Witch of Endor was summoned to impel him to return. Impervious to her influence, he refused, and as in the book of Samuel – where Saul asked the Witch to raise Samuel's spirit – the sorceress took it upon herself to conjure the ghost of Hellalyle, who she knew to be the one person whose command he would heed. It was Hellalyle Isengard had seen in the blinding light of the knight's chamber, placing her hands on his head, her gentle touch causing his repellent facial wound to begin to heal – his appearance restored, fraction by fraction, to its former undamaged condition."

Engrossed in Amora's narrative, she said to her awestruck congregation, "I want you now to form a single file, and come forward to obtain a view of one particular leaf of the manuscript. What you will see, on close inspection, will take your breath away: it is a finely illuminated picture of the miraculously transformed panorama we all beheld that morning when the Teutonic Knight set forth from our Monastery of Thorbjorg on his final journey.

"My sisters, we have had no instruction to finally bind the manuscript, so it must be assumed there are more developments to come in this fantastic adventure. Whatever they are must beggar the imagination, for everything so far described bears comparison with the poems of the Great Book!"

38

*The young Prince encounters the ghost of
his mother, Princess Hellalyle*

The whole story surrounding the circumstances of Crown Prince
Hagen's birth, and the death of his parents, was withheld on
explicit instruction of his grandfather the king, who considered the
facts too disturbing to relate to an impressionable young man. To
shield his grandson from reality, he had sent him abroad, to receive
education at a distinguished seat of learning.

After many years' absence, the prince, now fourteen, was about
to return home when a curious incident occurred while attending
his last lecture, on mythology. A bearded teacher of a foreign tongue,
with a faraway look, summoned Hagen to the front of the class and
with an impenetrable air, introduced himself, "My name is Taltos.
Your usual master is otherwise engaged, so today it is myself who
conducts this, your last lesson."

The individual was the very man whom Karl von Altenburg
had chanced to meet at the bridge over the ravine, many years
before. This unusual character, who had been perusing a beautiful,
illuminated manuscript of unknown provenance, summarily
requested of Prince Hagen, "I would like you to narrate these
pages from this document. Take your time, even study it for a few
minutes, as there is no hurry, but get it right."

To the young man, it appeared to be an epic romance concerning
an unnamed princess of the north and a certain English knight.

Trying to win a favourable response from an enigmatic mentor, the young man confidently declaimed the opening section of the work with bravura and rhetoric. His voice began to waver as he reached an obscure passage, chthonic and tragic, that seemed to infer some personal connection with events from his past. Breaking his recitation mid-sentence, he became lost in introspection. An eerie silence filled the chamber as his audience fixed their gaze on his fraught and pallid countenance. During Hagen's delivery, Taltos observed his protégée but did not seem unduly upset by the young man's perturbed reaction to the story.

As the scholars filed out past their tutor after the final lecture, once again Taltos singled out Hagen for attention, and with a warm, encouraging smile, touched him reassuringly on the shoulder.

"Well done, young man. Save for one hesitation, your delivery was satisfactory. I hope you learned something of interest?"

To which, Hagen replied, "Master, what are the origins of such a document? The script and the images I saw within seemed to stir within me recollections of times long ago, yet, my age dictates it cannot be so." Taltos said not a word, only indicating with a sweep of the hand, for Hagen to depart the classroom.

Not long afterwards, the chimerical Taltos disappeared, taking the manuscript with him.

His imagination fired, the young prince continued to reflect on the nature of the tale, whether it be a real account or fable, unaware his unsettling experience in the classroom had indeed been contrived to draw him, inescapably, back to a time in his early life.

With Hagen's education concluded, he bade his friends farewell and returned to the domain of his grandfather, King Thorstein. On his first night at home, unable to sleep, his disturbed thoughts wandered, trying to interpret the meaning of the manuscript and come to terms with the unforgettable Taltos, whose personality had left an ineradicable impression on him.

Later, in the small hours, he was sleeping fitfully when a nocturnal wind seeped into his chamber. In its seductive murmuring, the lines of a poem unaccountably came to him, animating his spirit, beckoning Hagen towards the bordering forest…

Go forth, brave prince, quit thy abode.
Spectral pica, escort thy road.
Press on, through the prodigious glade
To striking mirage, borne of shade
Where, from despair, in darkling straits
A soul, incomparable, awaits.

As soon as Hagen was awake the following morning, he felt an irrepressible compulsion to explore the surrounding woods, on his own, without his bodyguards. On the point of setting out, he reached instinctively for his cap, only to discover the familiar emblem attached to it had inexplicably vanished. In its place was pinned a pearl and silver badge with a bird-like device, in the shape of an ortolan, perching amidst blooms of *Mountain Everlasting*. Below this was delicately wrought the bright, metallic image of a young woman, juxtaposed with the heraldic device of lions passant, beneath an axe. The whole design was encircled with the striking figures of twelve knights.

The realisation unnerved him, and he wondered whether an intruder had entered his quarters, yet nothing appeared to have been disturbed. Then, bewilderingly, it was as if he was revisiting a dream. A precious jewel sprang to mind, flashing out of the vellum leaves of the illuminated manuscript he had been made to read aloud on the concluding day of his studies. Now, its significance struck him palpably, and with his face aglow in the reflection of its unearthly lustre, he drew the brooch to his lips and kissed it, unaware a magic ritual was preparing him for induction into an ethereal world.

The plucky young man rode into the wilderness, eventually reaching a clearing where he stopped to get his bearings. Without warning, a magpie darted down and, enticed by the glint of a bright object, furtively plucked the black velvet hat from the rider's head. Bearing the prize in its beak, it skimmed into the lower branches of a tree and, making sure the young man was in pursuit, led him a merry dance. Each time the rider drew close, the thieving crow would race ahead, hither and thither, flashing in and out of the leafy awning, emitting cacophonous squawks. The bird taunted the prince, in a frantic chase through unfamiliar territory, to an elevated position looking out over the surrounding forest. Then, as if its actions were predetermined, the feathered thief paused mid-air, and suddenly let go of the stolen bonnet, and flew away to settle in an aspen tree, keeping watch. As it did so, the aspen remembered its part in the crucifixion of Christ, and now witness to another unfolding dynamic, its leaves momentarily trembled.

Drawing in his breath, the prince dismounted to retrieve his cap. Castellated ruins on the horizon caught his attention, momentarily beguiling his vision, like a mirage of *Fata Morgana*. He stood there, spellbound, gazing at the fluctuating outline of a shadowy edifice.

Hagen was aware of a mysterious pinpoint of light, ghostly yet compelling, shining from the fortress. By a curious coincidence, the bird in its camouflage of greenery chose that moment to leave, winging its way, silently and inconspicuously, into the remoter parts of the hinterland.

Surmising that the king would have sent soldiers in search of him, the prince decided to return home. He was keen to research the history of the stronghold and would be careful not to mention the supernatural scene he had witnessed.

His questions were received evasively by the local people, who stared at him in stony silence. He went on to speak to his grandfather, but the monarch was enraged.

"Why do you want to know such things?" he shouted at Hagen across the room. "You are not to go back there – do you hear me!"

The servants, eavesdropping at the king's door, had never experienced such a violent display of their monarch's temper.

"May I remind you, young Hagen," Thorstein said impulsively, "I issued a decree many years before, banning entry to the old ruins of Preben on penalty of death, and I can assure you that even an heir to the throne is not exempt from such a forfeiture! Hagen, this is my last warning, now let the matter rest!"

Seeing the agitated state of his grandfather, Prince Hagen thought better of it, bowed to the sovereign and discreetly backed out of the room. As he opened the door, the listening attendants scattered in all directions. Hagen was not to know, that soon after, the king sent word to the Monastery of Thorbjorg that if they receive a visit from the young prince, they must refuse him access to Hellalyle's lexicon.

Later, Hagen in his room heard a faint knock at the door. On opening it, a middle-aged, peasant woman confronted him. It was Runa, his late mother's lady-in-waiting, and she stood there leaning on a stick – her old hip injury had worsened with the passing of time. When she introduced herself, he stood there for a moment open-mouthed in amazement.

"I cannot believe it!" he said, before throwing his arms around her in the warmest of embraces, while she held him tightly, and they swayed from side to side in the excitement of the moment.

"Oh, I am so glad you have come back, Hagen," exclaimed Runa.

"Please, you must come in," said he, assisting Runa into the abode.

They sat down facing one another, she with arms outstretched, holding the prince's hands, proclaiming, "Word had circulated that you had returned, and after all these years I had to see for myself." (It was partly a lie, for Thorstein had suggested this visit, to use her influence in deflecting Hagen from probing the history of his early years.) "My last, abiding memory of you was a baby in arms. Now, let me gaze at this handsome young man before me," she said as she cast her eyes over the youth. "Well, well, how proud your mother would be if she could see you now."

For a few moments, there was silence as each had so much to say, but did not know where to start. Then suddenly, both blurted out at the same time, sending them into fits of laughter.

Composing themselves, the young prince spoke first.

"Tell me, Runa, how are things? Are you managing to look after yourself?"

"Well, my prince, I am extremely indebted to your mother, for she had secretly made provision for me, in the unlikely event of her early passing, but tragically, I was only to learn of it at the tragic loss of the kind-hearted princess. The world must be bereft of losing such a beautiful woman, so artistic and cultured. She was without equal."

Choking on her words, she dabbed her eyes, unable to continue. Hagen placed his hand on her shoulder in empathy. Hagen attempted to lighten the mood, asking her, "Where are you living, Runa?"

To which she composed herself, and said, "Your mother, Princess Hellalyle, had left a will, requesting her father bequeath me lodgings in perpetuity, so the king, without question, gave me a small cottage on the edge of the hamlet that you can see from this castle's battlements. Although my infirmity has prevented useful work, the royal court looks after my interests. There is no restriction on my visiting the castle, and from time to time, the guards are sent to fetch me. The banquets held here are a wonderful experience – they lighten my life."

Hagen then circuitously broached the circumstance of his mother's death, but she, aware of Thorstein's wish that they should shield his grandson from the truth, stumbled for a moment in answering.

"You must not dwell on it," she said.

Hagen stood up, staring into the distance, and replied in a thoughtful vein, "On my last day at college I was introduced to a fascinating book, a manuscript of unknown origin, its leaves unbound. The teacher, a puzzling individual we had never seen before, had brought this document with him, and he requested that I read out to the class an extract from the vellum. The part I recited described a human tragedy occurring in the tower of a castle called Preben. It seemed so real, as if I was somehow connected, and it has haunted me ever since."

Runa interrupted him, repeating the maxim that his mother died in childbirth. "Do not doubt it, my young prince, your mother paid the highest price any woman could give. She passed away delivering you, her offspring!"

The prince then told Runa of his discovery the day before: the distant ruins of a castle.

"It was uncanny, but I am sure I witnessed a pinpoint of light coming from its structure, but when I came home, nobody would converse with me about the mysterious fort. My questions met with stony silence. When I raised the subject with my grandfather, he flew into an almighty rage. However, nobody knows, only you, of that light I saw at the edifice."

He looked surprised at Runa's reaction, looking up at him, listening with both hands to her face in trepidation and fear, his disclosure imbuing in her a feeling of terrible foreboding.

"Hagen, I know what you are thinking. Please put it out of your mind – you must! Do not go there!" she said earnestly.

"But why, what danger awaits me?" he said.

She implored of him, "There is something not of this world that inhabits the blackened fortress, souls of the undead that must not be disturbed."

Hagen, sensing Runa knew more than she let on, softly said, "Who was my father?"

Aware the boy was becoming suspicious, she looked at the floor and whispered, "He was a foreign soldier, a Prince of England, but that is all I know, so please do not press me further. You must not resurrect the past – it has gone, gone forever."

Aware she was becoming upset again, the young Prince changed tack to lighten her emotion.

Gossip was brought up to date, and the time passed speedily. When the moment came for Runa to depart, he assisted her to the door as she leaned heavily on her stick. In the passageway outside they expressed their goodbyes. He promised to visit her in the coming days and invited her to come and see him whenever she wished. She kissed him fondly on the cheek, and like a mother with her son, lingered, lightly sprucing the youth's attire, straightening the collar on his doublet, her hand tiding his hair. It was then she uttered in a serious vein, "Dear Hagen, will you promise me faithfully, here and now, that under no circumstances will you visit the old castle?"

He mumbled an inaudible reply as if reassuring her, while looking down, deliberately avoiding eye contact.

That evening, Runa in her simple thatched dwelling was sitting by a fire that had a cauldron suspended over it, the smoke curling up through a hole in the roof. Close by, a tethered nanny goat patiently pulled hay from a hanging net, while its newborn kid basked in the glow of the flames, lying on straw at the woman's feet. Above them, on a cross beam, chickens and a cockerel were roosting. It should have been a scene of utter serenity, except, instead of taking a nap, Runa could not relax, persistently stoking the fire, reflecting on her reunion with Hagen. Gradually her thoughts gelled, and a fantastic notion came to her: could the manuscript the prince had referred to have been Hellalyle's very own? However, on second thoughts she dismissed the probability, believing the document was secure at Thorbjorg.

A phantasmal vision of the ancient castle so preoccupied Hagen's imagination, it was that very evening before dusk, he went back in secrecy, drawing even closer to the ivy-clad walls, but there was no sign of the sinister light he had observed previously.

Diverted by the sudden appearance of an old woodcutter coming out of the trees, Hagen hailed him to stop. The prince quickly alighted, and leading his horse by the reins, he went over to question the elderly, bearded man, clothed in virtual rags. He stood there with a bundle of brushwood in his arms, mouth partly agape, revealing his only tooth. Hagen asked, "Excuse me, my man, can you enlighten me on the history of the castle ruins, or whether you are able to recall any unusual tales about it?"

The prince was shocked when the elderly woodsman snapped a grim warning. "Why do you want to know, young sir? Take my advice and stay well clear of this haunted site, and return home post-haste! The sorrows of the world seem concentrated here – surely you can sense it? The only reason our paths have crossed is I am an old man, I get confused, and gathering kindling I have unwisely strayed again, near to the walls of Preben."

The youth suddenly caught hold of the woodsman.

"Did you say its name was Preben?"

Chilled, Hagen listened to the grizzled rustic.

"Yes, Preben, you heard right. I once ventured into the fortress and my ears were assailed by the terrifying disturbance of knights in combat, and the blood-curdling screams of a woman in torment emanating from one of the towers. The sounds I heard that day, I hope never to hear again."

The woodsman crossed himself, then shook a gnarled hand in the direction of one of the castle towers as he watched an agitated flock of birds muster around the battlements.

"Look!"

The old man said, "The birds have gathered again, like before – their congregation augurs another manifestation of the spectral woman! What I say is not superstition, but is real!"

Undeterred, the prince put pressure on him to explain the significance of these dreadful apparitions, but the old peasant pulled away from the agitated Hagen and scuttled off into the woods.

These disturbing accounts served to remind Hagen of the impact that epic poem had made when he first read it, spurring the young prince to uncover the secrets of the ruins. He entered the empty courtyard as quietly as he could. Despite his stealthy approach, the heavy tread of his mount seemed to echo mockingly from the dilapidated walls of the fortress.

Then suddenly, out of the blue, there burst a violent cataract of clattering hooves. Eight phantom horsemen on the rampage, causing the throng of mysterious birds on the battlements to take flight, scattering in disarray in the encroaching dusk. Hurriedly tethering his steed, Hagen took refuge in an archway leading to one of the turrets. With his heart in his mouth, he struck a light before ascending a stone staircase, conscious only of the faint whisper of his flickering torch as it swung to and fro, casting shadows on the rounded walls. All at once, hair-raising screams ruptured the stillness. The pathetic cries of a woman's voice were succeeded by a deafening din, the fierce clashing of soldiers in savage combat. Suddenly, the flame of Hagen's lamp was blown out. Shutting his eyes, he froze in terror at the sound of martial clangour, thundering past him at breakneck speed, pitching headlong, down into the black abyss. Mysteriously, his torch rekindled, restoring a sense of calm.

Continuing to climb, he reached an open space below the ramparts, where only the pale gleam of stars perforated the gaping holes in the roof. Gripped by a feeling of unease as he reconnoitred the ghostly voids, he recoiled, aghast, as he picked out the spectral figure of a knight bearing down on him with brandished sword and a raised shield displaying heraldic images of an axe and golden lions. Inexplicably, at the last moment, the warrior faltered in his aggressive stance, staring blindly at the prince as if by a second sight he recognised him. Stunned that the young man had seen him seeking vengeance in this purgatorial setting, he lifted one arm to conceal his face and staggered backward, engulfed in Stygian shadows.

Overwhelmed by this terrifying encounter, Hagen steadied himself against the broken window. Staring dejectedly at distant stars, he tried to analyse what had happened. As he stood there, he slowly became aware of another presence, and called out apprehensively, "Who is there?"

He paused, then shouted his challenge a second time.

In the ominous silence that ensued, the young man's courage deserted him, and he longed to flee but was daunted by the forbidding, twisting shaft of the turret steps. Then, a woman's voice, tinged with sadness, whispered through the gloom, "Who has the temerity to enter a place the Lord has forsaken?"

Swinging around, the prince could make out the apparition's slim, vaporous shape. In the background, what might have been the spectral crania of seven warriors loomed, distinguishable by the inky outline of their protective helmets.

"I am Prince Hagen, son of Hellalyle, grandson of King Thorstein!" Hagen announced boldly.

His exclamation caused the figure to emerge into the flickering torchlight where it morphed into substantiality, and instinctively, the frightened prince knelt in front of her, timidly raising his eyes as she loosened her hood to reveal a woman of exceptional beauty, gazing at him in disbelief. A tense moment of silence ensued, and then with high emotion, with trembling lips, she spoke, "Your mother Hellalyle stands before you, refusing to leave this world before my scion – offspring of the knight Hildebrand – is returned to me, uncertain whether he be alive or dead. Now my prayers are answered."

Overcome, quavering and struggling to speak, she managed to stammer, "Divine Providence may have denied me knowledge of your childhood, but now I can look, with pride and joy, on my flesh and blood."

Gazing at him intently, she ran her hands over the young man's cheeks, tenderly brushing back his hair, searching his eyes, as if it were never so…

"All along, the agencies of the Lord were watching over little Ethla, who prevailed against the odds in the tasks I set her. She helped to deliver you from danger and safeguard the kingdom from conflict and destruction. Only divine authority could have been responsible for reuniting us on this momentous occasion, bringing the Prince of England's son, Hagen, face-to-face with Hellalyle, his mother."

Heartened by her powerful words, and now more at ease with himself, he embraced his mother tightly. He cried for joy, reluctant to release from his arms a woman whom he had only been able to conjure in his mind's eye, from anecdote and legendary stories about her.

He could see, in the darkness beyond, the mysterious black figures still gathered in a ghostly band, and gained the impression they were listening as Hellalyle began to relate her account of his father Hildebrand's life and death, and the brave exploits of her bodyguards – especially those of his friend Karl von Altenburg, to glean the significance of this restoration of their family ties.

Lovingly, she kissed his forehead. "For all these years, I truly believed the powers of righteousness had abandoned me, but seeing you here, I now realise how wrong I was."

She told how the tragic events at the castle of Preben were a prophecy of the spectacular coming of the *Wild Jagd*, which

Hagen's father and mother witnessed as they rode together by the shores of Lake Eydis; even if at that time, head over heels in love, they had not foreseen the consequences of the apocalyptic occurrence. How the cruel machinations of the diabolical Paulus tricked her brothers into believing they were protecting their sister's honour from the Englishman's attention. Yet the close bond between the young prince's parents was no cause for shame and did not contravene the teachings of the Scriptures.

In the tragic events that unfolded, Hellalyle related, her brothers proved no match against his father's ferocious assault, in which he, as an act of mercy, tried to induce them to surrender, before being incited by the unscrupulous prinz to take the fight to Hildebrand. In retaliation, Hildebrand reluctantly raised his sword again, and dispatched all her siblings, save Paulus, who treacherously stabbed to death the Prince of England. Now, the boy's father had become a cold-blooded executioner, set on vengeance. A prisoner of his divided world, deeply upset by Hellalyle's experiences – and, following his untimely death, powerless to help her.

The boy's mother described how Hildebrand's troubled spirit would resurface, only to vanish again, in its ruthless mission to bring retribution on her poor brothers, pursuing them relentlessly while their cries for mercy resounded in the space. She predicted the shades of Hildebrand and her brothers would live on, but cursed, for violating the Peace of God. It was forbidden to fight on the Sabbath, especially in a holy place. Thus, they were banned entry into the Kingdom of Heaven.

She related how Karl von Altenburg finally slew the villain, putting an end to his tyranny – even if his death came too late to save Hagan's mother.

All that she disclosed to her son confirmed what he had read in that mysterious Chronicle.

As Hellalyle's ghost drifted towards the window, the boy, observing her gazing trance-like at the night sky, became convinced that she was communicating with extra-terrestrial powers beyond his comprehension. When she came to herself, she voiced these words:

"Your presence puts an end to years of despair in this accursed castle, making it possible for me to take leave of this world, in the company of the king's now-pardoned champions. Although I am instructed to renounce Hildebrand for contravening the laws of chivalry, it was the benevolent forces of nature, by artful contrivance, who were responsible for bringing us together; and because of this, he will receive mercy...on the understanding that he remains here on earth for the duration of his son's life, until a time I am destined to come back and reclaim him."

In a voice strained to breaking point, she continued.

"Knowing you would never be able to forget your petrifying confrontation in this very fortress, when a demoniacal assailant bore down on you, hell-bent on striking you dead... I now reveal that this man was your father! I beg you, Hagen, return to this place, seal an enduring friendship with Hildebrand so that when you are king, he can become your counsellor...both in personal affairs and in military matters, where he excels in courage and the ability to command. Count on your father in everything. Rule your kingdom well, so that your reputation and good conduct will help him assuage all the heartbreak and desolation of this bleak stronghold."

Then, after an uncomfortable pause, Hellalyle, with sorrow traced across her face, said, "Farewell, young prince. I must leave you now."

As her elusive figure receded into a leaden backcloth to re-join the umbral shades, very softly, she made her last, enigmatic utterance:

"This castle is destined to look upon me once more, but not during your lifetime."

Young Hagen, in desperation, repeatedly called out after her, "Mother! Mother! Mother...!"

His plaintive voice echoed in the darkness, but there was no response.

Saddened, but no longer fearful, he descended the turret steps, this time without incident. He realised that the ghostly warriors responsible for the conflict and inextricably linked with his mother had vanished from the scene.

Hagen's emergence from the tower coincided with the arrival of the king, Princess Amora, and a party of soldiers. Before his grandfather could rebuke his disobedience, a phantasmagoric spectacle unfolded: the haunting apparition of a great white stallion, airily cantering high above the castle, escorting the transient figure of Hellalyle – who appeared to be conveying some vital message to the pale charger. With a fleeting kiss and encouraging pat, she bade farewell to the spectral mount, which, responding to her touch, sped off majestically in the direction of distant, wooded hills, ethereally shaped in the light of a rising moon.

King Thorstein, who had long disguised a suspicion that the broken spirits of his children still haunted the charred remains of Castle Preben, was overcome with emotion, weeping on the shoulder of his sister Amora at the vision of his daughter's remarkable metamorphosis.

Rooted to the spot, Hagen was mesmerised by the image of his mother, gloriously ascending into heaven at the head of seven knights, the shadowy figures he had seen in the darkness – her beloved brothers.

Hildebrand, watching from the ruins, witnessed the departure of the woman he held dear. Distraught that she was abandoning him, he ran agitatedly along the allure of the battlements, trying to keep track of her retreating figure, before it dissolved in the celestial sphere, leaving the warrior filled with remorse, heartache, and eventual isolation.

The years rolled by, and the forsaken ghost of Preben wandered forlornly through the fractured blocks of the old fortress. It was said, by those who chanced upon this eerie place, that one could make out the disturbing sound of heavy footsteps, the ringing sound of brandished weaponry, the clinking of polished silver spurs, and the anguished cries of one desperately calling for his lost love. The phantom's torment seemed unremitting when stony silence met his grief and lamentation.

The spectre's identity was known only to Hagen – now king, having succeeded his grandfather Thorstein – who was determined to honour the promise he had made to his mother: forging strong ties with his father, empathising with his spirit, giving succour to his forbear's abject loneliness.

During the years that followed, the monarch, returning to the ruins, often sought the advice of the legendary warrior. But he was never to see his father again, only the sound of his voice speaking to him from the shadows; the soldier's deep-felt shame inhibited him from direct interaction with his son. There occurred a melodrama in one of these early scenes, when Hagen attempted to advance, determined to behold once again the ghost of his ancestor – but immediately there issued a warning, a sharp riposte: "*Stay back.*"

For Hagen, born without a father, to find himself so tantalisingly close to him and yet be denied face-to-face contact caused bouts of melancholy, which would plague him for the rest of his life.

Over the years, at their talks, the English knight never failed to impress how his heart yearned for Hellalyle, still unable to believe she had deserted him. Hagen would reply that he should never give up hope of her returning one day, as she had foretold.

Imbued with his mother's wisdom and compassion, and with a flair for military leadership gained from his father, Hagen, steadfast in the face of adversity, ruled his people well.

39

The meteor

Seventy years on, the aged Hagen lay resting in his room at Yrian, knowing his end was near. He requested another chamber where he could gaze at the distant, wooded hills, beyond which he would be able to picture the immemorial remains of the castle at Preben, striking a spark in his weary soul.

Next day, shortly before dawn, the monarch passed away. At once, a brilliant shooting star of apocalyptic intensity broke from the constellation of Gemini, flashing across the sky to leave a visible trail in the heavenly vault. Incandescent rays flooded the king's chamber, allowing the mourners to observe an untroubled but intriguing smile on the ashen face of the dead sovereign. At the same time, beyond the ruins of Preben, a slender hooded figure, attired in a black, religious habit of coarse well-worn cloth, ragged at the hem and the sleeve, the individual emitting a faint, auroral glow, giving belief of an eternal, religious wanderer, could be seen moving restlessly near the edge of the woods. Alongside the mysterious nomad was the ghostly silhouette of a spiritual messenger from the Guardians of the Forest.

The unknown traveller stood motionless, glancing nervously up at one of the derelict towers, but no discernment of its features was visible, for the head covering of the frock was pulled forward. No one would have been aware that the stranger's anxious manner belied its terrifying recollections of bloody deeds, a premonition of an unwelcoming reception at the castle.

In panic and desperation, the cloaked figure knelt in prayer, seeking divine guidance in its moment of crisis, for the task it had now to accomplish, while the attendant angel offered reassurance and strength. Now fortified, the enigmatic stranger rose, gliding unhurriedly across the sward, soon enveloped in the charred and blackened remains of Thorstein's forbidding fortress. The Seraph of the forest, whose presence had brought such comfort, took its leave, returning to its mystic realm.

Meanwhile, inside, the grief-stricken ghost of Hildebrand, having witnessed the brilliant spectacle in the firmament, peered through an arrow loop on the turret stairway. Rainwater dripped on dank masonry as he waited impatiently for the final break of day. Without warning, the tenebrous scene lifted. The spent torches, attached to the stone walls, spontaneously ignited, illuminating the darkness in glorious radiance. Light footsteps he heard, the soft swish of a garment, as a figure slowly ascended the steps in his direction.

To the knight's astonishment, a woman's face emerged from the hood of the spectral silhouette; irradiate, serenely beautiful, almost saintly; wearing a blissful smile. He saw her blue eyes sparkle like sapphires as she held out her hand to him.

Here was Hellalyle in all her majesty, returning as she had promised. To think he had waited a lifetime for this moment, testing his faith to the limit. The emotional impact was so overpowering he broke down in tears, unable to look at her. He turned his face to the wall, feeling unworthy, his confidence exhausted after years of gruelling separation.

He stood speechless, in fear she might again forsake him, and now, at the very spot where long ago the knight made his overture, kissing the hand of the shy and reluctant Hellalyle, she grasped *his* hand, gently squeezing it as a signal of reassurance, bringing it to her lips in tender adoration. She turned the stricken knight towards her, easing his head onto her shoulder to soothe and comfort him. Then, in a state of emotional fullness, she exclaimed, "Hildebrand, the heroic leader of my bodyguards, let me embrace you. You are the only man I have loved, and as such will never renounce, but cherish you always with utter devotion. Our son, King Hagen, has now passed away, his reign complete, so my wanderings in Arcadia are finished. Come with me, my dear prince, and leave your exile in this castle of sadness, and I shall transport you to a sacred place, where the pain of parting will end, and we shall be united forever!"

The entwined figures, released from their ardent embrace, became invisible as Hellalyle took leave of the world, bearing the knight with her. The torches grew faint and were soon extinguished, reducing the fortress to cheerless, sombrous desolation. At long last, its wounds healed.

At that instant, the sun rose spectacularly over the outlying mountains, where Hellalyle's giant eagles still soared. From misty heights, the Four Winds gathered pace, and in their unaccountable force could be heard dulcet harmonies of a thousand women's voices, so pure and melodious the sound gladdened the hearts of all who heard it. The forest foliage gently danced and swayed to the rhythm, which, reverberating through the virgin landscape, induced inspiration and rapture in its wild inhabitants, assuaging their despair after long years of misery. An immense flock of birds ascended the morning sky to perform Hellalyle's dance amongst the billowing clouds, with aerobatic artistry of awe-inspiring grandeur.

Across the blue expanse of Lake Eydis – Hellalyle's Mare Nostrum – flashes of silver were visible as shoals of fish leapt wildly in the wind-driven swell, and white-tipped waves rolled in. The water, as it approached the land, was held back and jostled with itself, throwing spume from turbulent crests, to be miraculously transformed into beguiling figures of nymphs clasping garlands of *Mountain Everlasting* as they disported themselves in the spray, before evanescing, and allowing the tide to retake shape, tumbling and breaking on the shore.

This wondrous occurrence would influence what followed: the magical reinvigoration of the lifeless garden of Preben, which had become a burial ground for the plants that had stubbornly resisted growth. They now seemed to spring instantaneously from the soil, restoring to the place the long-lost splendour of nature. On a branch of fresh blossom, the familiar little passerine alighted, to join the throng and sing in jubilation before it sped across the boundless forest to land at a forgotten pagan grove, the resting place of Ethla's mortal remains. Perching on the most prominent boulder it could find, the bird chattered excitedly, then fell silent as it focused its piercing, searching gaze, to bring to light a rare heathen inscription, now becoming visible on the mossy surface of the stone. Translated, it said,

> *Summoned to this place by wraiths of the wild, I came*
> *To serve a pretty princess of legend and fame,*
> *Who stooped down to save me from penury and doom,*
> *Offering sanctuary, a welcoming room.*
> *She became the gentle mother I never knew,*
> *Inspiring devotion, which flourished and grew.*
> *In the spell of gratefulness, I seemed to unbend,*
> *Helped free her son from a grim, untimely end.*
> *And now, I shall rest, dwelling on this hilltop isle,*
> *Lost to the world, save in spirit of Hellalyle.*

The ringing sound of the tuneful choir ascended the steep to Castle Yrian, the echo of music spreading through the great hall, where displayed Dyonisius's sibylline masterpiece, *Lone Lady in a Landscape*, causing the picture to metamorphose supernaturally, by introducing into the composition the figure of an English knight lying alongside a noblewoman, in her sweet repose, to be united forever, by the shores of an inland sea.

In the gardens of the Monastery of Thorbjorg, the nuns were startled by the recurrence of the beautiful, strange choral unison. It was borne on the wind over the ivy-clad convent walls, causing fruit trees in its path to rustle insistently, before gaining the chapel, the repository of Hellalyle's manuscript. The gust blew open its devotional doors, disturbing the abbess kneeling alone at prayer as if some metaphysical force had invaded the sanctuary. She watched in astonishment as the iconic document vanished before her eyes, spirited out of the sepulchre by the angels of the forest.

The spirits of Nature regarded this holograph, written in part by the hand of Hellalyle, as a sacred document, and were determined that its unique message, and the secret covenant they had made with her, be under their control. The manuscript was taken out of the kingdom, carried across Asia Minor, and far beyond to a remote valley which lay beneath the snow-capped peaks of the Altai mountains. In the most isolated location, the polymaths painstakingly inscribed their final entries, and completed the Illuminated Chronicle. Their dedicated work might have been to no avail, for the ghosts of the steppes, grief-stricken at the passing of their princess, exacted revenge by tampering with individual illustrations in the text, altering Hellalyle's appearance. Her face now turned aside, denying the reader a glimpse of her striking features – adding mystery to her legend.

Before the phantasms of the steppes dissolved away, they saw to it that the manuscript be kept hidden by summoning the creatures of the wild – led by the fearsome tigers of the Caspian – to guard it against the outside world. In times to come, pilgrims would eagerly set out in search of the elusive icon, a sumptuously illuminated treasure of the mediaeval age, comparable to the Book of Kells or the Gospels of Lindisfarne. However, it was a work of unique conception, for Hellalyle's distinctive voice could be conjured from its leaves, faculties of sound, so reassuringly gentle and pure, her speech created emotional tranquillity in all beings of the earth. Her profound insight healing and instructing a troubled world. But that far away hiding place, in which her book was so securely concealed, retained its secret, so that, after the upheavals, century upon century, of human conflict, its questionable existence has become the very subject of folklore, even to lie in the long-lost library of the Russian Tzar, Ivan Grozny – Ivan the Terrible.

As this day of ceremony and jubilation ended, a breath-taking sunset lit up the skies, inducing in the joyous throng a heady mix of wonder and presentiment, as if the earth itself were ablaze, before the shifting of light caused this manifestation to melt into the ether. These memorable events set the seal on the veneration in which Hellalyle was held by the other division of the earth, awaiting her brief reappearance to take into heaven Hildebrand, her knight protector.

That same day, in Britannia, at the cathedral of Winchester, the reverential quiet of the precincts was shattered by the exploding sound of its chiming bells.

The prior, Adam of Farnham, summoned a monk. "Go up to the chamber and see who is causing the disturbance. Put a stop to it at once or the tower will come crashing down."

In some trepidation, the lowly cleric ascended the steps to investigate. As he got nearer the noise deafened him and, with hands pressed over his hears, he entered the chamber, only to find it empty of people while the large bells danced merrily away, seemingly out of control, the changes abandoned, furiously emitting their cacophony of music. Dumbfounded by this discovery, the frightened monk raced back down, meeting Adam of Farnham coming up.

"Brother Adam!" he shrieked, pointing rearward from whence he came. "The bells must be bewitched – they ring out themselves since there is no one there!"

To which the incredulous prior, at the top of his voice, exclaimed, "What magic is this? Has the world gone mad?"

But the world had not gone mad; every bell across the land, from the towns to the villages, the majestic abbeys, to the isolated church in its rural setting, all were ringing of their own volition. For the soul of England had risen, celebrating the union of its warrior prince with Hellalyle, the princess of a mysterious land, a joining never to be split asunder.

Chivalry is only a name for that general spirit or state of mind which disposes men to heroic actions, and keeps them conversant with all that is beautiful and sublime in the intellectual and moral world.

The Broad Stone of Honour (Pub. 1823) Kenelm Henry Digby (c 1800–1880)

Epilogue

The following autumn, on a day in the year of our Lord 1272, the woodlands were resplendent in their brilliant hues. The forest floor carpeted by discarded leaves, still falling from the woodland canopy, colours of burnished gold, orange reds, tans and russet browns, the colour tones of the earth all dappled with butter yellow, a visual experience so delectable, it etched itself upon the memory.

At the Abbey of Sunniva, two spectral figures glided along the cloisters and through a doorway, heading into the wilderness beyond. There, in the tranquillity of the sylvan tract, only broken by the sighing of the wind in the treetops, the wise owl flitted silently through the woods. The bird – symbol of the wisdom of Christ – was sent by Hellalyle to alert all those in the forest, and to tell them not to be afraid – for two ghostly figures would be coming.

A small group of deer, taking advantage of the quiet climes in the depths of the timberland, were quietly browsing on the flora and searching for food beneath the carpet of wonder, when they suddenly looked up and took note, as the apparitions of a man and a woman appeared amongst the trees. The shy *Cervidae* showed no fear and stood stock-still. The young deer looked to their elders as if seeking reassurance, intrigued as to why they did not flee; but they assuaged that this extraordinary vision, unfolding before them, held no threat.

For they were witnessing the knight, Prinz Paulus, whose purified soul was leading by the hand his mother, Queen Gudrun, now lovingly reunited in the afterlife, with the son so cruelly taken from her many years ago. Above them, the owl now nestled in the crook of an oak tree, and partly hidden by the ivy, watched intently as the pair reached a magical, silent waterfall. Its pure water made no noise, cascading down to the plunge pool below. Around this cataract, strange clematis vines, brilliant green mosses, and unknown, but exquisite, flowers still grew.

The wrongdoings of humankind were banished here, for the princess's spirit lived on in all things. It was a place distinct from the outside world, where eternal peace reigned, and all bathed in a most extraordinary light.

For a few contemplative moments, they stood at this sacred spot, before mother and son vanished forever. The owl then departed on its eerie flight, through the glades of the forest, sole witness of what had occurred in the secret idyll of Hellalyle's domain.

Lightning Source UK Ltd.
Milton Keynes UK
UKHW011848250920
370536UK00002B/156